Acclaim for ADAM

Monopol

D1043779

"Forces the reader to look at AIDS afresh without any of its usual emotional baggage [and to] examine the universal emotions of loss and grief and reverence for the dead."
—*The New York Times*

"[Mars-Jones is] a wide-ranging purveyor of the telling detail and a fine stylist to boot...A splendid book." —*USA Today*

"Takes the reader deep into the netherworld of AIDS, a world of hospitals, buddies, funerals. We see them, through taut, spare prose. In less talented hands these themes...would be unrelenting, but Mars-Jones's flashes of humor and his never-wavering compassion make it somehow bearable."
—*San Francisco Chronicle*

"Mars-Jones works with a precise eye and a style that is sharp and detailed. With subtle irony and wry humor, [he] details the ways in which the human heart is tested [and yet] never slips into pity or sentimentality." —*Houston Post*

"Moving and devastating.... Contains stories dealing with a range of poignant, funny, angry and desperate responses to AIDS." —*Lambda Book Report*

"A substantial achievement [of] taboo-breaking courage and tenderness." —*The Guardian*

"Without in any way mitigating the catastrophe of AIDS, these grim, funny, touching, eloquent and brave stories demonstrate that it is possible to salvage something of lasting value from the wreckage." —*Times Literary Supplement*

ADAM MARS-JONES

Monopolies of Loss

Born in 1954, Adam Mars-Jones was educated at Westminster and Cambridge. His first collection of stories, *Lantern Lecture*, won the Somerset Maugham Award in 1982. Since then he has edited *Mae West Is Dead: Recent Lesbian and Gay Fiction* and is the co-author, with Edmund White, of *The Darker Proof: Stories from a Crisis*. His novel, *The Waters of Thirst*, is being published in 1994. He lives in London, where he writes film reviews for the *Independent*.

INTERNATIONAL

Monopolies of Loss

MONOPOLIES OF LOSS

ADAM MARS-JONES

VINTAGE INTERNATIONAL

Vintage Books

A Division of Random House, Inc.

New York

FIRST VINTAGE INTERNATIONAL EDITION, MARCH 1994

'Slim' was first published in *Granta*, 1986; 'An Executor', 'A Small Spade',
and 'The Brake' were first published in *The Darker Proof*, Faber and Faber,
1987; *'Summer Lightning'* first appeared in the *Observer Magazine*, 1988;
'Remission' was first published in *Granta*, 1988; 'Bears in Mourning' was
first published in *Granta*, 1992; 'Baby Clutch' was first published in *Granta*,
1989; 'The Changes of Those Terrible Years' first appeared in *The Faber Book
of Gay Short Fiction*, Faber and Faber, 1991.

Library of Congress Cataloging-in-Publication Data
Mars-Jones, Adam, 1954–
Monopolies of loss/Adam Mars-Jones.—1st Vintage International ed.
p. cm.
ISBN 0-679-74415-0
1. Gay men—Great Britain—Fiction. 2. AIDS (Disease)—Patients—Great
Britain—Fiction.   I. Title.
[PR6063.A659M66 1994]
823'.914—dc20   93-42197
CIP

Manufactured in the United States of America
10 9 8 7 6 5 4 3 2 1

Contents

Monopolies of Loss

Introduction: Monopolies of Loss

Writing fiction about Aids calls for a sustained effort of adjustment, but then so does everything else to do with the epidemic.

A virus, being invisible, peculiarly invites the mechanisms of denial and paranoia. We can't see it, so we pretend it doesn't exist – and a teenager has unprotected sex under the politically correct gaze of a Safe Sex poster. We can't see it, so it acquires the power to turn up anywhere – and a widow who has slept alone since 1976 becomes convinced she is symptomatic.

Denial and apocalyptic brooding each has its attraction. Aids is an irrelevance: learn a few rules of hygiene and go back to living your life. That's one way of looking at it. Aids will depopulate at least one continent (Africa) and a number of cities. That's another. The present reality of the epidemic must lie somewhere in the middle, but it's hard not just to oscillate between extreme positions.

Writing about Aids should be a way of finding a truer picture, but it brings its share of problems. The novel seems the obvious form for so weighty an issue, but in any individual case of Aids the virus has a narrative of its own, a story it wants to tell, which is in danger of taking over.

In any novel about Aids there are likely to be rites of passage, hard to avoid but hard to reshape, retroviral equivalents of the Stations of the Cross: first knowledge of the epidemic, first friend sick, first death, first symptom . . . How do you tell a fresh story when the structure is set?

A writer attempting the subject is likely to feel like one of the spiders that was fed drugs in experiments in the 1960s, and ended up spooling out silk in frazzled doodles – except that Aids is not a disorienting drug but a superior spider, spinning its web from cell to cell and organ to organ.

Perhaps only a customized form of the novel could adequately represent both the reality of the virus and its irrelevance, its irrelevance even to those whose lives it threatens. Imagine for instance a story interrupted by a footnote that grows to book length, the text never resuming. Aids doesn't deserve to be promoted up into the body of the book. It's only a bug, after all. Why flatter it?

There is also, for a gay writer seeking to treat the subject of Aids, a particular political variant of denial. At a time when media coverage tends to push the issues of Aids and homosexuality closer and closer together, as if epidemic and orientation were synonymous, how can you justify writing fiction that brings this spurious couple together all over again? Surely the truly responsible thing to do now would be to write sexy nostalgic fiction set in the period before the epidemic, safeguarding if only in fantasy the endangered gains of gay liberation?

Well, no. Even when I thought that the problems of writing about Aids satisfactorily were insurmountable, for me at any rate, I still felt that it would be a good thing, even politically, if the trick could be managed. Fiction might create a psychological space in which the epidemic could be contemplated, with detachment rather than denial or apocalyptic fear.

In 1985 or so I read a story by Edmund White, 'An Oracle', published in the American gay glossy *Christopher Street*, which told the story of a man bereaved by the epidemic, and contained poignant flashbacks to the illness itself. I admired the story, and felt that it came as close to dealing with the subject of Aids – not very close – as fiction gracefully could.

It wasn't in fact fiction but a newspaper article I read in 1986 that made me abruptly able to deal with a subject that I had previously found intractable. This was an article that described Aids in Africa, where it goes by the name of Slim.

The problems attaching to the subject turned out overwhelmingly to be attached to the name. By suppressing that, I was suddenly able to write about the epidemic. My previous fastidious fear of writing in the first person also disappeared – since 'Slim' it has become an addiction – and the story was written in a couple of days from the time I read the article. Looking over 'Slim', though, I see that it contains at least one involuntary homage to 'An Oracle', since both stories use the image of a wind tunnel on their closing pages.

Having written my story, I realized that its indirectness could be turned to further account. If it was read on the radio, say Radio 4, it might reach people who would turn off by reflex if they heard the word 'Aids', but might hang on and, well, learn something if the trigger-word was delayed indefinitely. I imagined fingers actually frozen on the on–off switch, waiting in a sort of genteel torment for permission not to care.

In due course the actor Tom Wilkinson did read the story on Radio 4, occasionally using intonations so unearthly sounding I could only conclude they were based on my own.

Later in the year I had become so bold that I was contemplating a whole book of stories about Aids, though I didn't want to be sole author. Part of this was high-mindedness, a reluctance to annex the epidemic single-handed and become the *poète maudit* of HIV, and part of it was second-book paranoia, a matter of not wanting to face disenchanted reviewers alone. It seemed no bad idea to drag a hostage with me into the searchlights, using another writer's reputation as a sort of human shield.

Edmund White had in fact been a friend since I had reviewed his *A Boy's Own Story*, describing it as a cake that had been iced but not baked. (It is a peculiarity of this writer that a bad review can positively inflame his charm and goodwill.) He was then finishing his novel *Caracole*, but thought he had at least one more Aids story in him. He seemed to agree that there was a real advantage in tackling the subject in a short story, that the big issue and the little form had a paradoxical affinity. I for my part thought I could manage four stories in all.

Faber were responsive to the idea of publishing the projected book directly as a paperback, and soon. Edmund and I spoke to them first in November, I think, of 1986, and undertook to deliver the manuscript in March of the next year. The book could then appear in June or July. (In those days Faber referred to such projects as 'quickies', later coming to prefer the phrase quality-book-in-a-hurry.)

Edmund and I discussed what we were going to write only in general terms, anxious to avoid overlapping, though perhaps any overlap would only have highlighted our differences of background and temperament. As it turned out, there was only one area of convergence. We both wanted to write about a relationship between an HIV-positive person and a partner either negative or ignorant of his status, but we planned to address this issue from opposite sides of the antibody divide.

The programme of my four stories was, first, to look directly at Aids – with 'Slim' – and then to edge it into the background. I wanted to crown HIV with attention and then work to dethrone it. I struggled to turn Aids into a countersubject, to give it an appropriate status, neither ignored nor holding centre stage. That seemed the best way of rendering HIV its due, no less and no more.

It was at my suggestion that the suppression of the word 'Aids' was extended to the whole book. This involved only a little editing of Edmund's 'An Oracle', and presented no real problems. After the book was published, though, the device seemed to have served its turn, and in later stories I returned without a qualm to using the word that had once seemed to hold so much power.

As co-authors, Edmund and I were consulted by Faber about cover design. My instinct being solidly for commercial suicide, I suggested a non-pictorial cover, like an old-fashioned Faber poetry title, perhaps incorporating – on a subliminal level, and in a deconstructionist sort of way – the tombstone-and-marble imagery of the public-service adverts that had recently appeared on television in Britain. Edmund suggested instead an artist he knew in Paris, so we went with that.

4

The title was more of a problem. The usual solution with a collection is to choose the title of one of the constituent stories, but that wouldn't work when there were two authors. Eventually we settled on a phrase from the first volume of Cocteau's diaries, which both of us, tireless interveners in the marketplace, had recently reviewed.

After attending the dress-rehearsal of a play, Cocteau borrowed an image from print-making, telling the cast that everything was as it should be – they should just 'draw a darker proof'. I think it was I who suggested turning the indefinite article into a definite one, on the notably rigorous grounds that only books of poetry should have an 'a' in their titles.

The Darker Proof was published in the middle of 1987. Edmund and I were ready with a cod-Shakespearean quotation to explain the title – 'Friends in affliction make the darker proof of love,' or something of the sort, supposedly from *Measure for Measure* – but nobody asked. Perhaps people already assumed it was from a Shakespeare play that they weren't familiar with.

The reviews were generally kind. By then, it took a certain amount of effort to disparage a book with such liberal credentials, to attack its achievement without denigrating its intentions. One reviewer, admittedly, while summarizing the medical background, invented a new category of HIV transmission: a promiscuous and/or haemophiliac butcher with sores on his hands – I think I've got this right – could endanger his customers by supplying them with contaminated meat for the traditional Sunday lunch of steak tartare.

Some of the critics complained about the high per capita income of Edmund's characters as compared with mine, but he wasn't trying to impress any more than I had made a political decision to keep my feet on the ground. Neither of us knew much about Aids in Africa, Aids in Romania, Aids in Edinburgh, Aids as experienced by women, children, needle-sharers. We didn't even try to cover the whole range of the epidemic.

My stories as much as Edmund's are necessarily concerned with the generation that once referred to a well-built man as having 'the body of death', the generation that wore – if only blushing and on holiday – T-shirts with the message SO MANY MEN . . . SO LITTLE TIME, before finding out that for so many men, there was so little time.

A more judicious criticism was that there was perversely little fear in our stories, Aids without fear being *Hamlet* without the Prince, without the court, without all rotten Denmark. Maybe so. Gay men learned to live with fear before other communities acquired that appalling knack. I hope at any rate that my stories are free of fatalism even when they refer to fate, that they belong, rather to a tradition of Stoicism – which I will better be able to advocate when I have spent some time in a library and mugged it properly up.

Even before the book was published, I had taken part in training days at hospitals, and read stories in the afternoon to nurses whose mornings had been filled with immunology and diagrams. It seemed strange to be turning 'Slim', say, into a performance, trying to delay the first laugh while also milking it. The first laugh establishes that an audience is having fun of some description but also makes it feel guilty, the matter of the story being so demonstrably serious.

But the experience also reminded me that the story had been a performance all along, so perhaps I shouldn't be embarrassed about the manipulative, even positively deceptive, element in fiction. Certainly the stories after the first batch, starting with 'Remission' (included in the second edition of *The Darker Proof*, 1988, along with a further story from Edmund), seem somehow less conscientious.

Willingness to write stories that are deceptive as much as educational has sharpened in turn my appetite for performing them. These days I have to be dissuaded from delivering the last third of 'The Changes of Those Terrible Years' as a party piece on all occasions. My voice takes on a Gielgud tremor, my eyes become worryingly damp.

All but one of the stories I wrote in this period were concerned with Aids, and even the single exception ('*Summer Lightning*') is included here. It was commissioned by the *Observer* for a summer fiction series: 'something to read on the beach' – that was the brief, or something like it. I set out to write something entirely lighthearted, but it didn't quite turn out that way. The story is offered here as a sort of entr'acte, and perhaps it says something about the first decade of Aids, not just my reaction to it, that lightness of heart could become so much a relative notion.

Aids is a theme that won't let go of me, or else I won't let go of it. It isn't really a question of social responsibility. How often does a writer not have to go looking for a subject, but more or less have to barricade his door against it? There is a sweetness here not cancelled out by the bitterness of the subject itself.

By now my reaction to the epidemic is inextricably bound up with the experience of writing about it. There is nothing new, of course, about a writer's confusion between the world of words and the world of things. Early on in the epidemic I noticed that I had bizarrely high standards for journalism on the subject. True, there was often an all-too-detectable bias or tendentiousness in the reporting, but it was more than that. Even if there were no obvious errors or distortions, I was dissatisfied. It was as if in my fantasy the perfect article about Aids would actually end the epidemic.

Now, though, I have practised a different sort of confusion on myself. I don't imagine that the perfect short story about Aids could do as much as raise a single person's T-cell count. It's rather that I think of my stories as parasites on a parasite. I have to admit, even, that when I read an optimistic newspaper item about treatment, vaccine or cure, I feel almost threatened.

Part of it is simply the sense of having been fooled before. There is also a particular pang involved, the sense that impending reprieve adds unbearably to recent casualties – to my losses, which I make stand in for the world's. A sort of super-futility attends the death of a soldier on the day armistice is signed. Won't the last wave of Aids deaths be the first forgotten? I imagine the Aids quilt with all its names being folded up and put away, as the victory fireworks shoot up the sky.

There's something obscene about this resistance to good news, but I can't help that. It may be, for one thing, that fear is not apparent in these stories because it has settled in the bone. It is a shattering prospect to think of being free of it. Having made an adjustment to unnatural conditions, the adapted organism rebels against a further set of changes. How much reprogramming can the circuits take?

It must also be that I am wishing to mothproof my personal Aids quilt, the imaginary embroidered panels reproduced here, to protect it from irrelevance and decay. This may not be a particularly desirable piece of literary property, but haven't I worked to secure it? It took long enough for me to be at home with such dark colours and sombre patterns. No wonder part of me, against human instinct, wants to hold on to a monopoly of these losses.

SLIM

I don't use that word. I've heard it enough. So I've taken it out of circulation, just here, just at home. I say Slim instead, and Buddy understands. I have got Slim.

When Buddy pays a visit, I have to remind myself not to offer him a cushion. Most people don't need cushions, they're just naturally covered. So I keep all the cushions to myself, now that I've lost my upholstery.

Slim is what they call it in Uganda, and it's a perfectly sensible name. You lose more weight than you thought was possible. You lose more weight than you could carry. Not that you feel like carrying anything. So I'll say to Buddy on one of his visits, Did you see the local news? There was an item about newt conservation, and then there was an item about funding Slim research. But newts first. What's it like talking to someone who's outranked by a newt?

Buddy just looks sheepish, which is probably best in the circumstances. Buddy would rather I avoided distressing information. He thinks I shouldn't read the papers, shouldn't upset myself. Even the doctors say that. If there was anything I should know, I'd hear it from them first anyway. Maybe. Yes, very likely. But whenever they try to protect me, I hear the little wheels on the bottom of the screens they put round you in a ward when you're really bad, and I'll do without that while I can.

Buddy's very good. That sounds suitably grudging. He tries to fit in with me. He doesn't flinch if I talk about my chances of making Slimmer of the Year. He's learned to say *blackcurrants*. He said 'lesions' just the once, but I told him it wasn't a very vivid use of language, and if he wasn't a doctor he had no business with it. Blackcurrants is much better, that being what they look like, good-sized blackcurrants on the surface of the skin, not sticking out far enough to be picked. So now, if the subject comes up, he asks about my blackcurrants, asks if any more blackcurrants have showed up.

I do my bit of adjusting too. Instinctively I think of him as a social worker, but I know he's not that. He's a volunteer attached to the Trust, and he's got no qualifications, so he can't be all bad. What he does is called *buddying*, and he's a buddy. And apparently in Trustspeak I'm a string of letters, which I don't remember except the first one's P and stands for person. Apparently they have to remind themselves. But I've decided if he can say Slim and blackcurrants to oblige me, I can meet him halfway and call him Buddy. Illness is making me quite the internationalist: an African infection and some dated American slang.

Buddy may not be qualified, but he's had his little bit of training. I remember him telling me, early on, that to understand what was happening to me perhaps I should think of having fifty years added to my age, or suddenly having Third World expectations instead of First. I suppose I've tried thinking that way. But now whenever I see those charity ads in the papers, the ones that tell you how for a few pounds you could adopt someone in India or the Philippines, I think that maybe I've been adopted by an African family, that – poor as they are – they are sending me what they can spare from their tainted food, their poisoned water, their little lifespans.

Except that I'm not young by African standards. Pushing forty, I'd be an elder of the tribe, pretty much, and the chances of my parents still being alive would be slight. So I should be grateful for their being around. They've followed me step by step, and now I suppose I take that for granted. But I didn't always. Before I first told them about myself, I pinched the family album, pinched it and had it photocopied. It cost me a fortune, and I don't know what I thought I wanted with a family album and no family, if it came to that. But at the time I thought, no sense in taking chances. Maybe if they'd lived nearer London, if I'd seen them more regularly, it wouldn't have seemed such a big risk. I don't know.

My African family doesn't have the money for photographs. My African family may never even have seen a photograph.

I've been careful not to mention my adoption fantasy to Buddy. No point in worrying him. And, touch wood, I haven't cried while he's been around. That's partly because I've learned to set time aside for such an important function. I've learned that there is a yoga of tears. There are the clever tears that release a lot in a little time, and the stupid tears that just shake you and don't let you go. Once your shoulders get in on the act, you're sunk. The trick is to keep them out of it. Otherwise you end up wailing all day. Those kind of tears are very more-ish. Bet you can't cry just one, just ten, just twenty. But if I keep my shoulders still I can reach a much deeper level of tears. It's like a lumbar puncture. I can draw out this fluid which is a fantastic concentrate of misery. And then just stop and be calm.

I used to cry to opera, Puccini mostly. Don't laugh. I thought the best soundtrack was tunes, tunes and more tunes. But now I cry mainly to a record I never used to listen to much, and don't particularly remember buying: *Southern Soul Belles*, on the Charly label. I find records far more trouble to put on than my opera cassettes, but *Southern Soul Belles* is worth it. It has a very garish cover, a graphic of a sixties soul singer with a purple face, for some reason, so that she looks like an aubergine with a beehive hairdo. The trouble with the Puccini was that you could hear the voices, but never the lungs. On *Southern Soul Belles* you hear the lungs. When Doris Allen sings 'A Shell of a Woman', you know that she could just open her mouth and blast any man out of the door. Shell she may be, breathless she ain't. There's a picture of her on the back cover. She's fat and sassy. She could spare all the weight I've lost. Just shrug it off. Her lungs must be real bellows of meat, not like the pair of wrinkled socks I seem to get my air through these days.

I treat myself to *Southern Soul Belles* every other day or so. I've learned to economize. Illness has no entry qualifications. Did I say that already? But being ill – if you're going to be serious about it – demands a technique. The other day I found I was writing a cheque. I could hardly lift the pen, it wasn't a good day, not like today. But I was writing everything out in full. No numerals, no abbreviations. Twenty-one pounds and thirty-four pence only. Only! I almost laughed when I saw that *only*. I realized that ever since my first cheque book, when I was sixteen, I've always written my cheques out in full, as if all the crooked bank-clerks in the world were waiting for their chance to defraud me. Never again. It's the minimum from now on. If I could have right now all the energy I've wasted writing every word on my cheques, I could have some normal days, normal weeks.

One of the things I'm supposed to be doing these days is creative visualization, you know, where you imagine your white corpuscles strapping on their armour to repel invaders. Buddy doesn't nag, but I can tell he's disappointed. I don't seem to be able to do it. I get as far as imagining my white corpuscles as a sort of cloud of healthiness, like a milkshake in the dark flow of my blood, but if I try to visualize them any more concretely I think of Raquel Welch, in *Fantastic Voyage*. That's the film where they shrink a submarine full of doctors and inject it into a dying man's bloodstream. He's the president or something. And at one point Raquel Welch gets attacked and almost killed by white corpuscles, they're like strips of plastic – when I think of it, they *are* strips of plastic – that stick to her wetsuit until she can't breathe. The others have to snap them off one by one when they get her back to the submarine. It's touch and go. So I don't think creative visualization will work for me. It's not a very promising therapeutic tool, if every time I try to imagine my body's defences I think of their trying to kill Raquel Welch. I still can't persuade myself the corpuscles are the good guys.

One thing I find I can visualize is a ration book. That's how I make sure I don't get overtired. Over-overtired. I suppose my mother had a ration book before I was born. I don't think I've ever seen one. But I imagine a booklet with coupons in it for you to tear out, only instead of an allowance for the week of butter or cheese or sugar, my coupons say One Hour of Social Life, One Shopping Expedition, One Short Walk. I hoard them, and I spend them wisely. I tear them out slowly, separating the perforations one by one.

In a way, though, it's not that I don't have energy, it's just the wrong kind. My head may be muzzy but my body is fizzing. I suppose that's the steroids. But I feel like an electric razor that's been plugged into the wrong socket, I'm buzzing and buzzing but I'm not doing any work. It's so odd having sat at home all day, when your body tells you you've been dancing all night in a nightclub, just drinking enough lager to keep the sweat coming, and you're about to drive home with all the windows down, smelling your own sweat. And sleep.

I can't work. That should be pretty clear. But I've been lucky. I'm on extended sick leave for a while yet, and everybody's been very good. I said I had cancer, which I do and I don't, I mean I do but that isn't the problem, and while I was saying *cancer* I thought, All the time my Gran was ill we never once said *cancer*, but now cancer is a soft word I am hiding behind and I feel almost guilty to be sparing myself. Suddenly *cancer* had the sound of 'interesting condition' or 'unmentionables'. I was curling up in the word's soft shade, soothed gratefully by cancer's lullaby. Cancer. What a relief. Cancer. Oh, that's all right. Cancer. That I can live with.

Sometimes I'm asleep when Buddy visits. Sleep is the one thing that keeps its value. He presses the buzzer on the entry-phone, and if I haven't answered in about ten seconds he buzzes again. I know the entry-phone is a bit ramshackle and you can't hear from the doorway whether it's working or not, but when Buddy buzzes twice it drives me frantic. I don't need to be reminded that I'm not living at a very dynamic tempo right now. I'll tick him off one of these days, tear off a coupon and splurge some energy.

Then Buddy comes pounding up the stairs. Sometimes he

smells of chlorine and his hair's still damp from swimming, but I suppose it's a bit much to ask him to slow down, to dry off properly and use cologne before he comes to see me, just so I don't feel bruised by his health. I'll bet his white corpuscles don't need a pep talk. Crack troops, no doubt about it. I'll bet he drinks Carling Black Label.

I watch too much television. Television isn't on the ration.

Buddy's breaking in new shoes, which creak. Why would anyone crucify his feet in the name of style – assuming liver-coloured Doc Martens are stylish in some way – when comfortable training shoes are readily available almost everywhere? It's a great mystery.

Buddy likes to hug. I don't. I mean, it's perfectly pleasant, it just doesn't remind me of anything. It was never my style. I'm sure the point is to relieve my flesh of taboo, and the Trust probably gives classes in it. But when Buddy bends over me, I just wait for him to be done, as if he was a cloud and I was waiting for him to pass over the sun. Then we carry on, and I'm sure he feels better for it.

He's still got a bruise above the crook of his elbow, from his Hepatitis B jab. I really surprised myself over that. I wasn't very rational. He wasn't sure whether to have it done or not, and I almost screamed at him *Do it! Get it done!* If I'd had a needle handy I'd have injected him myself, and I don't think getting my own back was my only motive. I remember Hep B. That was when illness came up and asked me what I was doing for the rest of my life. That was before there was even a vaccine.

The back of his neck is something I tend to notice when Buddy visits. It always looks freshly shaved. He must have a haircut every week or so, every couple of weeks anyway. As if he would feel neglected unless he was being groomed at regular intervals. Neglect is what I dream of. I long for the doctors to find me boring, to give me one almighty pill and say Next please. But my case history seems to be unputdownable. A real thriller.

My grooming standards are way below Buddy's, but perhaps they always were. There's not a lot I can do about that now. If the

Princess of Wales was coming to pay me a visit, if she was coming to lay her cool hand on my forehead, stifling her natural desire to say Oh Yuk – I'm with you there, Di – I might even trim my fingernails. But not for Buddy. Fingernails are funny. They're the only part of my body that seems to be flourishing under the new regime. They grow like mad. But the Princess of Wales isn't coming any time soon. I happen to know that now, now as we speak, she's opening a new ward in a newt hospital. A new *wing*.

I think I'm entitled to a home help. I believe that's one of the perks. But I'd rather go on as I am. Buddy told me a story about a man he visited for the Trust – I'm sure he's recovered by now, ha ha – whose mother was jealous of his home help. Just for that, she said, just for Slim?

I couldn't believe it. I'm still not sure I believe it. But then Buddy explained that the mother was eighty-five, and when her son started saying, Sometimes I feel better but I never feel well, she must have thought, What else have I been saying all these years, fat lot of attention you gave me.

I think Buddy was making again the valuable point that getting Slim only involves being exiled from the young, the well, the real.

Buddy is always offering to wash up, but I'm happier when I don't let him. He doesn't do a great deal to help me, in practical terms, anyway. Tessa next door changes my sheets and does my washing, and Susannah still expects to hear my dreams, even the grim ones. It was Susannah who first suggested Buddy. She felt I was cutting myself off from real kin, that even if I was saying the same unanswerable things, Buddy would return a different echo. I even suppose she's right. I've earned my friends, but Buddy I seem to have inherited, though God knows from whom, and whether he served them well.

I sometimes talk to Buddy as if he was the whole Trust gathered in one person. I'll say, My father says you're not reaching him. Why are your collection-boxes massed in London? Why do you insist on appealing to an in-crowd?

But then I let him off the hook and say, Mind you, my mother thinks that anyone collecting for Slim research in Eastbourne or

Leamington would get a few swift strokes from a rubber-tipped cane, if nothing worse. And my father chooses to give love and money direct.

Cutting out the middleman, says Buddy. He smiles. He doesn't have a Trust collecting box, of course. I'm not sure I've ever seen one. In fact, on this visit he's brought me a package. It's in a plastic bag, and it seems to be a foil container with a cardboard lid, and foil crimped down around it. I'm very much afraid it's food.

I've fed Buddy once or twice, used a shopping voucher and prepared a simple but exhausting lunch. Those times it has seemed to me that Buddy eats suspiciously little. I mean, he eats more than I do, he couldn't not. And I'm not the best judge of healthy habits. But somehow I expect an earthier appetite. It's certainly true that a little company at table can make me eat more than I usually do, without even noticing, while any sort of greed will inevitably sicken my stomach. So does that mean Buddy is obeying another mysterious Trust directive, and suppressing his true eating self? Perhaps he filled up with food before he came, or perhaps he's going to dive round the corner the moment he leaves, and into a burger bar. Before he leaves I open my mouth to say, Here's some money for your real lunch, but I manage to close it in time.

And now he's returning my hospitality. Go on, he says. Open it. You don't have to eat it now. It'll keep good for a few days. Not that it contains any preservatives.

He has written a few deprecating comments about his cooking on the lid of the container. There's no wishing it away. I edge up the rim of the foil and see inside a startlingly pure green. On the green lies a row of small cigars.

Fresh lamb sausages, he explains, with mint and parsley, on a bed of green pea purée. An old family recipe, that appeared quite by chance in last week's *Radio Times*.

I lower my nose over the container and breathe in the smell, trying to think that it is a bouquet of flowers that I must express thanks for, from someone I like and want nothing to do with, rather than a plateful of food that will stiffen in the fridge unless I am stupid enough to eat it, in which case I will most likely be sick.

Thanks. Can you put it in the fridge for me?

But Buddy has more to say about his choice of recipe. They're skinless, he says. I thought that would be easiest for you.

He's right, of course, with my teeth the way they are now. But I'm sure I haven't complained, I'm sure I haven't moaned to him. Perhaps my habit of dipping biscuits in my tea – not to be looked for in a man of my class – is a dead giveaway to a seasoned Trust volunteer. Next time I feel the need to dunk a digestive I'll be more discreet. I'll do my dunking behind closed doors.

The doctors are trying to save my teeth at the moment, and the last time I went to pick up some prescriptions they were being altogether too merry, it seemed to me, about the dosage that would do the trick; 200 mg, one of them was saying, that sounds about right. And the other one said, Yeeeees, in a kind of drawl, as if it wasn't worth the trouble to look it up.

Buddy is still expecting something from me. Thanks, I say again. That looks very nice. Yum yum.

Kid gloves are better than surgical gloves. Perhaps I should say that to him. That would give him some job satisfaction. I'm sure that's important.

Buddy puts his present in the fridge and heads for the door. He stops with his hand on the handle and asks me if there's anything I want, says if I think of anything I should phone him, any time. He always does this on his way out, and I suppose he's apologizing for being well and for being free to go and for being free to help or not as he chooses. There is nothing I want.

He clatters down the stairs. I remind myself that he clattered up them, so there is no reason to think he is moving as fast as he can and is planning to put a lot of space between me and him, now that his tour of duty is over.

I could check, of course, if I move to the window. I could settle my mind. I could see whether he skips along the road to the Tube, or whether he's too drained to do more than shamble. Maybe a trouble shared is a trouble doubled.

I try to resist the temptation to go to the window, but these days it's not often that I have an impulse that I can satisfy without asking myself whether I can afford what it will cost me. So I give in.

Buddy is moving methodically down the street, not rushing but not dawdling either, planting his feet with care like a man walking into a wind. I know that when I tear out and spend one of my shopping coupons and go out on to that street, I look like a man walking into a wind tunnel. I can see it in the way people look at me.

I look down on Buddy as he walks to the Tube. In the open air the mystique of his health dissipates, as he merges with other ordinary healthy people. No one in the street seems to be looking at him, but I follow him with my eyes. There is something dogged about him that I resent as well as admire, a dull determination to go on and on, as if he was an ambulance-chaser condemned always to follow on foot, watching as the blue lights fade in the distance.

*A*n *E*xecutor

Of course the flat was empty. Gareth made noise on the stairs and crunched the key harshly into the lock, as if he had just bought the flat, and wanted the lock to know all about it. No one on a simple errand, no one who felt that his right to be there would go uncontested, would go to such trouble to avoid seeming furtive.

His business was with the bedroom, but he turned lights on in the flat generally, so that the lighting pattern as seen from the street would express matter-of-fact occupation, rather than a late-night lightning raid on an intimate chamber.

It was unlikely that anyone was looking at the building, which was in poor condition and had an untenanted air. When in recent months an old friend of Charles, full of good wishes but not quite brave enough for a visit, sent a bunch of flowers instead, the delivery squad returned the bouquet to Interflora, saying that a mistake had been made: the property was derelict. Charles passed this story on almost with amusement. He was spared the irony of physical decline in immaculate surroundings.

Gareth made a tour of the flat, putting off his errand. He was used to running errands: that was one of the reasons he had been installed in Charles's life. But this errand was a little different. The rooms looked unfamiliar with the central lights on; Charles had favoured softer lighting, from table lamps fitted with bulbs of modest wattage.

The sofa was still overlaid with a laminated tablecloth, for the benefit of Charles's cat Leopold. Charles had become expert at what he called 'riding the symptoms', blotting out all the reasons for misery and concentrating on something he was looking forward to, even if it was only a broadcast on Radio 3, two days distant, that he was planning to record on tape. He could keep depression at bay on his own account, but he couldn't extend the same service to Leopold, who responded to negative emotion by pissing on the sofa. So Charles would prepare for bad patches by covering the sofa with a waterproof tablecloth, and Gareth had learned that the placement of the tablecloth was the best indicator – indirect as it was – of Charles's state of mind.

The more orthodox place for Leopold's toilet was a long wooden tray, like a shallow unpartitioned knife-box, that fitted into a recess just inside the kitchen door. Gareth glanced at it. The shavings of impregnated wood that filled it were still swollen with urine, although Leopold had already been in Haywards Heath for a few nights, with neighbours of Charles's parents, where by Christmas – Gareth couldn't help imagining – his name would have been simplified or changed altogether.

Leopold's routine with his box was to climb regally in and turn right round – he was no small cat, and the manoeuvre was far from simple – so as to face the room. Being so near to the kitchen door, he could in fact be seen from most of the sitting-room. Charles would always stop what he was doing, even if he was in mid-sentence or on the phone, and lock eyes with Leopold. Excretion in cats involves the hoisting of the tail and the adopting of an intellectual expression. Charles, who found even the word 'cat' consoling and would sometimes say it a number of times in a row, got pleasure from watching Leopold at his business. Leopold's blink rate accelerated a fraction, but he showed no other sign of self-consciousness. He never failed to turn round again, through a full circle, to survey the reeking wood scrolls, with the calm of a master diplomat – a diplomat retaining his composure when served with a hideous local delicacy. Then he left the box, with just the token backward paw-scrape in passing of an indoor cat, who has never in his life had to regard the burying of waste as a serious feline project.

Gareth wondered why Charles took such pleasure in spying on

Leopold's visits to his box; perhaps because this was his pet's nearest approach in the day to a moment of embarrassment. If shame got no purchase on Leopold then, it never would.

Even the most earthbound moments of Leopold's day took place on a plateau of calm self-absorption that Charles was unlikely, in his day, to achieve, however rich the pickings on Radio 3. Gareth hoped this thought never occurred to him while he watched his cat at squat, blinking slowly back at him. But envy must have been a factor in his watching, since the contrast between Leopold's unforced motions and Charles's own, which called for a large plastic bag full of dressings from Clinic every fortnight, was very great.

Moving from that corner of the kitchen, Gareth had an urge to inspect the freezer compartment of Charles's fridge. He had set himself the task of clearing it out about a month previously, and had to to work with his fingers, with a knife, and finally, without much more success, with fingers, knives and a kettle. It was not the simple enterprise it had seemed at the beginning. He had suggested it because it seemed less servile than doing the washing-up, which Charles apparently found embarrassing and which in any case only amounted, these days, to a couple of cups and small plates. Cleaning out the freezer compartment was a more ambitious programme, but one that ran no risk of imprinting his personality on the kitchen in a way that Charles might find jarring.

It might even stimulate Charles's hunger to have the various freezer treats and Lean Cuisine delicacies that friends had brought him liberated from their moraine of crusted ice, where they looked as appetizing as mammoths in a glacier. Gareth brewed a pot of tea and started work, kneeling in the cramped space of the kitchen.

Leopold started pestering him from the moment he opened the fridge. Leopold could grasp the idea of food, and even the idea of food-not-his, but the idea of removing food from a box and returning it a few minutes later was clearly beyond him. Charles moved a chair to the corner of the kitchen and sat there with

Leopold held in his lap, but Leopold wouldn't stop squirming, with a violent patience that suggested he was being gentle with his master, now that their strengths were so nearly equal.

In the end Charles took him to the window and pushed him out on to the window-box, lowering the window to leave only a crack open, through which Leopold tried to thrust his head until the skin of his face was pulled back, and his eyes were turned into vertical stripes hidden among his other markings.

Some of the ice in the freezer compartment was granular, as if it had formed from frost, while other compartments – particularly between the top of the freezer compartment and the fridge proper – were clear and smooth. Neither type was particularly easy to dislodge, though the granular was attractive while he worked away at the smooth, and the smooth held the promise of a sudden breakthrough, a major yielding of encrustation, which seemed unlikely while he was scraping at the granular.

Watching Charles slumped in his chair, even without Leopold's tiring presence, Gareth knew he was longing for the bed. His bed was the natural home for the day's troughs: sitting in a chair was peak activity, not to be sustained beyond a short period. Gareth fell back for a moment from his relationship with Charles into routine, into pity, until he was recalled by the intervention of his knees, which were hurting, and of his hands, which were numb with cold where he hadn't burnt them on the kettle. He himself was dying for a sit-down, and would look with favour on any proposal that entailed slumping on a bed.

He prepared to make the suggestion himself, but a minor breakthrough in the ice-face forestalled him. A cylindrical fragment of ice from near the back came free. Then he saw that it was a small vial, of something that remained perversely liquid even at these temperatures. The label was bleached and faded as well as encrusted with ice, but the name of the product seemed to include a stylized lightning bolt. He looked enquiringly at Charles, who chose that moment to gather himself for the walk to the bed, without meeting his eyes.

The phone rang, and at that point Charles did look round, to signal his unwillingness to answer it. Gareth thrust the little bottle back in the freezer compartment, and picked up the phone.

At one stage, Charles had taken to letting the phone ring, or unplugging it from the wall. His parents had accepted this practice meekly enough, but his friends had overruled it. Phoning each other up for news, they touched up their worry until it became chronic. Then one of them would volunteer, or be deputed, to call on him at the flat. Charles was encouraged to feel that cutting himself off from those with a claim on him was a permissible stratagem for the worst hour of a bad day, but not for a bad day in its entirety.

Having Gareth screen his calls, when the phone rang during one of his visits, was a luxury that even Charles's friends would be prepared to accept. In practice, though, however much he shrank from the phone when it rang, he always interrupted Gareth's mumbled explanation that he didn't feel up to talking. He would reach across for the receiver and start to speak with a tiny new access of energy.

The voice on the phone this time was rich and smooth. The phrase *rich and dark, like the Aga Khan* arrived in Gareth's mind: he had seen it on an old advertisement in an antique shop, used to promote Marmite or Oxo or Bovril. The voice said only, but with an immense confidence, 'Charles?'

'Who is this please?' asked Gareth. 'Charles doesn't feel like talking.' He was already passing the receiver across, anticipating Charles' little ritual of refusal, then acceptance of the social world. The instrument was between them when the caller announced his name: 'Andrew Gould'.

Charles gave a tight shake of the head, and finished his interrupted journey to the bed. Gareth, caught by surprise at a time when he thought his switchboard duties were over, stumbled through the rest of the message. He promised that Charles would call back when he was feeling better, and hung up.

Charles was now wrapped up in his colourful coverlet, rummaging through a drawer that lived on the floor by the bed, where he kept his collection of cassettes. Gareth knew he should resume his assault on the freezer compartment, but found himself putting it off. He knew that just by sitting there he was silently pressing Charles for comment.

'Shall I let Leopold in?' he asked. The cat was still intermittently trying to squeeze himself into the room.

'Yes, do,' said Charles. Leopold streaked in, but showed no interest in the kitchen. Instead he hopped up on to the bed, and settled in the crook of Charles's knee.

Charles continued to clatter through the cassettes with his fingers. 'Andrew has been away. Not far away, but far enough. In prison in fact. You may have read about him in the Sundays a while back. They put him away for dealing drugs, but he seems to have carried right on. That's what the papers said, anyway. But he's out now.' He held a cassette up, to read its label. 'I broke off with him, years ago now. Wrote him a very sensible letter. For once. Even I could see he was bad news, utterly bad news. So I told him it just wasn't my style of suicide.' He clicked the cassette into the lolling mouth of the cassette player and pressed the button to play it.

'So will you phone him back?'

'Probably.' He leant back against the pillows, lifting Leopold up in a sort of momentary hammock of blankets. Leopold put his claws out for safety, but withdrew them when he was returned to bed level. 'Otherwise he'll only phone back. And I expect he needs help. He always needed help, come to that, help hot and strong, help here and now. But now he may really need it.' He gave a small smile. 'Put it this way. If the virus has missed out on him, it's missed a great opportunity.' A soft wall of music built up behind him. 'And that seems out of character.'

Gareth had not resumed work on the fridge that day; but now he took another look at the freezer compartment. The futile food was still there; ice had grown back to shroud the packets. He reached towards the back, and pulled out the little flask. It was stuck to the back wall, and brought a little ice away with it. He held it up to the light, and shook it gently. There seemed to him something actually obscene about its liquidity at this low temperature, its continued willingness to vapourize if its stopper were pulled, its frozen obedience to desires that had long since, themselves, evaporated.

He had put off his errand long enough. He turned off the lights in the kitchen and the sitting-room, and entered the bedroom. He tried to remember the exact words of Charles's instructions. He was to remove what Charles had described, using a wry all-purpose comic tone that would have done at a pinch for reproducing a Monty Python sketch or a Goons routine, a Gumby or a Bloodnok, as 'kinky relics'. The idea was to spare Charles's mother, the most likely person to clear up Charles's possessions. Responding to Charles's request, Gareth had to stop himself, there in the hospital, from using the posthumous word 'effects'.

Charles had made these stipulations not as it turned out on his final visit to hospital, but at a time when he had the first bodily conviction of death not far off. Gareth had noted down his instructions, and was all set to carry them out the next morning when Charles telephoned, having rallied in the night to an extraordinary extent. He was discharging himself, and wanted Gareth to contact his mother, who should now visit the flat rather than the ward. She should of course bring Leopold back from his exile.

In his instructions on that occasion, Charles had mentioned a leather waistcoat and some chaps, the leather overtrousers zipping up the inside leg that American motorcyclists had adapted from cowboys, and had had borrowed from them in their turn. There were also two pairs of leather trousers, one of which could be exonerated in the name of fashion. The other, of inferior hide and with a large rip at the knee, had to go. In Charles's sock drawer was a cap that would, apparently, break a mother's heart if found there.

He felt, as he approached the bedroom at last, more guilt even than grief. He felt, too, like a case history from Krafft-Ebing: *Deflections of the Amorous Impulse, Appendix I. A Fetish Burglar.* Perhaps Charles had removed the things himself on his last return from hospital. That would make life a little easier for

Gareth, though he could hardly visualize Charles in his weakness making the journey down three flights of stairs, laden with hides, and taking them to a skip, however near to home.

The waistcoat was easy to find in the wardrobe, and the chaps, neatly arranged on a hanger, were unmistakable. Did people say, a *pair* of chaps? Certainly they said a pair of kippers, and that was what the chaps really resembled. They looked filleted, as if they would need to be reconstituted in some way – soaked overnight, say – before they would be of any use. Without legs to fill them out, they looked peculiarly useless and desiccated. They didn't even have the familiar hang of trousers in repose.

Gareth slid them off the hanger and tucked them into his saddle-bag – he had come well equipped – next to the waistcoat. On the next hanger along in the wardrobe were the two pairs of leather trousers. He had no difficulty in discriminating between them, restoring the innocent pair to the rail in the wardrobe and tucking the guilty ones away in his bag.

There only remained the sock drawer and the hat. He located the sock drawer after a couple of false starts, but nothing lurid leapt to the eye. It seemed like an ordinary crate of bananas, he thought unsteadily, no tarantulas anywhere. Some of the socks were stridently coloured and others were widowed, but that was the worst thing you could say about the sock drawer. Then a little rummaging dislodged two caps that had been tucked away at the back.

One of them was a tall little cap with a downward-tilted peak, made of a grey felt-like material and modelled on the Confederate uniform cap from the American Civil War. What erotic message might this be sending? The other was of a black shiny material, but more like plastic than leather. In shape it was like a postman's cap, or a traffic warden's. If it had been severely plain, or else adorned with chains or some barbarian insignia, Gareth would have felt confident that this was the object that Charles's mother must not find. But round the brim, every few inches, were little polyhedral buttons that seemed – the light in the bedroom was not good – to be made of translucent red and yellow plastic. These seemed to put it out of the sexual running. It seemed hardly likely that Charles would invest in something so cheap-looking; Gareth remembered him saying that the chaps came from New York, and were good of their kind. But perhaps the second cap's aphrodisiac aura was profound, unaffected by the tackiness of its materials.

Only for a moment did he think of taking them both. That would have been exceeding his instructions, and it somehow seemed important not to take anything unnecessarily away from this bedroom, which was suddenly becoming a museum. He could see, here on a chair, a shirt of his that he had given to Charles, neatly folded and probably never worn by him. Gareth liked the shirt, had talked himself into parting with it on the grounds that its sleeves were too short, but would gladly have gone on wearing it in all weathers with the sleeves rolled up. It had probably been fingered by Charles only for a few moments since Gareth had washed it and handed it over, but it had passed absolutely into Charles's possession. It didn't occur to Gareth to reclaim it.

Likewise in the sitting-room he had seen not one but several books he had lent to Charles. They had been announced as loans and not as gifts, but he couldn't imagine taking them away, not just the one with the bookmark tucked in it, but any of them. Although these rooms would soon be cleared out, perhaps in a matter of days, everything in them was becoming somehow definitive.

He hesitated still between the hats. Then he noticed something else tucked away in the drawer. It was a wallet of scuffed black leather, with a zipped compartment for change, on a chain that ended in the sort of spring-loaded clip that the belt-loops on Levi's 501s seemed to feel incomplete without. On the front of the wallet was an emblem in macho embroidery, a yellow-winged eagle with a yellow scroll above it, reading HARLEY-DAVIDSON. He picked it up and unzipped the change compartment. Inside were a receipt from a building society's automatic cash-till and the ticket stub from a dry cleaner's.

This biker wallet was in some way exempt from the embargo that lay over the rest of the flat. Gareth felt free to take it away with him, although he had no real expectation of using it. He didn't tell himself that it was something that might upset Charles's mother; it would do no such thing. In its unfamiliarity it had none of the power to hurt her possessed by Charles's oldest, tattiest shirt. In a sense it belonged with the leather clothes, but they at least had been chosen, or even made, to fit Charles; this had no similar link. They were sombre in their pretensions to masculinity; this was simply preposterous. It was an object designed for rough times and the open road, but destined for a succession of sock drawers, Charles's and now Gareth's, with occasional expeditions to the shops in the high street, and no likelihood of ever coming near a motorcycle.

He came to a decision about the hats. The balance of probability implicated the black cap in sexuality, and cleared the grey. He put the black one in his bag, slipped the wallet into the pocket of his coat, and returned the grey cap to the sock drawer.

Then he remembered a further item of instructions. He was to remove a volume of pornography, which lived under something Indian in the sitting-room. That was all he could remember, the words 'under' and 'Indian'. Under an Indian print? Under an Indian book? He couldn't be sure. At the time he had been too busy making Charles's requests seem ordinary to pay the necessary attention. He had said, in a worldly way, 'It's a brave man who goes on a long journey without destroying his pornography.' The moment he said it, he had realized that it had the ring of a morbid fortune cookie, and he tried to think of ways to take it back, or to transform it into some other kind of statement. But Charles seemed unaffected. Gareth thought that perhaps only people on the skin of misfortune can be encouraged to forget or be brutally reminded, spared by tact or pained by tactlessness. Charles was well below the surface.

There seemed to be nothing Indian in the sitting-room at all. There was only a limited number of things for an object to be placed under, come to that, and he looked under them all. He hoped that Charles had disposed of the book himself, during his last days in the flat, or else that the hiding-place would be as impenetrable to everybody else as it was to him. This failure to complete his mission made him nervously unwilling to leave. He was able to get moving at last only because his bladder was asking him to urinate, and using Charles's lavatory would have been obscurely a trespass. He turned the lights out, and stumbled down the stairs in darkness. Then the thought came to him that one of the *rugs* in the sitting-room might be Indian. It seemed unlikely that there was anything underneath them, but he had to go back and check, whatever his bladder had to say about it.

The rugs might well have been Indian, but were concealing nothing but dust and cat hairs. By now the demands of his bladder were insistent, and overrode his qualms about using Charles's lavatory.

Yet he was right to be reluctant: he had been able to foresee the other rooms, and prepare himself for Charles's absence from them. The lavatory hadn't entered into his calculations. He was always on his own in that room, after all, so there was no reason to expect any special sting of absence to be felt there.

Once inside the lavatory he was able to keep his eyes away from Charles's last massive issue of dressings, but there were limits to his self-discipline. He couldn't help expecting the noise of the flush, as it died slowly away, to be replaced by the continuity that Charles borrowed for his life, as it faltered, from the radio. He found himself listening out for an aria, a sonata, or at least a sonorous précis of the events of Act III. He had braced himself to face absence in the rest of the house, but not to have absence sneak up on him here.

After this small fresh climax of loss, he trotted down the stairs with relief, and without any more nagging thoughts about failing exactly to obey Charles's instructions. He had done everything he could. In fact as he left the flat and turned his thoughts to his new destination, a wholly different set of feelings and expectations cut in. He wasn't satisfied, exactly, with what he'd managed to do in the flat, but it was behind him now, and he found himself becoming for a short time at least an altogether more purposeful person, although his errand for Charles was over. Now he was on a different style of errand, one that filled him with a certain anaesthetized confidence.

A taxi was passing the entrance of the building as he emerged from it, and he hailed it. He would not have been particularly surprised if a taxi had been waiting for him at the foot of the steps, the driver patiently reading an evening paper.

He gave the name of a hospital which contained a ward not in theory given over to a particular illness. The secret was not particularly well kept. Children on the main road outside would shout, 'Fifth floor! Fifth floor!' at suitable men visiting the hospital, in hopes of being rewarded with a grown-up's mysterious tears.

In the taxi, he relaxed. He had no fears of being late. He had the strong feeling that nothing could happen without him at the hospital. However unwillingly, he was deputizing, and his authority though borrowed and temporary was real.

He made his way directly to the ward. For once the lift was waiting on the ground floor, and contained no wheelchairs or wheeled baskets of linen. On the fifth floor there was, as always, a notice requesting visitors to ring the bell and wait to be met by a member of staff, but he ignored it. Tonight he could not imagine being challenged. There had been a recent hardening of attitude among the staff, since the popular press had discovered that this floor of the hospital was not a ward at all, but a unique horizontal mine of horror stories, all of them with morals. The patients' notes were no longer hung outside the doors of the rooms, but on the ends of the beds. There was a chance that even the most public-spirited reporters could be deflected, if they had to penetrate the rooms in order to riffle through the notes at the foot of the beds. But tonight Gareth couldn't imagine being challenged, even if no one who knew him was on duty.

He looked through the glass window in the door of Charles's room before he entered. Charles's mother, he could see, was sitting at the side of the bed. She was leaning forward and

30

seemed to be offering her son a last flower, from which, eyes closed and with only the most sluggish movement, he was turning away his head.

Charles had always complained about her failure to grasp the concept of 'treats'. Illness had separated him into two distinct bands of personality, as if illness were a centrifuge and Charles a hitherto cloudy solution. He was now a child who understood affection best in terms of presents, as well as a sophisticated adult, with an adult's full-sized contempt and impatience, who knew the child better than anyone else.

Charles had forfeited the idea of pleasure except as episodic, and needed to have emotion properly dramatized in objects. His mother, however, came on her visits to the flat and to the hospital empty-handed, while he hinted with increasing crudity that she could do better. Finally he had sent her down in tears to the hospital shop, to buy something, anything, a potted plant, if she was to have any prospect of exchanging another word with him. After that she performed better as a bringer of trivial gifts.

Only with a great effort of will had Gareth been able to stop himself from bringing presents, but his overriding priority was a different one. He needed to keep himself in a category separate from friendship.

Gareth entered the room and tucked his bag away carefully in a corner, unnecessarily concerned to make sure it didn't tip over and spill its contents. At this range he could see that the object in Mrs Hartly's hand was an oxygen mask, though he hadn't been mistaken in thinking that Charles was slowly turning away from it. She would follow him with it as he turned, until he arrived at the end of his neck's reach and turned back towards her again. Then she would follow his head with the mask as it moved slowly back towards her. Charles's gesture much impressed Gareth, being both instinctive and opposed to survival. It seemed to show a sort of vegetable will, as though a flower was turning consistently away from the sun.

Gareth was acutely aware that Charles was badly shaved, with crumbs of stubble in some areas of his face and sore-looking patches elsewhere, and that this bad shave was his doing. It had been the first and last time he had shaved Charles, the day before. As a wet shaver himself, he had failed to get the measure of Charles' electric razor. He had failed too, or so he assumed, to give Charles a sense of himself as groomed.

Charles's mother turned her head to see Gareth, without loosening her grip on the oxygen mask, and without any real change in expression. She reacted as if he was returning after a short absence; she incorporated him directly in her preoccupations. 'He won't wear this,' she said submissively, indicating the oxygen mask. 'He won't keep it on his face. I put the loops round his ears, but he just shakes it loose.' She seemed to be asking for guidance.

Gareth felt uncomfortable with any approximation to the role of adviser, since he would not have enjoyed having her hear the advice he had tendered to Charles over recent months – not advice as such but cumulative suggestions, hints that Charles should keep an open mind on some issues (but only in a certain way).

He had detected in Charles a suppressed desire, which every fumbling phone call from his mother brought nearer the surface, to backslide into reconciliation with his family. He was not especially estranged from them in the first place, as such things go, but illness seemed to bring with it a growing temptation to relapse into absolution. People whose ill health could be guaranteed not to dissipate entered a special category so far as their loved ones were concerned, in which without ever apologizing they were forgiven, as if repentance was actually a stage of physical collapse.

Quietly Gareth had opposed this programme. He had pressed Charles to resist a creeping amnesty which came into effect without even being announced. A person with limited energy owed none of it to anyone. Playing Camille was an exhausting role; only a healthy person should attempt it. Being Camille was something else again, and no audience was entitled to watch.

He had kept chipping away with these arguments from day to

day, and when Charles finally said, without actual prompting, that he couldn't help having a child's mobility, and a child's strength, but it would be a nonsense to aim at a child's submissiveness as well, Gareth had felt enormous relief.

There was quite enough presumption, he now felt, in the part he had played. He found it impossible, now, to imagine intervening between the two people in the room with him. If he had committed the impertinence of interfering with someone's destiny, perhaps that was only because he was well placed to do it. He had better not compound the impertinence by seeking to advise Charles's mother. He leant over, all the same, to hear her better. He decided that she was speaking so softly in order not to be heard, not by Charles – that must surely be an extinct fantasy – but by the nurses. He found it hard to read her expression, since he had only seen her in extremity and had no idea how she functioned in real life.

'They said he's chain-stoking,' she said. 'What can that mean?'

'It's a type of breathing.' Above the faint hiss of the oxygen mask and its compressor, he could hear a rasping of irregular breath.

'Well, what has it got to do with chains or stoking? At first I thought they said *chain-smoking*, and I almost laughed. Because he never has. As you know.'

Gareth had a reflexive impulse to correct her by rephrasing her statement in a more appropriate tense – 'No, I know he never did' – but fought it successfully. 'I think perhaps it's someone's name,' he said. 'Chain-Stokes. Or perhaps it's two people's names. Chain and Stokes.'

'You wouldn't think it'd take two people to hear someone breathing, would you?'

'No, not even if they're doctors.'

Mrs Hartly winced. She seemed to be upset by the implication that Gareth had found in her joke, that doctors were not necessarily superior beings. He felt the need to backtrack. 'It's a particular sort of breathing.'

33

'Yes, I can hear that,' she said. She was slow to take his comment as placatory.

'It means there's not far to go,' he said, as gently as he could.

She was quick to take this comment as inflammatory. 'That's not for us to say. It's not up to us.'

This was true, strictly speaking, and certainly served to shut Gareth up. But he couldn't help feeling that two recent events in Charles's life, quite apart from the new breathing, pointed to closure: his being received back into the Catholic Church, and his asking for an obliterating dose of painkillers.

It troubled him that Charles, having placed no hopes in the shredded safety net of family, should have clutched at two others, faith and anaesthesia. He also felt an emotion almost like pique that the dispositions he had scribbled down in his diary a few weeks previously, at the time of the kinky-relics conversation, no longer applied. The choice of priest to officiate still held good, but Gareth would now have to withhold an announcement to which Charles had given much weight, weight represented by underlined capitals in Gareth's diary: DID NOT DIE A BELIEVER. He felt his custodianship of this not-quite-final testament, this redundant intimacy, as oppressive.

There was a knock on the door, and after a few tactful seconds a nurse came in. That at least was what, a few moments later, Gareth realized had happened. At the time, his attention was so tightly focused, underneath his other preoccupations, on the man in the bed that it didn't immediately occur to him that the soft knocking could have any other source than that body on that bed. He found his head jerking towards the bed, giving him a twinge in the neck. Only when the nurse made her rustling entry did Gareth properly interpret the sequence of events. From the expression on Mrs Hartly's face, she had experienced a similar moment of disorientation.

The nurse's voice was gentle. 'We need to turn him now,' she said. There was a second nurse behind her. 'You can come back in just a minute.'

She spoke directly to Mrs Hartly. 'Do you want us to wake your husband, and Charles's brother?' Gareth knew that Mr Hartly and his son Arthur were being put up in a room down the corridor. Mrs Hartly shook her head.

Gareth led her by the arm along the corridor, to a small waiting-room that contained two old travel magazines and a vase of dried flowers. He waited for her to sit down.

'Sally and Jerome said they'd try to look in later on,' he said. It was meant to sound like a peace offering, though if there was any little rupture between them Mrs Hartly seemed to have forgotten it. His sentence came out, in any case, trivially social.

'Charles has such wonderful friends,' she said. Irony didn't seem to be in her conversational nature, but still there was something faintly accusing about her tone, as if having friends was just another estranging refinement of her son's personality.

The nurse came back to them. 'You can go back in now.'

The atmosphere in Charles's room had undergone a change. At first Gareth thought that the nurses had opened the window. He looked over at the window, but it was closed. Perhaps they had opened the window and then closed it. Then he realized that the change was profound, and in Charles. His head was turned away from the door, and his eyes were now half open.

Gareth moved round the bed so as to be in Charles's line of vision, if any, but without approaching too closely to him. Mrs Hartly followed him. Charles's half-open eyes gave him a look, a sly look, that was not in his repertoire as a person. Gareth for one was terrified, not of death as it might happen to him, but of whatever had been substituted in Charles's body for the familiar. He found that he was holding his breath. If he breathed at all he was afraid that he could speed up his breathing, breathe faster and faster and then collapse. When he had reached his limit of endurance, he let go his breath. At the same moment Charles too breathed out, breathing out his tongue a little distance as he did so. It took Gareth a few moments to realize that Charles was leaving him to inhale on his own.

Charles's mother grasped Gareth by the elbow but made no

35

nearer approach to the bed. 'I'll get the nurse,' Gareth said. 'No, I'll get the nurse,' said Charles's mother. They stayed where they were. Gareth was very willing to take the cowardly option, but could not at the minute remember which it was. Was it cowardly to avoid being alone in the room with someone who was dying if not actually dead? Or was it brave for either one of them to leave, and miss any possibility of being with Charles at the moment of a vital transition?

He realized that if it was brave to fetch a nurse, it was a bravery that claimed too much status for himself in the event. He had better go. 'I'll go,' he said. Mrs Hartly let go of his elbow but stayed exactly where she was, as if retreating would be a betrayal of her son, but advancing more than she could manage.

On his way out, Gareth noticed that the flap of his saddle-bag had fallen open. He closed it nervously, but dared not waste time by actually strapping it shut.

The doctors' room was empty except for one of the nurses who had turned Charles, in a way that now seemed to have been decisive, to have given some mortal enzyme its signal. She had a cigarette in her mouth and was looking at a list of patients on the wall, their names written in marker-pen on a sort of white blackboard. There was a sponge in her hand, and Gareth couldn't help thinking that she was just about to wipe someone's name out. He knew she might just as easily be changing a room number, or the name of the doctor assigned to a particular patient. Then the appalling idea came to him that she had already rubbed a name out, and that the name was Charles's. He had to check the list for Charles's name before he could speak, and it took him several moments to find it.

Even if she had been about to make some final deletion, the nurse had the grace to put the sponge down, and stub her cigarette out with a single gesture, thumb down and twisting in the ashtray. On the way back down the corridor Gareth tried to explain what had happened, until he realized that the nurse wasn't listening. Either she was thinking of something else, or she dealt with illness on a level deeper than narrative.

Charles's mother was still standing in the same spot, but Charles had moved, in the sense that he could no longer be said to be on a borderline of any description. The nurse walked rapidly to the bed, and closed his eyes. She said, 'It's over. He's gone. He's dead,' leaving a little pause between each version of events, so that the phrases seemed like three separate wedges of increasing thickness, for opening a crack. Then she tried to lead Mrs Hartly from the room.

Mrs Hartly stayed where she was.

'My son,' she said, then cleared her throat. 'My other son. And my husband. They're in room 25.'

'I'll bring them,' promised the nurse. 'But why not come along to the doctors' room, and we'll have a cup of tea.'

Charles's mother almost smiled at the weakness of this lure. 'I'll stay here till they come,' she said.

The nurse went on her errand. Tactfully she ushered Charles's father, and his elder brother Arthur, into the room, and then withdrew. Gareth would have liked to do the same, but found himself installed at the heart of the family group. Mrs Hartly was already talking, saying 'There was something strange about his breathing, and I left the room so the nurses could turn him, and when I came back he wasn't breathing, or he breathed just the once, rather. It must have happened while they were turning him, but they didn't say anything, and I was out of the room. That's when it must have happened.' She seemed to focus her sense of the injustice of the death on its manner and its moment, as if a returned Charles, dying slowly here and now, would have left her satisfied.

Her husband held her stiffly and said, 'It's no one's fault, baby. It would have happened anyway.' But when he had fully absorbed her impulse to cry, he was unable himself to contain it, and then it came round to Gareth. Charles's father stepped sideways from his wife as he started noisily to cry, and reached his arms out wide. Gareth, startled, hugged him, and could see over his shoulder Arthur moving to embrace his mother.

He wondered, and was ashamed but kept on wondering, if he

was receiving Mr Hartly's emotion because that way, passed on outside the family circle, it would have no repercussions: if the emotion was to be discharged, rather than expressed. But he himself had feelings to hide, notably his spasm of selfish terror when he entered the room and saw the changed Charles, and he was glad enough to be treated with warmth, whatever its source and exact composition.

The nurse, who had perhaps been watching through the room's square porthole, tapped and came in. On this second attempt she was successful in tempting the bereaved group down the corridor to the doctors' room. This time, Gareth was careful to pick up his saddle-bag, and strapped it shut at last.

Gareth helped the nurse with the kettle and the rituals that devolved from it, the fetching from a cupboard of a carton of milk, the scraping up of the last spoonfuls in a sugar bowl. Even those with no love for tea and coffee as drinks are compelled to admire them, in crisis, as generators of trivial catechism. Gareth established who liked what and how, and how they liked it, and prepared the drinks. Only at the last minute did he spot that the milk, which he had not taken the precaution of sniffing, was floating in small bricks at the top of each cup. Carefully he ferried the cups in convoy to the sink, poured them out and started again. He tried to give the impression by his calm and concentration that he always made a round of dummy cups by way of rehearsal, or that cups of tea and coffee were like pancakes, and the first one always a failure. He thought he could feel everyone's eyes on him, and his hands were shaking by the time he brought a fresh carton of milk from the fridge. When he had finally delivered the hot drinks, he sat back in silence.

'This foul illness,' said Arthur suddenly. 'This bloody illness.' 'It's an awful thing,' said his father, and Mrs Hartly just said, 'Terrible.' Gareth felt nearer to peace than he had been since he had arrived at the hospital. Listening to this moment of acceptance between denials, he could feel almost at ease.

The nurse said in a business-like voice that there was business to be done, but that this was no time to do it. It was too late at night for a death certificate, so they would have to come back the next day. It made sense to do everything then. 'The best thing you can do is have a good night's sleep,' she said, and made her tone sufficiently prescriptive for them not to protest, as if she was speaking from a vast body of medical knowledge uncontaminated by common sense. As a group, the family went back to Charles's room, and then returned as a deputation to give Gareth formal thanks.

It distressed Gareth to think of the three Hartlys in a huddle in the room where Charles lay dead, discussing forms of thanks. He had an image of them as people wrangling over a tip, for a porter who had carried bags unduly heavy, or unreasonably far.

'You've been so wonderfully kind,' said Mr Hartly. 'We all owe you so much. Living away from London as we do, it hasn't been easy, but it was a comfort whenever Charles said you had paid him a visit. I hope you can come to the funeral. I don't know when it'll be, we'll let you know. But it won't be complete without you . . . I mean, I hope you'll come.'

Again Gareth caught the odd social tone, and guessed at the reason for it. They were operating under conditions of intimacy without familiarity, trust but no knowledge.

Arthur Hartly gave Gareth a double-handed handshake and his own few words of thanks. It seemed to Gareth from the faint sidelights he had gathered from Charles's conversation that Arthur was a reassuring disappointment to his parents. He had not stuck with either one career or one wife, but they were grateful to him for remaining intelligible in his faults. Charles had baffled even in his virtues.

After the Hartlys had gone, Gareth threw away their plastic cups, predictably full of cold liquid, and the nurse put the kettle on again. Gareth tried to remember if she was called Angela or Eileen. He was too tired to manage it. Was it Angela that had the red hair? If so, this was Eileen. The nurses' schedules changed from time to time, just when he had got used to them, and a new set of shifts, a new set of relationships, would be there to baffle him. On this point he could feel that he had the beginnings of a patients' ritualistic querulousness, demanding that the nurses be the same every night, and three clean pillow-slips before sleep.

He was exhausted. 'Bad day?' he asked.

'Just awful,' she said as she dropped tea-bags in the pot. 'We're all very down. We lost number 11 earlier on. He was twenty-six.' She poured tea without waiting for it to brew. 'That's my age. We're going to have an extra Support Group meeting.' She drank from her cup. 'We need it.'

Gareth blew on the surface of his tea, not really because it was too hot but because he couldn't think what to say. Selfishly he resisted the widening of context from Charles's single death to include other lives and other deaths, and it took him a little while to absorb what the nurse had said.

In the past he had socialized somewhat with nurses, not with this particular batch but with others met in similar circumstances. He had enjoyed the cheap meals in Chinatown, in restaurants where all the main courses cost £1.50 and the threads of meat hidden among the noodles could have been anything. But he found their taste in entertainment baffling. They loved films, and so did he, but their preference was for the soppy or else for the horrific. After a day at work, dealing patiently with the failures of the body, they enjoyed a romance, in which reality was made up of emotions, and the body only a house for emotion.

But they also favoured brutally violent horror films, which made Gareth sweat and keep checking his watch, waiting for the film to be over. After a day at work, dealing patiently with the failures of the body, they seemed to relish seeing flesh mauled, mangled and generally beaten about, treated as if it was fully as sacrosanct as pizza, and with no one – or at least someone else – to clear up afterwards.

There was a creaking from the door by the lift, and Gareth turned to see Charles's friend Sally, who to judge from her dress had been to a dinner party. 'I'm sorry I'm so late,' she said, 'and Jerome couldn't make it, I'm afraid.'

Gareth had a sudden horrible vision of a long conversation – long even if it lasted only seconds – in which he struggled, against the grain of social reality, to introduce the fact of Charles's death. He tried to say, 'I'm afraid I have bad news,' but that would be usurping the medical style, and it seemed in any case cruel to draw out a long-expected announcement. So he said simply, 'Charles died a while ago.'

Sally burst into tears, said 'Thanks a lot,' with what seemed to him bitter resentment, and stretched out her arms to be embraced. Gareth hugged her, thinking that in her place he would have hugged the nurse, hugged a passing stranger, hugged anyone rather than the person who had passed on the news, as he had.

Soon she quietened down, and said, 'I don't know why I'm crying. All the way up the stairs I was saying, 'Please God let him die tonight, please God let him die tonight.' She tightened her grip on Gareth's shoulder, with an appeal that was almost amorous. 'Can I see him?'

Gareth had no authority, and no idea either, but he could see over Sally's shoulder that the nurse was nodding assent. He said, 'Of course,' and then modified that to, 'I'm sure you can, isn't that right, nurse?'

He escorted Sally to the door of Charles's room, and waited outside. He didn't want to look in through the porthole, nor be seen through it. He paced up and down a bit, but the soles of his shoes made startling squeaks from contact with the rubberized flooring, and it seemed sensible to avoid that in a place where the few sounds that weren't sombre were sinister instead.

When Sally came out she said only, 'There'd just better be an afterlife, that's all.' Already she seemed quite composed. 'Will you call me a taxi?'

The appeal to his gallantry gave him his cue to leave the hospital; without it, he might have stayed there until he passed out. He hadn't thought of making a move, though nor had he given a thought to where he would sleep if he stayed. By leaving the hospital he would be cutting one more fibre in the ganglion of desperate experience that bound him to Charles, and he was grateful to have the rupture disguised by Sally and her errand. He picked up his bag from the doctors' room, and they took the lift down together. He decided, once they had hailed a taxi, that he might as well share it with her, so they travelled together to Sally's flat in Camden Town. Then the taxi took him on home alone.

Gareth had come across one of the few of the city's cab-drivers uninterested in conversation, at a time when he needed distraction and was willing to work for it. He tried what were in theory foolproof openers, about getting the Knowledge, about the inconvenience to the driver of London cabs, hot in summer, cold in winter, awkward turning circle and ruinous price (£15,000 these days, wasn't it?). But the driver seemed willing to give up the prospect of a tip if the loss at least won him some silence.

Finally Gareth gave up, and slid shut the glass compartment between himself and the driver. Leaning against the upholstery, he found himself murmuring the phrase, 'I'm all right,' with different readings and emphases, as if he were giving individual answers to a whole battery of voices – tender, anxious, exasperated – that were asking him how he was.

He was all right. He was thrown back, as Sally's perfume dispersed from the cab, on memories of Charles, and particularly the last part of their kinky-relics conversation. 'Get rid of them for me, would you?' he had said. 'Just throw them away.'

'Well, let's not be hasty,' he had said. 'Wouldn't you rather I gave them to someone who would appreciate them?' In itself this was the weakest of suggestions, prompted only by the primitive need to meet gesture with gesture, to say for instance, 'That'll look lovely in the bathroom, thanks so much,' of a plant that won't live to see the weekend. But he had also felt, and did still feel, that for Charles to throw anything away at this stage of life was in some degree an act of self-rubbishing. He was anxious to prevent that if he could.

'Yes, all right,' Charles said, with the minimum of breath.

'Well, I don't have to. It really is up to you.'

'No, I'd like you to.' Charles's voice was stronger. 'Do what you can, anyway.'

Gareth now felt himself bound by this wisp of a promise. But he recognized that there was such a thing as excess of scruple. When in a dimly lit street not far from where he lived he saw the huge yellow hulk of a skip looming up, he tapped impulsively on the glass and asked the driver to let him down.

It took no great ruthlessness to cast the leather trousers into the skip, among the broken chairs and broken bricks. They were acknowledged to be of low quality, and the tear at the knee made it impracticable to pass them on. The verdict on the cap was no different: heads varied in size to an almost absurd degree, and he had in any case never seen such a cap before, even in Earls Court, so he felt safe in judging its second-hand value as low.

But as he picked it out of his bag to sling after the discarded trousers, something small and heavy fell out of the cap and dangled at the end of a wire. He squinted at it in the poor light. It was a metallic package which he eventually identified as a battery. Wrapped around the first wire was another, ending in a wedge of cardboard the same size as the battery top, with a small raised ring of metal on it, clearly for electrical contact of some kind. Gareth pressed the cardboard against the top of the battery. To his horror, the polyhedral buttons round the cap, red and yellow, lit up and started flashing in a festive sequence, like so many oranges and lemons in a fruit machine, flashing out the good news of a jackpot.

The hat was clearly no item of darkness, but a souvenir of a birthday party in Oxford, or of Mardi Gras 1975. He had chosen the wrong hat. Asked to remove incriminating evidence, he had left the gun and taken away a fruit bowl.

There was no going back for it now. He disconnected the battery, and threw the cap into the far end of the skip. As he walked the short distance home, he excused himself by thinking of his state of mind, and how much stress he had been under, must still be under. If he could find the right word for his state of mind, he could excuse himself. But what was the right description? Was he blank? Hysterically calm? Simply sad? He felt no affinity with any of these descriptions. But if he couldn't name his state of mind, perhaps he was guilty of neglect after all. Still he couldn't do it. Was this the burn-out he had heard so much about? His own responses seemed to him pinched and ungenerous, but he dimly remembered that too as normal.

There remained in his bag the chaps and the waistcoat. There had never been any question of throwing either of them away. Back in his flat, he hid them, but not where he would have hidden a secret thing of his own. They were a secret, but they were someone else's secret, and he put them in a second-order hiding-place. He stowed them under his bed, in other words, and threw there also Charles's keys, which were no secret of any sort, but which he couldn't bear either to throw away or to leave anywhere that he could see them. Not having a sock drawer as such, he put the biker wallet among some shoes that he didn't expect to wear any time soon, so that an interval would pass before it could mug him with memories.

He had assumed that he would fall asleep instantly, but just as he was dropping off he thought *I'm falling asleep*, as if it was something he was dreading as well as counting on; in any case the idea of sleep, solid and specific, for long moments blocked off the thing itself.

Mr Hartly, as promised, gave him due notice of the funeral service. Gareth didn't know the area where the church was, and spent some time trying to find it, losing his sense of direction and failing to co-ordinate reality with the map. He found his failure in this respect entirely galling. Apart from anything else, it was not the sort of confusion that Charles ever felt, and he found himself mourning with an almost ridiculous timeliness the loss to the world of Charles's particular cerebral strengths, that enormous brain laid low by a know-nothing mould. Charles had an unerring sense of spatial relations: he could remember maps, could visualize a route from Johannesburg to Seoul, and could memorize a grammar or a family tree with equal ease. Consequently he displayed a dazzling command of languages, and a mild but definite snobbery which Gareth found dismaying, but would have been unable to imitate – so meagre was his memory for cousins and collaterals – even if he had admired.

Wandering through the streets, with his mental compass starting to spin whenever he thought he had got it fixed, Gareth at last arrived at the church and the funeral. Mr Hartly shook his hand warmly as he made his entrance. Arthur's handshake a few seconds later was even warmer and firmer, and contained an extra squeeze that represented apology. Immediately following the apology was the statement that made it necessary: 'I wonder if I can ask you, my parents and I have been thinking, not to mention the cause of death?' His smile was urgent. In imagination Gareth snatched back his hand from Arthur's with its compounded pressure; but still it remained there, while Arthur continued to mould it to the shape he wanted. Arthur went on to explain that some of the relatives were from the country.

It seemed to Gareth that they might as well have put a trapdoor under his pew and flushed him down into the crypt, as invite him and then, once he had arrived, ask him to suppress his reason for attending. He wondered how far the Hartlys had thought things through. Was he really supposed to use the time, while the ritual part of the event went ahead and before the social element took over, to construct an inoffensive basis for his relationship with Charles? Since people spent a fair amount of time at funerals asking each other precisely how they came to know the dead person, he would have to devise a whole false history. The effect was to isolate him altogether. It was hard not to feel he was himself being treated as a contaminated agent, who must be prevented from infecting the healthy with unwelcome knowledge.

Consequently he looked on the ceremony with a cold eye. It was apparent, for one thing, that there was a tension between the versions of Charles being perpetuated by his family and by his friends. The friends had arranged for an expensive soprano – announced as such by the usher who escorted Gareth to his place – to sing an anthem. She was stationed for effect in the organ loft at the rear of the church, so that when she rose to sing, the people gathered beneath were offered a choice between two diverging identities. They could continue to look ahead of them, and be defined as a congregation attending a rite, or they could shift round in their seats ever so slightly, indulging themselves in a better hearing or an oblique view of the singer, and slide into being an audience at a concert.

The Hartlys and their immediate neighbours continued to face ahead of them. Those friends of Charles who had come up with the combination soprano/Mozart sat sideways in their pews without embarrassment. Most of the people in the church, as the singing went on, moved slowly out of alignment with the altar, though a handful whose attention was drawn bit by bit to the organ loft fought the attraction, like iron filings choosing between two magnets, and turned their heads to face forward once more.

The Catholics in the congregation stood and sat and knelt with practised smoothness at the appropriate points in the service, not needing to be prompted by the priest. The others were more ragged in their drill, seemingly puzzled by the artificial informality of the priest's commands, which were always phrased with the question 'Would you like to . . . ?' Sometimes he started on a prayer without inviting the congregation to stand, so that the faithful rose to their feet and the less well trained wobbled upwards when they had regained their bearings, and once they were satisfied that standing was not fervent in itself. For most of the time, standing and sitting seemed morally neutral activities to these non-Catholics, and admittedly they were part of a customary social range: people stood up on formal occasions when a newcomer arrived, sat down when told to by their hosts. Kneeling fell outside that range, and so some non-Catholics contrived a kneel that said 'I don't mean this, I'm just being polite', leaning forward and resting their elbows on the back of the pew in front, but bringing their knees no nearer to the floor. Gareth half-expected to see people crossing their fingers behind their backs as they mouthed Amens to the prayers, falling back on the less adult way of doing things and not doing them at the same

46

time. It was an extraordinary tribute, he thought, to pay to
something that had no power over you.

Less calmly, almost with a twinge of hysteria, he thought that
what with the choice between sitting, standing and kneeling,
plus the errors of rotation introduced by the soprano, Charles in
his box was probably the only person present whose posture was
beyond criticism.

Gareth had the unbeliever's high standards for religious
services. It seemed to him that if a funeral service was to be
effective as ritual, it required no element of the personal. And if it
wasn't effective, then no element of the personal could save it. So
when the time came for the funeral address, he was thoroughly
prepared to be unmoved. He resented the intrusion of secular
consolation into sacred, and although he asked for nothing better
than secular consolation this was not a setting in which he could
imagine receiving it. He did think it extraordinary, nevertheless,
that a man speaking to a large audience on a subject of great
interest to them all could offer them a version of the dead man, a
roll-call of qualities broken up with small humanizing anecdotes,
that sentence by sentence excluded his listeners. It was like a
sophisticated effect of theatre lighting, in which a stage-wide
dazzle of illumination faded almost imperceptibly to a dim
spotlight trained on the speaker, narrowing to black-out.

The priest threw Communion open to all comers, whatever
their denomination, saying that all were welcome. This didn't
prevent the approach to the altar rail from being an occasion for
politeness and deference, the exchange of neutral smiles and the
allowing of ladies to take precedence on their way to the Host.
But perhaps it inspired the last communicant, a young rockabilly
with a quiff and something that clanked on his jacket, or possibly
his belt. He sauntered down the aisle just when it seemed that the
sacrament was over. Communion was being given in one kind
only, but the rockabilly seemed not to have grasped the nature of
the set-up. He received a wafer from the celebrant and then
stayed where he was, as if there might be more on offer
something perhaps to wash the wafer down. His model for the

eucharist was apparently the buffet lunch. He seemed to Gareth the living spirit of try-anything-once as he waited there for service. In the absence of a chalice, he seemed willing to settle for seconds of wafer, brown perhaps as a change from white. The celebrant gave him a look that remained grave and formal, but was nevertheless the nearest possible priestly approach to a frown. The rockabilly returned to his seat with a shrug.

After the service Gareth turned down an invitation to the funeral itself, although the invitation seemed sincere and included the offer of a lift to the crematorium. But it seemed to him that to go any further was to lay claim to belonging to an inner circle of bereavement, and he could not then avoid the question of how he came by so much grief. The fact that he did want to spill his secret, and denounce the little knot of refusals that was to blame for its being a secret, only turned it into an act of virtue not to attend, and so not run that risk.

He went instead to the buffet lunch that Sally had arranged for after the service. There were not many people there when he arrived, perhaps because there was an unstated assumption that people should attend both service and cremation to merit the lunch.

Gareth brewed himself a cup of tea in a kitchen crowded with last-minute preparations; Sally's helpers concentrated on arranging food on plates, and left him largely alone. He strayed from room to room, wondering if by his very cup of tea he was being pretentious about the damage he had suffered, making it look as if he alone was still in shock, in need of hot restoring drinks, and not trusting himself with alcohol. Certainly all the other lunchers, as they arrived, helped themselves to wine from a sideboard or asked for whiskies or gins.

The first person to arrive that he properly recognized was an actress called Amanda (Amanda Pitt? Amanda Palmerston? Something resonant, anyway) with a mane of hair and huge hoop earrings. Gareth moved across to her immediately, hoping she was going to be the person he Got Back this time. It was late in the day to be Getting someone Back, but not perhaps too late. He couldn't help seeing these things in terms of exchange. Otherwise in the assignments he took on he was simply setting himself up for loss. If he could get someone back, establish a friendship with someone he would not otherwise have met, then there was something he could set against the wear and tear. So he had found himself, for instance, gazing across a rain-drenched crowd in Highgate Cemetery at a handsome man crying into the shoulder of a man reassuringly less handsome; or striking up a conversation in a hospital lift with a chain-smoking woman whose visits happened to coincide once or twice with his own.

Amanda seemed to have the makings of the person he got back this time. For one thing, she was wearing with a sort of defiance the hiking boots, brown with vivid red laces, that she had worn when she had done a sponsored walk in aid of research into the illness. Every sidelong glance from the more greyly dressed made her prouder and more vivacious, and she bubbled over with talk.

Gareth was aware of his voice rising in volume, out of its own animation and from competition with the other talkers in the room. He tried to rein himself in, since he and Amanda were breaking almost with every sentence the taboo laid on Gareth by Arthur Hartly at the beginning of the service. There was a sort of satisfaction to be had, or so he found, in defying human pressure, after months spent railing against nature's strong extinguishing push.

At the same time his gaze kept returning, all the time he was talking with bright defiance to Amanda, to Mr Hartly's head bowed down in the act of receiving sympathy, and to the bald eroded hinge where he must always have set his parting. At this distance only pity was operative, a pale wash of background feeling; at closer quarters stronger and more personal emotions would come to the fore.

Gareth's view of Mr Hartly, over Amanda's shoulder, was abruptly blocked by a slackly handsome man in his thirties, who stood there with an air of expectancy and of suppressed triumph of some sort. Idly, thinking that this man was perhaps waiting for an opportunity to chat with Amanda, Gareth wondered what might account for this air of triumph, of vindication. This person must have surprised others by performing some action assumed to be beyond him, and had surprised himself into the bargain. Looking more closely, Gareth thought that the action assumed to be beyond him might well be shaving without help, or at any rate shaving without a shaking hand doing damage to the neck above the bow tie. Gareth was slowly coming to realize that this person was waiting to speak to him rather than Amanda, coming also to feel a strong dislike in anticipation of their talk. The man's face and manner were carefully controlled, but he was like an actor who has played a drunk, night after night, month after month, in a long-running play. A sort of blur had settled on every gesture, and when he spoke, on every intonation.

'Your name is Gareth,' he said, 'and mine is Andrew Gould. Am I interrupting?' Amanda with tact retreated, depriving Gareth of his chance to ask for her phone number, or give her his, and so make sure that he got her back. He called after her that she could reach him through Sally, and she nodded brightly as she moved towards the drinks table.

Andrew Gould was not a possible candidate for getting back. Gareth bristled with antagonism before he had even properly begun to speak. 'I'm one of Charles's oldest friends,' he said, 'and from what I hear you've been very good to him.'

'I'm very glad I met him,' Gareth said.

'Well, I'm grateful to you,' said Andrew Gould, on exactly the proprietary note that Gareth had hoped to deny him. 'I'm one of his oldest friends, but I haven't been able to do as much for him lately as I'd have wished. But we always kept in touch.' He produced from his pocket a weathered postcard bearing a single line of Charles's handwriting in its last, most ragged phase: *I think of you often with much fondness.* 'He sent me this.'

Gareth by now was in a rage of disgust at the crassness of brandishing this postcard after a funeral, as if it was a testimonial. From the smoothness of Andrew Gould's gesture, it seemed that he had produced it more than once already. Beneath Gareth's feeling of disgust was a feeling of betrayal that Charles should have made even so mild an overture after what he had said about Andrew Gould. He buried the feeling of betrayal under the disgust, and then felt the need to work on the disgust also.

His first impulse, of course, was to denounce. But Andrew Gould's bid for status was so shameless that it made any conventionally harsh response seem itself unbalanced. Gareth tried to muster his charitable resources. There was little point in specializing in one brand of misery if it made him sneer at every other sort. There was nothing to be proud of about kicking away someone's crutches and shouting, 'See! You can't stand up!'

The alternative to rudeness was leaving the party altogether. Andrew Gould seemed to have much more to say, and to be beginning to say it, but Gareth affected to catch someone's eye, at the same time thrusting his teacup ahead of him, and then following it as if it had a massive momentum. He murmured, 'I'm late, I'm afraid, I must be going,' while still possibly within earshot.

He coincided with Mrs Hartly just inside the doorway of the flat, and struggled to find something to say to her. 'How is Leopold?' he asked, adding irrationally, 'Charles's cat, I mean.'

'Well, of course he misses his master,' she said meekly. 'I think animals understand so much, don't you?'

'They could teach us a lot,' he said on his way out. It was the blandest thing he could think of to say, but still it had an all-purpose asperity that he would have taken back if he could.

Mrs Hartly wrote him a letter a few days later, a letter that began 'Not being good with words . . .' She thanked him one more time for the help he had given Charles, said she knew he liked music, and wondered if he would care for a tape or a record from Charles's collection.

Gareth had not of course expected to profit in any way from being assigned to Charles, but had visualized things in terms of the non-acceptance of a piece of furniture, perhaps an antique mirror he had always liked, with a pelmet and little velvet curtains, rather than the non-acceptance of a record or a tape. He had the feeling that his stake in the mourning was being scaled down, though if he put his mind to it he could make a case for his deprivation being the more intense. Everyone else, after all, had memories of Charles that antedated the illness. They at least had good years to set against the bad, and a mellow auditing of accounts to hope for.

In practice, he knew that things didn't work like that, not for anybody. With the person gone, the memories attached to the person died their own small sort of death. They had no independent existence, any more than Christmas tree lights had a function when the Christmas tree was gone. Sooner or later they had to be tidied away. Gareth wrote to Mrs Hartly saying that he had never had much time for contemporary music, but that listening to Charles he had begun to think that perhaps he should think again, so perhaps – if she really wanted to give him something – a record or tape of contemporary music would be a suitable token. He was a little mortified to hear nothing from her after that.

It distressed him more that Amanda hadn't phoned him. It began to look as if this time he wasn't going to get anyone back. He phoned Sally and asked for Amanda's number, but Sally didn't have it. Amanda wasn't in the directory, certainly not under the name he remembered. He thought of going to the library and leafing through *Spotlight* until he saw her picture, and contacting her through her agent if need be, but that seemed pushy even to him.

He was left with the chaps and the leather waistcoat under his bed. Sometimes while making the bed he would step in a slithering puddle of hide, an unexpected texture which took some moments to identify. He had not abandoned his intention of passing them on to some appropriate party. It didn't seem particularly odd to him to take his obligation so seriously. If gay people like himself and Charles had unacknowledged unions and divorces that made no social echo, it seemed reasonable enough that they should dispose of their property, when they could, in their own way, with by-wills and sub-testaments separate from the public arrangements.

He himself had never found it possible to wear clothes that had once belonged to someone else. He had snapped up bargains once or twice in Camden Passage or the King's Road, and not been able to bring himself to wear them, once he had got them home. And yet here he was, proposing to find a new owner for a dead man's sexually implicated clothing. He had argued himself into finding this reasonable. It was partly that leather was non-porous rather than porous, and might be assumed to take on less of its wearer's substance than a textile would. One of the belt-holes of the chaps was a little ragged, true, and had lost its ring of metal reinforcement. But the clothes were impregnated, as it turned out when he sniffed them, with no essence more carnal than mothballs. But beside that, it seemed to him that black leather could not take on associations because in some way it *was* associations. Even its practicality was largely a matter of symbol-ism: a leather jacket didn't keep its wearer dry in wet weather, it just turned him into a person who found an umbrella's protection insulting. Leather was less a fabric than a set of meanings. To sum up: anyone who bought black leather was buying its image, and made no addition to that image during his ownership.

The new owner would have to be slightly built, like Charles even in his prime. Gareth tried the waistcoat on, idly, for size, and found it was taut across the back even if he kept his shoulders hunched together. He made no attempt to try on the chaps, which would have been much too short as well as tight at the waist and in the leg.

As a volunteer, Gareth was entitled to a month off after a death. It seemed like a macabre bonus for seeing someone off. There were regular support-group meetings for volunteers, and he supposed he should give them another try. When he had first heard about these meetings, he had assumed they would be events in the style of encounter groups, and had thought that on balance he would rather be traumatized than embarrassed. But he went along, and as he came to want something from the meetings, he began to think that a little psychobabble would come in handy. There was something about the phrase used at these sessions, 'Any other business?', that failed to draw out confusion and trouble. There was, admittedly, an elderly man in a corner who remarked, at every meeting Gareth had attended, that the Chinese ideogram for *crisis* combined the ideogram for *danger* and the ideogram for *opportunity*, but he found he didn't warm to that approach either. His attendance had never been regular.

More promising than the prospect of exorcizing his difficulties in front of his equals was the hope of showing off his competence, to someone who would be impressed by it. At one time new recruits for voluntary work had gone for weeks, or even months, while waiting for their rudimentary training – a baffling medical lecture, some tips on law and social services, a few bouts of simulated counselling – without contact of any sort from the organization to which they had pledged their time. This had happened to Gareth. A new arrangement was now being tried, whereby a new volunteer was assigned to a seasoned one, whose job was to make the newcomer feel he belonged, even before the baffling lecture, the tips and the counselling.

To date he had only talked on the phone to Adrian, the young man assigned to him. On these occasions he greatly overplayed hs *savoir-faire* and expertise. He didn't deny, in fact he strongly emphasized, that this was an area where no one had any answers, where there were only degrees of amateurism: you couldn't hope to do no harm, you could only hope to do less harm than good. But the absence of answers could also mean that everyone had an equal claim to be considered an expert, and a little experience could be made to go a long way.

He had been startled when it had come out, in the course of one of their conversations, that Adrian was only a year younger than himself. He had assumed a much larger gap between them, though this imagined gap was only in part chronological. It was as if there was a death virginity over and above the regular one, and those who had lost it looked on those who still had it with envy, and no inclination to take them seriously.

His own losing of the death virginity was made more definite by the way he had seemed to seek it out. He had met death half-way, if that was ever a possible way of meeting death.

But this time he thought that he and Adrian should actually meet. He hoped to benefit from this himself, but passed it off as a favour to Adrian, who seemed pleased and even flattered. Perhaps he had wanted a meeting earlier on, but had been shy of suggesting it. 'It's like having a substance when you arrive at school,' Adrian said, rather fancifully, 'you know, an older boy to show you around. Substances and shadows.' Privately Gareth thought that this was a school where the old lags were more shadowy than the new boys. It was exactly substance you lost as you learned.

Between them they agreed on a place to meet, a newly opened coffee shop run as a co-operative and radiant with correct attitudes. Just before he rang off, Gareth asked Adrian what he looked like. He didn't really think they would find it hard to locate each other, even in a gay milieu where everyone had a generalized alertness to signals, and everyone looked expectant most of the time; but he was feeling a late-flowering curiosity about Adrian, now that he was about to be more than a voice on the phone.

'Well, let's see,' said Adrian. 'I'm not tall and I'm not fat, in fact I'm definitely on the skinny side. And I've got red hair. And I'll be wearing a leather jacket. Will that do?'

That would do. Gareth felt something almost like excitement. Here was his chance to scoop up the waistcoat and chaps from under the bed, and to set about finding them a new home. It seemed to him that no one could be offended by the offer of a leather waistcoat; he had noticed them being worn as fashion items by a number of men, of no particular denomination. Then, when the waistcoat had prepared the way, it would be possible to ask a question about chaps, a trickier question admittedly but a safe one, he thought, in the atmosphere of a good will by then prevailing. He realized that it was perfectly possible that he would still be curator of the chaps at the end of the day, but he had high hopes of seeing the back of the waistcoat.

He arrived at the café ten minutes early and sat sipping a coffee, wondering if its high price represented a radical policy of paying food workers a living wage, or a further tired attempt to milk the pink pound. His attention was caught by something at the edge of his vision, and he turned his head to catch a glimpse of a man with a cruelly foreshortened arm, a neat row of fingertips arranged where an elbow would have been expected, trotting downstairs to the basement. He was shocked and embarrassed by this evidence that underneath his relaxation, his air of being different and accepting difference, he was constantly patrolling the boundaries of the normal.

He was still more shocked when the man returned from the basement, where the lavatories were, advanced towards him, smiling, and was Adrian. Adrian explained that he had been afraid he was late, and had run the last part of the way. Hence his sweaty face and hence also, Gareth assumed, the leather jacket draped over his arm rather than worn, as he queued in his turn for coffee.

Separate detonations of social shame combined to produce a firestorm of embarrassment in Gareth. For one thing, it shamed him that his first reaction was brute disappointment that Adrian was not after all going to take Charles's legacy of leather off his hands. In second place, he bitterly regretted having asked someone with a deformed arm to describe himself so as to be recognized, forcing him to crank through a whole series of redundant distinguishing characteristics, to produce a self-description of what must have seemed enviable anonymity. Then too he was ashamed of the thought that occurred to him when he realized that this was Adrian: *your disability will be a real asset when you're dealing with people who are so sick. You'll be such an example to them.* There seemed to him to be something badly wrong with this thought, and he filed it away for worrying at on a later occasion.

Adrian, meanwhile, was very much at his ease, and so by degrees became Gareth. Adrian's little fingers began to fascinate and, oddly, to charm him. He tried to find a way of both watching them and not watching them that wasn't a furtive stare, but

Adrian had perfected a calm that imposed no conditions. Without showing off exactly, he demonstrated the dexterity of his finger-lets. Having torn the top off a sachet of brown sugar crystals, for pouring into his coffee, he folded the sachet, using only his fingers, into a delicate pleated concertina. He watched his fingers, as they worked, with a cool appreciation shared with a greater warmth by Gareth, also watching. It was only when they were narrowly defined as fingers, Gareth thought, that they must be marked down. As toes, which they more closely resembled, they were clever and extraordinary.

'I think I'll train for the phone lines,' Adrian was saying. 'I'm not brave enough to do that sort of thing face to face. I don't know how you do it. Of course I may turn out to be too much of a coward even for the phones. I may end up stuffing envelopes. Making cups of tea.'

Even before Adrian had disqualified himself from doing voluntary work face to face, Gareth had puzzled out why he could in fact be at a disadvantage. Someone like Gareth could offer someone like Charles company, and a sort of queasy second-hand knowledge. He could offer advice, not all of it useless, not all of it stupid, and get in return a look that said, unmistakably, 'easy-for-you'. It was an important part of his assignment to receive that look; Adrian would inhibit it. But more than that, people like Charles had to develop a ramshackle, post-Modern bravery, that had nothing in common with previous braveries: a series of bargains from a position that ruled bargains out. Adrian's all too traditional version of the virtue would be disheartening and even irrelevant.

He was distracted from these thoughts, and still further from what Adrian was actually saying, by the passage past their table of the café worker who had served them their coffee, now wearing black rubber gloves and carrying a tray of dirty crocks. His expression was seraphic, as if this cyclic demotion – the co-operative workers performed all the tasks in turn – was freighted with revelation, like a king's visit to the abattoirs that supplied the royal kitchens. But Gareth could only be reminded, by the rubber gloves, of the cleaning staff in what he would continue to think of as Charles's hospital until it acquired another set of associations. The cleaning staff had been robust and cheerful, but had not come close to the bed, perhaps for fear of disturbing Charles. They had spent a lot of time polishing the radiators.

Adrian was still talking. He had moved on from material that was familiar to Gareth, about how he came to volunteer, to an interrogatory note that forced him to focus. 'Why do you do it? You personally. Have you . . . lost somebody? Perhaps I shouldn't ask.' His voice became hesitant and tactful.

Gareth floundered. 'No. I haven't. I don't know.' He shifted his coffee cup and adjusted the little vase next to it, which contained a single tiger-lily. 'I heard once, maybe it was on the radio, that you should never run uphill from a bear. A bear's front legs are short, you see, so it can run even faster up a slope than it can on the flat. But going downhill, a bear has real problems.' This was turning into an unenlightening anecdote. 'That's what you should try to do. Run downhill.'

'Never run uphill from a bear,' said Adrian. 'Right, I've got that. How does that help?'

'Well, I just think . . . people try to escape from this thing in the obvious way. Run uphill. You have to do something different. You have to walk right up to it.'

'Run downhill from it, you mean.' Adrian was doing his best to help.

'Well, yes.' He gave a snort in spite of himself. 'I haven't worked out a method of doing that yet. So in the meantime I walk right up to it.' He had to admit, now that he was trying to rationalize his position, that it held no particular water. If it was irrational to think you were immune from disaster as long as you ignored it, it was irrational in a different way to go right up to a slow terrible bear that nobody knew anything about, and think you could buy a little safety on your own account, just by surprising it for a moment.

'Perhaps you could blow up its nose,' Adrian suggested. 'You know, like animal-trainers do. Breathe up its nose and tame it.' By now Gareth was wishing he'd never mentioned bears in the first place. He should just have said that yes, he had lost someone, when Adrian asked. That way he would have seemed a little more heroic, and a lot less confused. 'Rather you than me,' Adrian was saying. 'I think I'll stick to the phone lines. That's close enough.' He picked up his leather jacket and shrugged himself into it. 'Wish me luck.'

'I'm sure you'll be good at it.' Gareth was being more than merely polite. But being attached to the same organization, while it encouraged camaraderie, ruled out real friendship, and Adrian didn't quite qualify for getting back. People needed to feel the same downward suction to have the same need to claw themselves upwards and out.

Gareth shouldered his saddle-bag with resignation. When he got home he slung the whole bag under the bed, without bothering to unpack it. He tried to forgive himself. Even at his point of maximum embarrassment with Adrian, he had at least not actually mentioned the waistcoat.

The saddle-bag was still under the bed when the phone rang two days later. A voice said, 'You don't know me,' in a way that was embarrassed rather than sinister. 'But I'm the friend of a friend.'

'Go on.'

'He's abroad at the moment, is Andrew, but there's something he asked me to find out.'

'Who is this Andrew?'

'Andrew Gould. He was a great friend of Charles Hartly, as I'm sure you know, and he needs to know something about Charles's estate.'

Gareth was puzzled. 'I'm not a lawyer, you know.'

'Yes, I know.' The voice cleared its throat. 'But there are things that belonged to Charles that Andrew thinks won't have been dealt with by lawyers. He thinks there may have been special arrangements.'

'What sort of things?' Gareth had a dim idea.

'Some clothes.'

'Go on.'

'Some leather clothes.'

'And?'

'Charles wanted Andrew to have them.'

'How does he work that one out?'

'Pardon?'

'I said, how does he work that one out?'

'Well, they were old friends.'

'And how about you? Are you an old friend of Charles's too?' He couldn't stop himself from sounding bitter.

The voice hesitated. 'No.'

'Did you know him at all?'

'I met him.' The voice was defensive. 'Look, I don't know why you're being so heavy about this. It's got nothing to do with me. I just said I'd ask a question.'

'All right. Ask your question.'

'Do you know anything about what I'm talking about?'

Gareth found himself unable to lie. 'Yes.'

'What do you know?'

'I know that Charles had some leather clothes. And I know he asked me to dispose of them for him.'

There was a short silence. 'So . . . have you got them?'

The conscientious part of Gareth, a part unaffected by anger, took over. 'I got rid of a pair of trousers and a cap.' He stopped himself from going into details about the mistake with the cap. 'I still have a waistcoat and a pair of chaps.'

'Well, that's something. Andrew will be pleased to hear that.'

'But what makes you think he has a right to them?'

'I told you, Charles wanted him to have them.'

'I don't think so. He asked me to get rid of it all. And I said, Why not give it to someone else instead? And he said, Fine.'

'So it's up to you, is it?'

'It seems to be, yes.'

'Well then, Andrew has rights. Charles wanted him to have them.'

'You keep saying that.' It maddened him to be dealing at so

many removes: in the first place with the husks of a dead man's obsession; with the friend of a friend, perceived by him as an enemy, and in any case through an intermediary; with a voice on the phone. But still with live issues of loss and possessiveness. 'You haven't said anything to convince me yet.'

'They were old friends. They had been lovers. They went back a long time. And they bought that leather together.'

Gareth had a mad impulse to ask for the receipts. Then he gave up. 'Then perhaps he'd better have it. But not because Charles wanted him to have it, because he didn't. Because he let me decide, and it might as well go to Andrew as anyone else.' He managed to suppress the surname, to grant Andrew at least the bare minimum of status. 'Not because Charles wanted him to have it.'

'He'll be pleased to have it anyway. Should I tell him to phone you when he gets back?'

'No. You started as a go-between, you may as well carry on.' His voice softened in spite of his instructions to it. 'I'd like you to. Tell me when you want to pick up the stuff. But make sure you tell him . . .' He didn't finish the sentence. He realized by now that any attempt to stamp the gesture with his meaning, and no other, was more in the nature of a murder than a resurrection.

A Small Spade

Bernard adjusted quickly and well, so well in fact that he began to think it said something rather odd about him. Or perhaps it was something to be proud of. After he had met Neil a couple of times, he told friends that he was willing to act as a support group for this sweet-seeming stranger, this so young stranger, so far from home. He also said that if you were going to offer support, it might as well be to someone you fancied. Then he started to cut down on the self-mocking pronouncements altogether, partly because he was seeing less of his friends, and more of Neil.

The circumstances of their meeting smoothed the adjustment. The place was a pub in Nine Elms which hosted an evening, every two weeks, for people who had been exposed to a virus. The great advantage, of course, was that the subject of illness, or potential illness, could be taken for granted and need never be mentioned, except where the context demanded. It could also be taken for granted, human nature permitting, that no further risks would be taken by the people who gathered there.

Consequently it was Bernard who needed to do the explaining. When it came up in conversation that he was negative in the matter of antibodies, he felt almost exposed as a fraud, as if he had been caught stretching his legs after sitting in a wheelchair, explaining feebly that there had been nowhere else to sit. In theory, those evenings were for anyone who put a high priority on healthy sexual living, but Bernard thought he could detect a whiff of disapproval – not from Neil – for the relatively assured future which branded him as not a serious person.

Neil was from New Zealand, very tall and young enough to make Bernard uneasy, twenty-four as against Bernard's thirty-two. He had been told of his antibody-positive status two months before his projected trip to London, and had not let it upset his plans. He wrote home more regularly than he would have otherwise, that was all, or that was what he said was all. He made sure that he didn't look any skinnier, in the photos he sent back to his parents, than his naturally skinny self.

Bernard found Neil's calm eerie, and guessed that Neil found his awkward animation wearing. But he took the trouble to write his phone number on the back of a raffle ticket – raffles for relevant charities were a big feature of those evenings – and to tuck it into the back pocket of Neil's jeans as he left. An absurdly elevated pocket. Neil laughed and went on talking, to a softer, furry-edged person whom Bernard thought was probably much more his type.

He was right in this assessment, or at any rate he learned later that Neil had gone home with this other person; any fidelity in their relationship was likely to be approximate, and that was all very grown-up and reassuring. But Neil had phoned the next week.

At close quarters, once he got to know him, Bernard could see that Neil made more concessions to his doubtful health than frequent letters home; but they were concessions that somehow suited Bernard. If Neil was tired, he lay down and made no apology for it. If he was hungry, he ate right away. Bernard enjoyed this programme of snacks and siestas during the time they spent together. It was never an effort to take a nap, or at least a lie-down. It was odd, but not unpleasant, to be the older man and have the junior energy. He ate whenever Neil ate, and if he didn't imitate Neil's moderation that wasn't really an issue. Long before this illness had shown up, love affairs had been divided for him into the ones that made you fat and smug, and the ones that made you skinny and neurotic. He was quite content, for a change, to put on a few pounds.

He found Neil's profession harder to adjust to than his

compromised health. Neil worked as a hairdresser, and hair-dressers in Bernard's mind were necessarily fatuous people, whose fatuousness extended to their choice of lovers. Never mind that he himself had regular haircuts at an establishment which, if not exactly up-market – it stopped short of consultations, conditioner and cups of coffee – charged at least enough money to command respect for those who had earned it. Bernard's prejudice remained. To compensate for it, he announced Neil's profession in conversation far more often than was necessary, as if unless he kept mentioning it he might be suspected of a liaison with a royal duke. This went on until a friend asked, without malice, 'Which hairdresser do you mean, the one who cuts your hair or the one who messes it up?' Bernard found himself blushing almost to the point of haemorrhage, and promised himself to do better in future.

Neil did yoga every Wednesday, with a group of similarly affected people, and swam several times a week. Bernard joined him in the swimming when he could fit it in. Neil had a relaxed antipodean style of crawl, but his stamina was only moderate, so Bernard could outswim him, though not by the same generous margin that he outate him.

Neil's shortness of breath was also noticeable in bed, where it had, again, a reassuring aspect. Hearing his lover's breathing return to normal after climax so much more slowly than his own, Bernard was at least free of fears that he was being sexually humoured. On a purely cardiovascular level, Neil's experience was the more intense.

He worried about Neil, of course, seeing him only two or three times a week, but then worrying had always been the great romantic privilege, and it was a pleasure not to have it resented. He thought that perhaps romance always had a basis in fear; it was just that this time the fear was clearly defined, and external.

Bernard's worry for himself took the form of an increased superficial cherishing of the body. He had begun by shaving more carefully than usual on days when he would be seeing Neil, and put plasters on any cuts he incurred even if the results were unsightly, until Neil confessed to a labour-saving preference for at least a hint of stubble. Now Bernard stayed unshaven on the days of their meetings. His growth of beard was modest, so he could skip a day without particular comment from his colleagues. He was spared the routine questions of whether he was growing a beard, as if that was a matter of educational policy and might be controversial.

Bernard kept his worry within bounds when, as now, Neil was late for a meeting. Neil wore no watch; his character had been shaped to some extent by a late strain of New Zealand hippyism, based round sunshine, cheap dope and free rock festivals in remote areas. Giving up Smoking, with the capital S, when he found that the habit was immunosuppressive, was the hardest sacrifice his new status had yet required of him.

Bernard had bought tickets for the train, and spent the time while he waited for Neil trying to identify gay couples engaged on the same ritual as himself: the weekend in Brighton. He hadn't himself visited Brighton since he was a schoolboy, and hadn't made an expedition with Neil any further than the cinema. It seemed to him, as he spotted couples mustering for their expeditions, that he could spot at least as many fun-hungry types stepping out of trains from Brighton, intent on the opposite ritual, of getting back in the sexual swim.

At last he saw Neil moving towards him, at a pace too slow to be described even as an amble. At first he had found this exaggerated leisure of pace irritating; there seemed to him little point in being an agile man of six foot four if you moved more slowly than someone plump and four foot tall, in a hobble skirt. But gradually he had retarded his own speed of walking, and Neil had slightly accelerated, not so much to meet him half-way as because the cooling air made sauntering less and less rewarding a style of motion. Already in early November there had been days, apparently, as cold as New Zealand ever got, and Neil had a respect edged with panic for the colder months to come.

He was carrying, all the same, only a small nylon holdall. Neil had a flair for travelling light, and had much to teach Bernard, who was ballasted by any number of magazines and library books, in that department. Neil was proposing to tour Europe late in the coming spring with very little more luggage than he was carrying now, and Bernard was persuaded he would manage it. He might even still be carrying the same book, *Grandchildren of Dune*, which he wasn't actually reading but carried as emergency rations, a sort of literary pemmican. His home library was equally basic: *Budget Europe*, *On Death and Dying*, and a grainy-paged paperback of pornography entitled *Black Punk Hustler*.

Any discussion of Neil's European trip, or the possibility of Bernard's changing jobs, or – as they started to trust each other's interest – a party a few weeks off, required the formal closure, originated by Neil but now spoken by either one of them, of the phrase: 'Oh, we'll be well over by then.'

Neil carried his liking for paring things down, for travelling light, to the point of naturism. He had found, after a couple of months in London, a couple of swimming pools, one in Stockwell, one in Hornsey, which held weekly naturist swims, for men only. At one of these sessions, Neil had met someone who had subsequently become his landlord, in the upper reaches of the Bakerloo Line.

Bernard and Neil had agreed to meet at midday, without reference to the times of trains; Neil's strong preference was for relaxation over efficiency. By the time that Neil arrived, a few minutes late, they had in fact missed the first train of the afternoon; they would have to wait half an hour for the next one. Bernard was a little irritated, in a way that gave him fresh evidence of the satisfying disparity of their temperaments, and looked around for one of the expresso-and-croissant stalls that nowadays brightened some of London's main line stations. Victoria seemed to have escaped such brightening, and offered only hamburger-joints, without the distorted grins and hair-trigger service, honed against their competitors, which made similar places in high streets entertaining.

Neil took it in his slow, unhurried stride. He ordered a fish sandwich and a cup of hot chocolate, while Bernard settled for coffee. As Neil raised his cup to his lips he said, 'Nice to have two days free, eh, before it all starts again. It's been flat stick all week.' Bernard had a mild romantic fetish for that mid-sentence *eh*, which for all he knew was a mannerism Neil shared even with the sheep in New Zealand, but was unique in his experience.

Neil singled out the idea of the weekend for praise and appreciation because it was a characteristic of his new job; he had been fired from his old one – where he had worked on Saturdays but had Wednesdays off – for being antibody-positive. He hadn't announced the fact, but a colleague had spotted a badge with the phrase Body Positive on it, when Neil had unzipped his holdall to retrieve a pot of yoghurt for his lunch. Neil's colleague seemed enlightened, and mentioned several friends of his as being in the same condition. He promised discretion. Then one Thursday, after Neil had dealt with a couple of clients, he was summoned to the basement by the manager. Did Neil have something to tell him? Neil was mystified and asked what this was all about. Then the manager said that three juniors had left work in tears the day before, and had phoned in to say they weren't willing to work with him any more (their mothers seemed to have played a part in this decision). He asked if Neil denied being a 'carrier'. The money that Neil was owed, plus a week's wages, was ready in an envelope, so he didn't even bother to argue. He had to leave on the spot, walking out through colleagues who seemed to be focusing on their clients rather more narrowly than usual. He took with him a fleshy-fingered little cactus that Bernard had bought him, and entrusted it to a friend who worked in the salon of Dickins and Jones.

Again, Neil reacted to this disturbance with relative calm. He was angry for about an hour, depressed for about a day; he swam a little more than usual, slept a little more than usual, ate a little less. The sentence that took the longest to break down into inoffensiveness was the manager's last word: 'It was very foolish of you, you know, to pretend you didn't know what I was talking about.' But it was Bernard who worked the incident up into a party-piece, and into an indictment of hairdressers. He couldn't help feeling that Neil was overdoing the British phlegm, or perhaps it was yogic indifference. There was such a thing, he knew, as burying toxic waste so deep you poisoned the water table. It was a possibility he sometimes mentioned to his current affairs class.

Neil seemed utterly free of poison. Closely examined though, he looked a little different today, in a way that would prompt Bernard, with anyone else, to ask if he had had a haircut. But life for Neil was one continuous haircut; he and his co-workers were forever giving each other trims in the quiet times between busy times. Over the months Bernard had known him, his hair – black with a haze of grey at the crown – had followed a general trend from crew cut to a fuller look, but with countless adjustments and accents. His beard went from stubbled to almost full, before being trimmed recurrently back.

Bernard had to admit, though, that Neil was by some way the least narcissistic person in the salon. It seemed to him that the other employees, male and female, straight and gay, would have done any work that involved their being surrounded by mirrors. If being a butcher had met that condition, most of them would be wearing blood-stained aprons by now, pleased to have them-selves to themselves in the mirrors, without human competition.

Bernard checked his watch all the more because Neil did without. He started to get restless when they had fifteen minutes in hand before the train, exaggerating the effect on their progress of Neil's slow pace. Neil consented to set off at last, using his tongue to press the last of the hot chocolate from his whiskers. Then it turned out that of the two trains to Brighton every hour, one was departing from Croydon, so that repairs could be carried out on the line. This was the one they were now set on catching; they would have to take a suburban train to Croydon to meet it. Bernard shepherded Neil on to the platform, where Neil found himself a baggage wagon to sit on.

Almost immediately an abraded voice on the Tannoy announced a change of platform. Bernard couldn't make out the message itself, but could reconstruct it from its instantaneous effect on their fellow travellers, who picked up their bags and ran. By the time he had convinced Neil that this was more than a piece of random British eccentricity, and that, yes, you had to play hide-and-seek with the trains in this country if you wanted to get anywhere, they were at the rear of a long queue, backed up outside the entrance to the platform proper.

There were few free seats left on the train when they reached it. The nearest they could get to sitting together was to be in sight of each other, occupying aisle seats, with two rows of passengers intervening. Bernard could see a newspaper sticking out of Neil's holdall, but was too far away to identify it. Neil bought a different paper every day, and was never satisfied, since he had to confront the highest concentration of distressing nonsense about the illness that threatened him, if he was also to find a reasonable minimum of the stories he liked (royalty features, pop gossip). Whatever his particular choice this Saturday, he wasn't reading it. His eyes were almost closed. He might very well be meditating, or practising autogenic training. Or just falling asleep in the normal manner of people on trains. Bernard had a book with him, which a strange isotope of loyalty would have prevented him from reading if Neil had been sitting next to him, so he turned their separation to good account.

At Croydon there was the same co-ordinated rush to the waiting train. Neil trailed behind without embarrassment, and Bernard forced himself to accept the idea of standing for the rest of the journey. In fact, this new train was much longer than the suburban one, and they were able to find seats in the buffet car, which was deserted. After about ten minutes, Bernard walked down the car and found to his joy and amazement that the buffet was staffed. The steward was standing in the shadows rather, and doing nothing to advertise his presence; perhaps he had eased up the grille of the buffet inch by inch in its groove of grease so as not to attract attention. But he was certainly there, and even on duty. When his bluff was called, he was willing to dispense refreshment.

Bernard knew he had no prospect of explaining to Neil his

sense of the extraordinariness of this coincidence of serving-counter and steward, but his heart was wholly lifted by it. For the first time he had the sense that this outing would be a success, and he almost pranced back along the buffet car, carrying another coffee for himself and another hot chocolate for Neil.

'It's made with soya milk,' he said as he put Neil's cup down.

'Really?'

'British Rail have always used soya milk. And the bread for their sandwiches is made from bulgar wheat. That's why people are always complaining about the catering. People just aren't ready for progress.' As he spoke, Bernard adopted a patently ironic tone so that Neil could know he was being teased.

The tease was undermined by the fact that Neil was no doctrinaire vegetarian, as the fish sandwich at Victoria rather tended to prove. He ate meat when it was prepared for him, and his avoidance of it when he could choose had more to do with being poor, and disliking cheap cuts smothered with sauces, than with any moral stand. He no longer bothered to explain the distinction, and acknowledged Bernard's teasing only with a broad smile. As Bernard noticed a little guiltily, he did remarkably little teasing himself.

Bernard had no idea why he teased Neil, or anybody else. Perhaps it was some evolutionary leftover, like an appendix, and he should only worry if it filled up with poison.

As the train approached Brighton, Neil became more and more perky, though he was too accustomed to ocean from New Zealand – and blue ocean at that – to be more than moderately pleased when the sea hove into sight. At the station he vetoed Bernard's suggestion that they buy a map, but this turned out to be less hippyish a gesture than Bernard first thought. He had looked at a friend's map the day before and thought he had a reasonable idea of the general layout of the town.

They set off in the direction that Neil indicated, at his preferred pace. The day was bright but with a chill to it. Neil was wearing gloves, but fingerless ones which emphasized his long, beautiful fingers, and the jacket of a suit inherited from his grandfather, long enough for him and actually a bit broad in the shoulder. It was rather too thin for the weather. Neil's grandfather, by dying when Neil was six, had given him his only example of a dead person, with the result that death seemed to have acquired the status of an optional event, almost a distinction. After a few minutes Neil fished out a knitted woollen watch-cap from his holdall and put it on. Bernard was wearing an identical cap, bought for £1.80 from Laurence Corner at the same time as Neil's, and he found growing in him the urge to take it off. He was content to be part of a couple, but he strongly resisted being part of a matching pair.

Since Neil rolled his cap down to cover his ears, while Bernard rolled his up into the smallest practicable shape, so that it clung to the back of his head only by fibrous tension, they were already taking steps to differentiate themselves. There was very little chance of their being mistaken for each other. Still Bernard unzipped his jacket and wore it open, as if the effort of sustained walking had warmed him up, and under cover of that pretext took off his cap a few minutes later. He took long refreshed breaths of sea air. He scrabbled at his hair with both hands to restore it to a roughly human contour, so that it looked at least like a loved haystack rather than a despised one.

They had only penetrated a few yards into Brighton before they were offered their first second-hand clothes shop. In theory Neil's needs were the greater, since his wardrobe was scanty and his fear of winter real, but it was Bernard who dived in and started riffling through the racks. Neil had set aside the coming Saturday, rather than this one, for buying The Winter Coat, an item for which he had drawn up almost arctic specifications. Half-heartedly he tried a couple of coats on, but each time asked Bernard to feel their weave and weight. Would this one be an adequate defence? How about this one? Bernard didn't want to swear to it, not being in a hurry to shoulder blame at a later date. Neil had shopped impulsively for The Winter Boots and was regretting it. Neil's feet were size twelves, and The Winter Boots were size elevens; their waterproof days were over already. But

size twelves never showed up in sales, and even size elevens – or
so Bernard gathered – weren't common enough to pass up.

Bernard bought a string vest of sea island cotton after trying it
on in a changing-room so small – a dirty curtain held a little away
from the wall – that it reminded him of the dressing-rooms for the
school play now in rehearsal (*Twelfth Night*, with Viola and
Sebastian played by a pair of Pakistani twins, their resemblance
not yet botched by puberty). This was not a welcome thought,
since he was supposed to be devising the costumes for it –
designing was too grand a word for what he had in mind, which
would include found objects and black plastic bin-liners as
important elements. But however modest his responsibilities,
today would have been a logical day to devote to them.

A little further into town, the moment Brighton made any sort
of impersonation of a resort, Neil started taking photographs. He
didn't waste film on views, but took a couple of photographs of
Bernard. More important was for Bernard to take the camera from
him and to take photographs suitable for sending home. He gave
Neil plenty of warning, so that he could blow out his cheeks a
little, and push out his tummy. He was holding weight well, as
far as Bernard could see, but from Neil's parents' point of view
there was no such thing as overdoing it.

For the first photograph Neil puffed out his cheeks almost to
bursting point, until laughter broke his lips open. But he was
undoubtedly happier when the camera contained a good stock-
pile of fat photos. He could put the camera away and start
enjoying himself on his own account, and not for the benefit of a
mantelpiece in suburban Auckland.

Neil liked to look in the window of every hairdressers they
passed, which in a town as dedicated to grooming as Brighton
seemed to mean crossing from side to side of the street more or
less non-stop. He got satisfaction of some sort from what he saw
through these windows, but made no comment. Bernard tried to
decide whether he was simply gloating over these people who
had to be cutting hair when he was free, or checking the tariffs to
reassure himself that his Brighton equivalents earned even less

than he did. The only certain thing was that he wasn't engaged in industrial espionage. He wasn't serious about hairdressing, and Bernard took comfort from that. It enabled him to construct two categories of hairdresser, the casual and the committed, with all the stigma attaching to the committed.

Neil was casual about his job, but well short of slapdash. Bernard had seen him more than once cutting a little girl's hair, kneeling on a towel by the chair – a chair made in Japan, for no known reason – although there were stylists much less tall, whom Bernard thought would find the job less awkward. Patiently, he cut the merest centimetre from her hair, combing her soothingly, so that she seemed not to realize she was no longer crying, though her posture was still sulky and she still held her doll in the combined crook of her elbows.

But he certainly had no great respect for his profession. The only hairdresser he admired was a friend called Joel, now working freelance, and that was because of what he managed to get away with. Joel still used the pair of scissors he had had at hairdressing school, the cheapest pair of Ice Gottas on the market, and turned up for magazine shoots – he did make-up as well as hair – with an old plastic bag bearing the motto 'That's the Wonder of Woolies', full of Outdoor Girl cosmetics. The magazine put different names for the cosmetics next to the pictures they printed, but then they did that anyway. But Joel's great achievement, so far as Neil was concerned, was to give ordinary cuts at enormous speed and inflated prices to a few selected clients in his own home, a small, shabby and disorderly flat. It was one thing to do a bad job in a pretentious salon, quite another to do a bad job – and get away with it – where the client could see his old tea-bags and underpants. Once, Neil and Joel had been about to go out for lunch when a client arrived whom Joel had forgotten. She wanted highlights, and Joel obliged in ten minutes, rather than the usual three hours, simply combing the lotion on to the hair. The results, according to Neil, were highlumps rather than highlights, and Joel charged £55 for his labour, but the client was highly delighted.

Among the hairdressers of Brighton were health-food shops and whole-food cafés. Bernard and Neil chose one that looked quiet, The Pantry, for a sit-down and a snack. It was narrow, with chunky tables of rough wood, and crammed with self-consciously tacky 1950s artefacts, some free-standing, some stuck on the walls, and some even hung on utility coat-racks: advertisements, sculptures, jokey ashtrays given a different status from the working ashtrays on the tables. In a tiny alcove there was even a mobile disco, twin turntables with a microphone attached, though it was hard to imagine anyone dancing there. Queuing for food was quite awkward enough in the cramped space, and a lot of apologizing went on even with relatively few people ordering and collecting food. Perhaps the disco was only kept there off duty, and was set up somewhere else; but it was difficult to imagine any of the helpers – three women of different generations and perhaps actually a whole-food dynasty, a matrilineal succession of carers – acting as DJ. The youngest, an early teenager, seemed to have her duties confined to clearing up and, to judge by the frequency with which she dropped things, would not be trusted with the boxes of scuffed singles sitting next to the disco.

When Neil had finished his salad and Bernard his wholemeal lasagne, they carried on towards what Neil's homing instinct or memory for maps told him was the historic city centre. Neil had picked up the word 'historic', which he used with deliberate lack of discrimination, from his least favourite client, an American woman who would smoke a cigarette and put on make-up while being blow-dried. Neil's boss had followed his usual practice of over-charging tourists, but this tourist was not to be deterred from returning, and always asked for Neil. He punished her by taking on this particularly hated element of her vocabulary.

Brighton showed no great increase in historical interest as they walked on, but to judge by the air of escalating chichi they were on the right track. Finally they came in sight of the Pavilion, which they had agreed on as their obligatory piece of sightseeing. It had for the time being a complex façade of boards and scaffolding, but was still open for business. By taking the tour they would be treating Brighton as a city in its own right, not just as a collection of gay-oriented businesses with a reasonably pleasant climate.

There was no tour of the Pavilion as such. If there had been, or if they had invested in one of the expensive guide books from the gift shop, they would have been given a definite idea of the Pavilion to accept or reject. As it was, they had to come to their own conclusions. It dawned on Bernard, as they entered a ballroom containing a grand organ, that he was now in one of the most piss-elegant environments in the world. 'This is certainly historic,' said Neil.

'Worse than that. In its own way it's actually Otaran.' Otara, as he had gathered from Neil, was some sort of Maori heartland, and therefore a sort of New Zealand shorthand for tackiness. Neil himself, of Yugoslav blood and unpronounceable surname, had been the only white person in his class at school. All the Maori boys were called Rangi, or so he claimed, and all the girls were Debra. He had ended up saying things like, 'J'wanta come down the Spice Inviders in my Veliant?' Thereafter, he had fallen in eagerly with his friends in their dismissal of anything Maori, though he had also had one or two affairs with Maoris not called Rangi.

Neil seemed thrown by Bernard's borrowing of a Kiwi expression, as he was on the rare occasions when Bernard said *obliverated* to mean drunk, *rapt* for pleased, *crack a horn* for acquire an erection. Neil's own accent, if his family were telling the truth on their occasional phone calls, was now pure Oxbridge. 'Well, I don't know, that place we had lunch was Otaran. This place is a bit different.'

'What then?' asked Bernard.

'This place is . . . Papatoetoan.'

'What's that?'

'Papatoetoe. It's not as far as Otara.'

Bernard laughed, and they moved through the preposterous rooms in a rare daze of unanimity. It turned out that there was an alarm system installed in the Pavilion, which gave off a series of electronic yelps if anyone infringed on the velvet rope, or even approached the edges of the aisle permitted to visitors. Each time the yelping sounded, the guard in whatever room it happened to be would intone, 'Please don't touch. Keep your distance.'

In one room the guard, who wore a stylized moustache, was young and busy with his eyes. Bernard nudged the rope, so as to make him deliver his recorded message. Then he couldn't help murmuring to Neil, 'What are the odds he turns up to a bar we're in tonight? Except he won't be saying *keep your distance* then, I'll bet.'

'Keep your distance, please don't touch,' said the guard again, as someone else triggered the alarm. Neil was normally resistant to Bernard's line of banter, but this time they were on a wavelength, and he laughed, in one little burst and then another.

They passed through to the kitchens, where Bernard saw the first things he actually admired, the endless rows of copper pots, all the way up to Moby Dick fish-kettles; the lids were sensibly provided with their own handles, raised above the rest of the lids for coolness' sake. Neil found further fuel for his laughing jag in a stuffed rat caught in a trap, and displayed under one of the kitchen tables. It was almost absurdly unlifelike, perhaps to avoid frightening schoolchildren, and the plastic fruit and veg on the broad pale-scrubbed tables would be a suitable diet for it.

Once the Pavilion had loosed its historic hold on them, they started to think about finding their hotel. There Neil's memory for maps, however impressive, couldn't be expected to help them. Bernard remembered the address as Derbishire Place, and they asked passers-by where that was. No one knew. Bernard didn't check the advertisements in *Capital Gay*, from which he had got the phone number. One reason for his reluctance was the name of the hotel, which was called Rogues. He had phoned another hotel first, advertised in the same journal but with a nudge-free name. It was full. He had asked the receptionist to recommend another establishment, relying on impartiality now that distortions of rivalry could be discounted, and it was then that Rogues was suggested. With a heavy heart he made the call, and would have put the phone down if he had been offered the Scallywag Suite, or been told about the cheap cocktails during Naughty Hour in the Vagabond Room. He wanted to stay in a hotel called Rogues every bit as much as he wanted to have a lover who was a hairdresser, though he hoped for similar compensations once the sacrifice was made.

Another reason for wanting to leave *Capital Gay* in his bag was the sheer depressingness of the paper itself. This was hardly the paper's fault; the journalists did their best to make up jaunty headlines. But every week there were more obituaries, and the obituaries became more flippant. The conventions of obituary-writing, either that death had set the seal on a long and useful life, or that death had cut off young promise in its prime, began to break down now that untimeliness was becoming the rule. Many of the casualties were too young even to be promising. The boss of a gay business wrote of a dead employee, in the issue that Bernard was keeping in his bag, 'He told us he did not expect to live after Friday. Punctuality was never his *forte* and it came as no surprise to us that he was 2¾ hours late.' The dead men weren't ready to die. The obituarists weren't ready to write obituaries.

Derbishire Place continued to ring no bells with the people he asked about it. When people asked what exactly he was looking for, hoping that would give them a clue, Bernard became very tight-lipped, while Neil gave him what was not a look of forgiving superiority, but which if fed and watered would grow up to be one. Finally they gave in and bought a local map from a stationers, but Derbishire Place was missing from it, along with all other places beginning with Derbishire. He went back to the stationers to check other maps of greater price and detail, but Derbishire Place was missing from them all.

At last Bernard fished out *Capital Gay* for the lowdown on Rogues. The address turned out to be Devonshire Place, which was not only marked on every map, however rudimentary, but which they had passed a few streets back.

Devonshire Place was a steep little street, and Bernard felt quite tired as they reached its upper end. To his relief, the frontage of Rogues was plain, its name appearing only on a small brass plaque. He had been bracing himself for black balloons and pink neon. The man who opened the door was a further relief. He was wearing socks and sheepskin slippers, and underneath his green polo-shirt could be traced in relief the outline of a thermal vest. Not for the first time in Bernard's experience, but much to his reassurance, gay life promised the depraved and delivered the cosy.

Their host led them into a lounge with a television, which was showing the omnibus edition of a soap opera which Neil followed, without fanaticism. It seemed to be one of the few British programmes which wasn't exported to New Zealand, and that gave it, in Neil's eyes, a slight extra kick. Their host left them at the mercy of the television, and promised them a cup of tea in a couple of shakes. They sprawled on the sofa, and Neil gave Bernard one of his trademark kisses, an amorous stubbled plosive full on the ear. In a world where bodies had unrestricted access to each other, this would come near the bottom of Bernard's list of favourite gestures. He braced himself for the detonation. In essence, he thought it was about as erotic a gesture as dropping a firework through someone's letter-box. But he could not now afford to despise any permissible act, and he had worked on his reactions until the symbolic sensation gave him pleasure. Now, on the sofa, he welcomed it.

'Who's that?' he asked, pointing at the television screen. 'Is that what's-his-face's boyfriend?'

'Don't know.'

'Didn't you see it on Tuesday?'

'Yes.'

'Well, who is it then?'

'I don't know.' Seeing Bernard's expression he tightened his hug a notch or two. 'Don't worry, I'm not going gaga before my time, I'm not getting the dementia. If I am I've always had it. I've always had a short attention span.'

'You have?'

79

'Yup. I think I've had a little snooze in every film we've been to, and you didn't notice, eh?'

'Can't say I did.'

'Maybe your attention's not so hot yourself. And if you work out who these people are, don't bother to tell me. I'm not that interested.'

'Do you think we can turn it off?' The lounge might in theory be the guests' terrain, but it was full of the landlord's presence, not to mention his cigarettes and two planks of a KitKat, half-unwrapped from their foil.

Before they could decide, the landlord came back with the promised tray of tea, a register and some leaflets. He needed some details for the register, and offered in exchange a map of Brighton with its gay attractions marked in. A number of venues had been deleted; it was, after all, off-season. There were, though, still places to go, and the hotelier made out little passes for them, vouching for their status as bona-fide visitors, with which they could get in free at a number of key nightspots. Then he left them to their tea and the television.

A little later he returned with two bulky keys, and showed them to their room. Rogues was a modest private house lightly disguised as a hotel; Neil's and Bernard's room, at the rear of the first floor, corresponded to the master bedroom of most terraced houses. There couldn't, Bernard thought, be more than three other rooms.

The underside of the door scraped on the thick carpet, almost to the point of sticking, as it opened. Inside were posters of exhibitions at the British Museum, and a colour scheme of striated greens hinting at leafy bamboo and derived from the Brighton Pavilion. It occurred to Bernard that there must be easily one or two hotel rooms in Brighton untouched by the Pavilion in decorative scheme, but he accepted that they would cost rather more than the others, and would need to be booked some months in advance.

The hotel owner padded out and left them alone, and they tried out the bed. Neil was unswervingly loyal to his futon, but Bernard had no great love for it. This was a little squashy, squashier than his own at home, but it would do. Neil seemed to think so too, whatever his stated position: he fell asleep almost immediately. Bernard tried as a general rule not to bombard him with concern, and had managed not to ask him, earlier in the day, if he was tired. Now he began to feel, from the avidness and depth of Neil's sleep, that he should have been more tender.

Bernard wondered if perhaps at some stage he and Neil would have to decide whether 'antibody-positive' was not now an understatement of Neil's condition. Perhaps that was a secret they were keeping from each other.

Neil was curled sweetly against him in sleep. Neil's sexuality seemed to Bernard altogether caressive rather than penetrational; that was certainly the role he played with Bernard, and the role Bernard played with him. Neil had called him 'cuddly' on one occasion, meaning fond of hugging, until Bernard broke it to him that in Britain cuddly was just a friend's word for fat, so would he please retract it. Neil had even given Bernard a teddy bear for his birthday. Bernard had slept with it one night, so as to atone for his embarrassment when it was handed over, and so that he could mention its usefulness without lying. He was rather appalled to wake up freezing in the middle of the night, still clutching the bear, in a shipwreck of bedclothes. The bear's stitched smile had a vindicated smugness about it.

At an earlier stage, of course, Neil's persona had been a little different. About five years previously, while still in his teens, he had gone through a phase of anal shenanigans; that must have been the time of his exposure to infection. He still had a sharp nostalgia for oral sex, which was not these days categorized as particularly risky; but Bernard hesitated, and seeing his hesitation Neil changed the sexual subject.

Bernard rolled quietly off the bed and went for a walk. He would have liked to find a café where he could have a cup of coffee and read, but the only café that was at all promising seemed to be mutating in some mysterious way into a wine bar. It had been open until a little while before, it would be open in a little while to come, and even now it was not exactly closed; but when he suggested to the waitress that he might sit in a quiet corner with a book and a cup of coffee, she wouldn't hear of it.

Thwarted of his civilized interlude, Bernard walked down to the sea front, then headed back to the hotel, not wanting to experience anything too distinctively Brighton without the partner that the whole weekend was arranged around.

Neil was stirring when he returned to the hotel room. He rolled slowly off the bed and started doing yoga exercises, hardly even opening his eyes. Bernard took his turn at lying on the bed, but after a moment he couldn't resist peering over the edge at Neil's slow smooth complex movements, and the quickened roughened breathing that went with them. He felt like an Indian scout creeping to the edge of a cliff to spy on the war games of a rival tribe.

There was one exercise that particularly appealed to him. Neil lay on his front and stretched back his head, arms and legs, giving his body a bowed shape and a resemblance to a parachutist in free fall. Bernard had an impulse to lean over and tickle one of the elongated feet, themselves sharply bowed, outstretched below him, an action which would have shattered Neil's calm – he was extremely ticklish – beyond the power of any mantra to reinstate. It was only a distantly mischievous impulse and he was able to rise above it with a small flexing of willpower.

Neil finished the tempting exercise, and moved on to the next. Yoga was known to benefit the immune system. It was agreed between Neil and Bernard, without any basis in evidence, that Neil was unlikely to have been exposed, as long ago as 1981 and as far from the centre of the gay world as New Zealand, to the full grown-up horror of the virus. It was much more likely, surely, that he had encountered some nasty intermediate form, some mid-mutation that was no fun to have aboard but bore no real grudge against him.

There were factors that worked against this theory. Neil had had affairs, in that distant period, with not one but two airline stewards. He was some way from the capital of danger, but he wasn't exactly in the provinces. Bernard had an image of airline stewards (flight attendants, whatever euphemism you cared to choose) as sheer vectors of sexual transmission, their buttocks a blur all the time they weren't actually handing out soft drinks and headphones. He reacted with relative sanity to press coverage of the illness, screening out the idiocies and focusing on the few scraps of undistorted information, but he had a little obsession of his own. If any political party had included in its platform the compulsory fitting of chastity belts to airline stewards, he would have thrown his full electoral weight behind it.

Neil finished his exercises, and lay back on the floor in feigned collapse. He was hoping for a hug to revive him, but Bernard thought he could offer him something better. The advert in *Capital Gay* had mentioned a shower in every room. It was simply a matter of locating the fitted cupboard that contained it. He strode towards the cupboard nearest the window and flipped the door open. Inside were the dark green tiles and gleaming fitments he had been hoping for.

Neil was pleased, and only took a moment to take his clothes off as he walked across the carpet to the shower. Bernard noticed again his furry thighs and the dark skin tone (Yugoslav blood) that he had at first assumed was a tan, and would fade. His preferred colour for his own skin was slug-white, and he still felt the same spasm of involuntary sympathy for tanned flesh – artificial or the real thing – that he could feel for the flayed tissue of a crocodile handbag.

Neil used soap only once a week, and washed his hair only about as often, in marked contrast to his colleagues at the salon. This was down-under hippie simplicity, to be sure, but it was also mild superstition. In his teens he had suffered so terribly from acne that he had become little short of a hermit, dropping out of school and shunning company. He had once been beaten by his Physical Education teacher for refusing to take his shirt off. Now that he was clear of acne, except for the high-water mark it had left on his shoulders, he left his outside alone as far as possible.

Acne had affected him profoundly, or to put it another way, on the surface; the virus in his bloodstream seemed to have changed him less. He seemed surprised, even now, to be a survivor of acne. He had suffered nothing worse at the hands of the virus, so far, than the loss of a margin for error, once the defining privilege of youth. He remained calm when possible treatments of the virus came up in conversation, but his voice took on a glow when he mentioned Roacutane, the desperate drug that had finally seen off his acne. He said he would be willing to endorse Roacutane on television, make a pilgrimage, carry a placard in the street, testifying to its healing powers. At the time it had made his bones ache, turned his lips yellow and given him bleeding from the nose and the rectum, but he regarded that as the smallest of payments. Roacutane had made his skin dry where once it had been extremely oily, but he was grateful to have working skin back, of whatever description.

A fan had switched itself on when Neil pressed the light switch to the shower, but steam was still drifting into the room. Bernard remembered, then put it out of his mind, that Neil had had one anomalous outbreak of acne after Roacutane, which suggested that his skin was having its ability to police itself undermined in some way.

Neil emerged from the shower with a small towel round his waist, dripping shamelessly on the carpet. He lay down on the bed after the briefest period of towelling, enjoying the hotel guest's privilege of treating the facilities to mild abuse. He beckoned Bernard towards him.

Bernard hung back a little. He had brought no finery for the weekend, but he had not intention of getting what he was wearing wet, just as they were going out to dinner.

Neil tried a different nuance of flirtation. 'Do you want a fashion show now or later?'

Bernard thought for a moment. 'Later.' Neil had promised to show him the costumes he had devised for the gay naturists' fancy-dress party, to be worn by his landlord and himself. The theme was Rude. Bernard was proud that he had kept his curiosity within bounds, so that Neil would satisfy it without making him wait too long. In fact his mind was ablaze with the need to know what Rude Naturist Fancy Dress could actually look like.

Neil didn't seem displeased by the prospect of a few more hours' mystery-making. 'Get dressed and go to dinner, eh?' he crooned up from the bed.

Bernard entrusted the choice of a place for dinner to Neil; it turned out to be a lengthy business. There were plenty of restaurants to choose from, but it seemed silly to walk into the first one that offered. Bernard had spotted on his walk a place that offered Genghis Khan barbecues, served by waitresses who seemed – from a peer through bottled glass – to be dressed in rags of Mongolian cut, but once that option was discarded, it was a matter of choosing from the competitive clamour of good taste, and deciphering a plausible menu from pages of scrawled French. Most of the restaurants, which after a few minutes seemed almost continuous, had permanent menus in their windows and blackboards with the daily specials out in the street, so a certain amount of cross-indexing was called for.

Finally Neil plumped for a place that seemed spacious. They were immediately shown up a narrow staircase to an upper room full of little tables; it turned out that the main dining-room had been booked by a large party. One beneficial side-effect of the cramped conditions was that they had to sit with their legs meshed together, in a way that would have got them thrown out of the main dining-room.

Neil ordered a rare steak, mildly to Bernard's irritation, since he had vetoed a number of places that had appealed to him personally, on the unstated grounds that they offered nothing to vegetarians, beyond salads that might just as well have had stencilled on their drooping leaves No Fun But Good For You. Bernard ordered mussels. He had a weakness for meals that needed to be processed as much as eaten, for spare ribs and artichokes, for foods that needed to be eaten with your hands, for dishes that left a satisfying pile of debris. It gave him a sense of occasion to be engaging in an almost adversarial relationship with food, instead of simply placing it inside him.

As he levered open the savoury hinges of the mussels, taking an almost philistine pleasure in the destruction, he became aware that another hinge, Neil's knee, was pressing against his trouser-fork with a force that went beyond affection. Bernard looked up, startled. Neil laid his knife and fork down neatly and leaned forward, putting a hand on each side of the table. His voice was dark with anger, angrier than Bernard had ever heard it. 'Do you hear what those people are saying?'

'No. Which people?'

'Behind us.'

Behind Neil were two ordinary-seeming middle-aged couples. The only fragments of conversation he had heard from that quarter had concerned schools and horse riding.

'What are they saying?'

'Listen.'

Bernard did his best to screen out the sounds of crockery and actual eating, the thick soundtrack of conversation. He thought he was able to focus on the offending quadrant of chat. The sentence he thought he heard was: 'And then of course that starts off a chain.'

'I think they're talking about moving house,' he explained, 'you know, someone makes an offer for a house, but they can only come through with the money if someone else buys their house, and *they're* in the same position. So it's called a chain, and sometimes people can get snagged up for ages.'

Neil was still gripping the table, and his voice had not lost rage. 'That's not what they're talking about.' Bernard couldn't help dropping his eyes to Neil's plate, wondering if this aggressive-ness was what happened when a habitual vegetarian dabbled in rare meat. The idea, as he could see as soon as it was fully formulated, was ridiculous, and in any case Neil had made only minor inroads into his steak.

'So what are they talking about? Why are you so angry?'

'They're talking about a certain . . . infection and its – what do you call it – methods of transmission.' He relaxed the grip of his fingers on the table. 'They're full of ideas. Ignorant fuckers.' He rested his hands on his lap for a moment, then took up his knife and fork again.

Bernard, finally, was in touch with his anger. 'That's outrageous. That's the last thing we need to hear.' Now that he had started to feel anger, he felt the need to work it up into action. He couldn't stop the virus itself from playing gooseberry, but there was a limit to what he had to put up with. There was no reason why he should sit back while these people broadcasted their idiotic editorials. 'Do you want me to talk to them?'

Neil gave a small smile, his mouth full of his steak's unaccustomed juiciness. 'Don't bother.' Bernard was forced to realize that if he made any protest, the people he ticked off would feel only that their rights were being violated: their right to make no distinction between public and private, their right to have the world remain as it was advertised to be. He returned reluctantly to his mussels, which had cooled off almost as quickly as Neil had, and were nowhere near as appetizing as they had been when he had last looked at them. They were no longer sending up steam to signal their deliciousness.

Neil's burst of temper hadn't lasted long, but it was still out of character. His personality held very little of the aggressive. Only in one family story that he had passed on to Bernard was there a trace of hostility mixed in with the warmth, and even there the aggressiveness was sweetened and made palatable. As a boy he had dreamed that New Zealand was stricken by a famine. At a family conference it was decided that they should eat Neil's elder brother Robin – who had been weeping quietly throughout – since he was made of trifle. Neil and the others took small spoonfuls from the place they felt would be least painful, just above the hips.

Bernard pushed away the graveyard plate of mussels. 'I'm stuffed,' he said. 'How about you?'

Neil looked startled. 'I'm not too stuffed, I've still got some inergy left,' he said. He used the same pinched vowel that made the word 'sex' on his lips sound like the number after five. Bernard didn't grasp for a moment the reason for Neil talking about energy, when he himself was asking about food. Then he remembered that 'stuffed', in the Kiwi lexicon, meant tired rather than full.

'I'm not stuffed either. What I meant to say was full up. Could you manage something else? I saw trifle on the menu.'

Neil seemed indifferent to trifle, in a way that suggested he was still upset about their fellow diners, who were now greeting the sweet course with a round of hushed exclamations, gasps of complicity in sugar and resolutions to take exercise. One of them was saying, 'As long as I ride enough, I don't have to worry. It just shakes off.'

For form's sake, Bernard enquired about the composition of the trifle. Neil would touch only teetotal trifle, since for some reason possibly to do with the virus, alcohol and sugar collaborated to make his teeth sing at the time, and screech the next day. The message came back from the cook by way of the waitress, who gave a proud grin, that the trifle was full of good things. 'You could wring the sponge out and fill a liqueur glass with it,' she said. 'A real Saturday night treat.' Bernard asked for the bill, and they left.

The nearest gay pub marked on the map that their host at Rogues had given them was called The Waterman. As they entered, their novelty ensured them the equivalent of a ticker-tape welcome. The Waterman had the usual amenities of a gay bar that had evolved stage by stage from a straight one, that is, no chairs, so that turning round to stare involved no violence to furniture. The pub was too crowded for conversation actually to stop, but everyone there gave them an aggressively searching look in their first ten seconds in the pub. Bernard knew the commercial gay scene well enough to realize that interest and approval were often signalled with a coldly accusing stare, but it still seemed strange to him. You would have thought that The Waterman was playing host to a convention of bounty hunters, he thought, who couldn't help comparing any unfamiliar faces with the Wanted posters in their minds. Neil and Bernard felt Wanted all right. It wasn't particularly pleasant.

When they had been served Neil took a single sip from his orange juice, narrowed his eyes and said, 'This should give you some idea of gay life in New Zealand. Imagine this being the only bar in Auckland. Those boys over there, eh, the cream of the local talent.' He nodded his head towards a group of bleached-blonds in multicoloured tracksuits, drinking gin and tonics. 'About the same number of punch-and-pricks.'

'What are punch-and-pricks?' asked Bernard, wondering if this was a word from the Kiwi lexicon or a term of gay argot that he was too old to be familiar with. It turned to to be professional slang.

'Punch-and-pricks? You know,' he lowered his voice significantly as a man passed between them on his way to the lavatory, 'hair transplants.'

'How do you rate that one?'

'Five out of ten.' He leaned forward against Bernard's ear, so that he expected a public version of Neil's trademark kiss. Instead he murmured, with the same moist intimacy, 'Yip yip yip.'

'What's that mean?'

'Don't look now.' He nudged Bernard's head into the appropriate alignment. *'Keep your distance*, remember? *Please don't touch?'*

Neil was right. The attendant from the Pavilion, now wearing jeans and a check shirt, was standing guard, with the same paranoid glint, over a pint of lager. 'Sharp eyes,' said Bernard. 'You must have been pretty good in Ye Olde Kiwi Gay Bar.'

Neil didn't deny it. 'Well, you don't want to drag home anyone too soft or tragic. Not with your friends watching. And they didn't have anywhere else to go either.'

The man who had been identified by Neil as a punch-and-prick paused on his way back from the lavatory. He was short enough for Bernard to be able to see his head from above; for Neil this was presumably the normal angle of vision, since he was so tall and spent his professional time hovering about people's heads with scissors. The punch-and-prick gave a broad smile. 'When you've had enough of these tired provincial queens,' he said, 'come over and talk. I'm with friends. You'll like them.'

There wasn't a lot Bernard could think of to say to that. Neil nodded amiably. When they left the pub, a little later, on their way to a nightspot marked on the map from Rogues, they could only hope not to be too visibly passing up this invitation. Given Neil's height and the pub's single exit, which meant passing near where the punch-and-prick and his party must have set up their rampart of masculinity, there was not much chance of their going unnoticed. At least they could hope that the punch-and-prick wouldn't turn out to be the owner of the club they were heading to now, or the little free admission vouchers from Rogues might not be enough to smooth their passage.

Vouchers or no, they had to wait quite a while on the steps heading up to the club. Bernard spent the time inveighing against the name of the club, Stompers. Why did every place that offered even the mildest pleasure after dark need to call itself by some idiotic plural: Stompers, Bumpers, Bangs, Rogues, Spats? Why did pleasant pubs called the Churchill Arms install a few spotlights and reopen as Churchills? Did it bother Neil as it bothered him?

Neil said, 'I can live with it.' Bernard was about to back up his objections when he realized he was only inches away from one of his classroom tirades, against crimes like Grocer's Apostrophe (Apple's and Pear's). He shut himself up.

The vouchers from Rogues, which Bernard had been nervously locating in his pockets at intervals throughout the evening, turned out to entitle them only to half-price admission. This would have taken the gilt off the gingerbread, except that no one waiting on those narrow stairs, after being buzzed through the street door, could have been expecting gilt or even gingerbread. There was something eerily familiar, Bernard thought as he explored with a drink, about the layout of the club, its chain of undersized rooms. Then he realized that like Rogues, the night-club was the smallest possible conversion from a terraced house.

He had been briefly fooled by the staircase, which caused them to enter where the top landing would have been.

The upper bar had taken the place of a back bedroom; the lower one was substituting for the front parlour. Eventually Bernard and Neil found their way to the disco dance-floor, which had once – perhaps even recently – been a kitchen. Bernard was pleased to see that the oldest man in the club was dancing with the best of them, was dancing in fact even when he was the only one on the little dance-floor, though he seemed to need little twists of tissue paper stuffed in his ears to make the experience bearable. From time to time he adjusted the paper-twists to block out more of the music that gave the dancing its excuse, before going back to his interpretative movement.

Bernard kept examining Neil for signs of fatigue. The whole visit to Stompers was something of a token gesture, to prove to themselves that they had gone to Brighton and done the whole bit, and he didn't want Neil tiring himself out for a gesture's sake. He asked Neil to dance as a preliminary to suggesting that they might as well think of going home, but neither of them was particularly light on his feet. Neil, when he danced, betrayed the awkwardness he must have had in school photographs – assuming they had such things as school photographs in New Zealand – towering year after year above the massed Rangis and Debras. Bernard for his part was kept well below his normal modest level of competence by thoughts of the primal kitchen which the disco had supplanted. The kitchen lurked reproachfully under the thin crust of night-life. He tried to make up his mind about what exactly the DJ was replacing. Would it be the fridge or the draining board?

When they had finished dancing and were sweating lightly in the kitchen passage, Bernard suggested they go back to the hotel. 'Do you want to?' asked Neil.

'Yes, why not?' Bernard was moved partly by consideration for Neil. Neil suffered from social strangury, though the word he used was *piss-shy*. He was unable to urinate in public; even taking turns in the bathroom with Bernard after sex, he couldn't perform at the bowl with Bernard there. He needed a couple of minutes to himself before his inhibited duct opened up again.

Bernard was pleased by this foible in such a sturdy naturist, Neil's bladder living by a more reticent code than his pelt's. But by now it must be several hours since he had been to the lavatory, several hours of taking in liquid without any alcohol to drive it off. He had been for the last time in the hotel before dinner, using the shared facility with a little difficulty.

Back at Rogues, Neil made no obvious dash for the bathroom; in fact he insisted on putting on his fashion-show at last. Bernard obediently faced the window while Neil undressed, and then made intricate adjustments. Bernard thought he could hear a snapping noise, either of elastic or some sort of fastening, as well as the faint dry swish of material on skin. Then Neil announced, 'You can turn round now.' His costume was worth waiting for. Rude, naturist, fancy dress; it fulfilled all the requirements. Neil was wearing a jock-strap with the pouch cut out, so that his genitals dangled freely; the jock-strap was held up – though this was purely a visual touch, the elastic waistband being perfectly adequate – by a pair of braces. Hanging diagonally across his chest, in the manner of a beauty-pageant sash, was a strip of towelling that Bernard recognized as being a strip cut from a corporation swimming towel, bearing the woven legend BOROUGH OF CAMDEN 1986. Neil advanced towards him to be embraced. 'It's wonderful. Really,' Bernard said. 'And is your landlord's just the same?'

'Yes. Except he's Mr Borough of Islington.' Neil's embrace became more rhythmic; he rocked their combined bodies from side to side. Bernard needed to do some marking, and broke the embrace to say so. 'I should have done it earlier on,' he said, 'I know. But I can't work on trains.'

Neil made no protest. He took another shower, calling from the misty cubicle that it wasn't a cold one, not by a long stretch, while Bernard did some perfunctory, guilt-appeasing marking. Then Neil brushed his teeth with his usual thoroughness. Bernard had conscientiously left his toothbrush at home, so as not to do the same through force of habit. Neil's gums had a tendency to bleed, and even when they weren't affected Bernard had been led more than once to the ultimate inverted-Judas gesture of withholding a kiss. Sometimes his tongue stood aside from a kiss even when he wanted to involve it. Neil, it had to be said, even at his most passionate, was not a great one for tongue-stabbing, and his reticence increased, understandably enough, when thrush made his saliva soupy.

Bernard's fear of going to the dentist had not long survived the onset of the health crisis. It had been quite a big fear until then, and he sometimes wondered where it had gone. It seemed likely that he had the same total quantity of fear in him, only now it was salted away in little packets rather than gathered in a single large consignment.

The dentist had become tolerable once Bernard had realized that kissing was the only possibly dangerous thing he intended to go on doing. The safety of kissing seemed to be assumed and disavowed almost by turns in the publications he consulted, but either way it was only sensible to have his mouth's defences regularly seen to. He had confessed to his dentist that he avoided brushing when he was going to be kissing soon after, expecting to be told not to be so silly. He had been disconcerted when the dentist had said that of course there was only a possible risk when his partner was 'shedding virus' (whatever that meant), but yes, brushing the teeth could abrade the gums and lead to bleeding. Brushing was a necessity in the long term but did involve a tiny risk, a really tiny risk, in the short. Not brushing before, er, intimate contact might be a realistic precaution.

So it was that Bernard smelled mintiness and freshness on Neil's breath, and Neil smelled whatever Bernard had been eating. This hardly seemed a fair exchange, except that the smell of toothpaste had come to seem definitely sinister to Bernard, even when he was brushing his teeth in the morning, in total security.

Bernard was still hanging over his marking, but had not been taking it in for quite a time. Neil, meanwhile, was already asleep. Bernard packed away the pile of exercise books, turned out the light and went to join him. He approached the bed from the near side, but as he lifted the duvet and prepared to slide in he encountered a large, heat-filled leg. He went round to the other side, but Neil was there too. He had the habit, when he went to bed before Bernard, of stretching out like a starfish, or at least of occupying the diagonal, so that Bernard would be certain to wake him.

When Neil reached a deeper level of sleep, Bernard knew, his personality would change, would lose this responsiveness. He would turn into a warm elongated bobbin and gradually wind the bedclothes around him, winding the warmth off Bernard. He was the last person on earth Bernard would have suspected of being a blanket-fascist, but there it was, you could never tell.

Bernard nudged his way into the bed, triggering Neil's reflexes of welcome. Neil shared his hoarded heat. His body offered a wide variety of textures, not just the ghosts of acne on his shoulders and the back of his neck, but the little fleshy pebbles seeded across his face and forehead which he said the doctors called *molluscum* – a term which Bernard refrained, as an act of love, from looking up in the medical encyclopaedia. On Neil's back were the extraordinary parallel scars he had acquired as a schoolboy athlete, his speciality inevitably the highjump since it involved a modified fall from his embarrassing height to the enviable equality of the sandpit. Once he had practised a Fosbury Flop over a barbed-wire fence, and the long striations of scar tissue on his back were the result.

Neil's scars had a sentimental value for Bernard. Neil had mentioned them in an early conversation in a way that Bernard had found inexplicable. Then he realized that Neil was disposing of embarrassment in advance, and was anticipating, consciously or unconsciously, a conversation in which the subject would necessarily arise if it hadn't been dealt with already: a conversation in which both of them would be naked.

Lower down on Neil, the textural variety continued. He

invariably wore bedsocks; night for him was always a cold country no matter what the temperature of day. Since mid-October he had taken to wearing two pairs, and no amount of central heating could coax his feet out of their coverings.

Neil's embrace was semi-conscious now, but Bernard couldn't resist asking, 'Neil, is there anywhere you've been in the world where you haven't worn bedsocks?'

Neil grunted faintly into the pillow but admitted it. 'Yeah.'

'Where?'

'Hawaii.'

Something else struck Bernard as odd. Neil hadn't actually been to the bathroom since they had got back from the disco. 'Neil . . . have you had a piss since we got back?'

Neil grunted again. 'No.'

'I thought you'd be dying for one.'

Neil thought for a moment, still muffled against the pillow. 'Is that why we left so early?' He struggled to the edge of the bed. 'I need a piss now anyway.'

When he had come back and settled back under the duvet, Neil said, with a deliberateness that was almost the same as sleepiness, but not quite, 'You really piss me off when you decide things for me like that.' His voice slowed down and lost definition. 'That really makes me . . .' on the edge of sleep, he found the appropriate Kiwi word, '. . . ropable.'

'Now you know that's not the way it works,' Bernard said. 'It's not me that pisses you off, it's you that pisses you off. Remember Re-birthing? You told me that was the whole principle of the thing. Taking responsibility.' There was no answer. 'So what you mean is, you really piss yourself off when you let me decide things for you like that. Isn't that right?' Even while he was saying all this he was wondering why he was fighting so dirty, using heavy ammunition – and more to the point, irreplaceable ammunition – in the smallest little squabble. He could only hope that Neil was fully asleep. He waited a few moments for a reply. Then he stretched out next to Neil, turning his back so their buttocks touched lightly.

95

He still wasn't satisfied that Neil was really asleep. There was only one way of telling for sure. Thanks to some aberration of the New Zealand educational system, Neil spoke good German, while Bernard was only now studying the language at an elementary level with an evening class. Neil didn't waste his academic advantage. So now Bernard breathed a simple sentence, knowing that if Neil was less than deeply asleep he would inevitably surface to correct Bernard's pronunciation, which he found laughable in its exaggeration. '*Der Friseur liegt hinter dem Lehrer,*' he murmured, but making the consonants clash like sabres in a duel. There was no answer, and this time Bernard was satisfied. That made it official.

Bernard himself slept well, except for a dream which had no characteristics until he diagnosed it as a dream, and decided to leave it. Then it became intensely confining. He tried twisting his arms and legs to be free of it, but they were dream arms and legs, and powerless. He started to cry out instead, and was so afraid they would be cries only inside the dream that he kept on making them. He produced, in reality, four low shouts. Neil put his arms round him and said, 'I'm here.' Bernard was now fully awake, while Neil had surfaced only long enough to give out that single breath of assurance.

Bernard lay awake for a while, thinking that in Neil's place he would have wanted to give reassurance too, but the phrases he would have used for the job were 'Neil . . . Neil . . . Neil' and 'You're having a nightmare.' Not very helpful. It would never have occurred to him that it would bring comfort to say, 'I'm here.' But Neil's sleeping self seemed to include, as well as the blanket-fascist, a sweetly competent disperser of nightmares that Bernard could only admire and find mysterious.

He was woken in the morning by what he thought was rain, until it turned out to be the sound of Neil getting his money's worth out of the shower. The time was 10.15. He stretched under the duvet, remembering what the hotel-owner had said about breakfast. Breakfast lasted from nine to eleven. 'So I'll turn the toaster on at five to,' he said.

'Oh, Neil and I were thinking of having an early breakfast and going for a walk.'

The hotel-owner nodded. 'Yes, people do say that.'

Bernard protested feebly. He didn't know whether the implication was lechery or laziness. He remembered a friend telling him about a weekend in Brighton with a new boyfriend, when they had broken a bed on their first night. The landlord had been very understanding. The next night they broke the other bed. Bernard wondered if perhaps he should reassure this hotel-owner that his furnishings and fittings were likely to survive the weekend. He settled for simple repetition. 'Oh, I think we'll have breakfast early and go for a walk.'

'See you then, then,' said the landlord politely.

Neil had dried himself by now, and returned to the bed. Bernard hugged him. 'When I heard you in the shower, I thought it must be rain.'

'Rain, eh? In England? At a weekend?'

'It was a wild idea and I bitterly regret it.'

'Have you looked out of the window?'

'No.'

'Raining. Just thought you'd like to know.'

Bernard took his turn in the shower. By the time they reached the dining-room, it was a little before eleven. Their host made no reference, even with a smile, to the planned walk, didn't for instance produce plates of shrivelled food, vintage nine o'clock. It was some consolation that the other breakfasters – there were only four of them – were just being served their test-tubes of orange-juice, and so couldn't have been down much before them.

After breakfast, Bernard settled the bill. They could still take their walk, but now they would have to take their bags with them. It seemed a good idea, all the same, and when Neil had wrapped around his neck his collection of Oxfam-shop scarves they set off down the hill to the seafront.

They took a turn along the promenade. One bus shelter in two seemed to be open to the sky, asserting in the teeth of the evidence that a resort once favoured by royalty could never run out of sunshine. Looking out to sea from the promenade, they could see the weather being formed some way offshore. Beyond a certain distance, the sky was an undifferentiated grey. On the near side of an invisible barrier, clouds appeared and were driven towards land. It was bad weather, but at least it was new weather, and there was some status in that. At least they had got to it before anyone else.

Bernard wanted to get down to the gravel beach, not because he wanted a paddle or a chance to make gravel-castles, but because somehow there was no point in going to Brighton and doing anything else. Neil hung back, either because the sea shore didn't meet his spoiled southern-hemisphere definition of beach, or because the going underfoot would prove too tough for what was left of The Winter Boots. 'We could have a swim, though,' he suggested. Bernard stared. 'In a pool,' Neil added.

'On a Sunday?'

'Why not?' Neil was optimistic.

'We'll have to break in.'

'I don't think so.' Neil held up the map. 'We can try, eh?'

It took them a few wrong turns, all the same, to find the swimming pool, but when they got there it was open. It was also called The Prince Regent Swimming Centre. 'Isn't that just as piss-elegant as you'd expect,' said Bernard as they queued for tickets. 'Other people have pools. The Prince Regent has a Swimming Centre.'

'I think it looks stunning. There's a water slide.'

The changing rooms were certainly well equipped. Because of their bags, Neil and Bernard had to use a relay of lockers, locking each key in the next compartment along to avoid pincushioning their trunks with safety pins.

Besides the water slide, the swimming centre had a separate diving pool, and a supervised lane for serious swimmers. Neil and Bernard included themselves in this category, and had the goggles – guaranteed against misting and leakage – to prove it. Bernard admired Neil's efficient unflustered crawl, his progress through the water in a series of easy windmilling shrugs. Once, as they passed each other in opposite directions, Neil slid his hand between Bernard's legs, breaching lane discipline for a moment in order to do so.

Afterwards, when they had dried and dressed themselves, Bernard said, 'I enjoyed that.'

'Yes, there's nothing like a good swim.'

'I don't mean that, quite. I mean when you touched me.'

Neil smiled. His face had a badger's-mask look to it, from where his goggles had left their shape on his skin. 'I couldn't be sure it was you. So I had to touch up everybody in the pool.'

When Bernard regained his bearings after leaving the pool, he realized that they were only some little way from The Pantry, where they had had such a pleasant snack the day before. Why not go there again, or try it anyway? If they were now in a town where swimming-pools were open on the Sabbath, perhaps they had been transplanted bodily to a universe where – in spite of its resemblance to Britain – anything you wanted might be had when you wanted it. Neil fell in with the suggestion, and Bernard obliged him by falling in with his lazy pace.

The Pantry was indeed open, though almost empty. The only addition since the previous day was a lavish spread of Sunday papers; the only subtraction was the middle generation of the staff. Today the old lady served, and the young girl once again cleared up.

Neil had a small salad and an orange juice – he always asked simply for 'juice', since he was now in a country where no one would think of looking for juice in anything but an orange, or rather a can of orange juice. Bernard ordered a coffee and some garlic bread, which took a little time to arrive. When it did, it repeated, he felt, the triumph that the mussels had had the day before, until they were obscurely sabotaged by the people at the next table: the bread was thick, the way Bernard liked it (and Neil didn't) and so saturated with garlic butter it might have been injected with it, like a Chicken Kiev.

Neil had already nearly finished by the time the garlic bread arrived, but Bernard felt no need to hurry. 'I should have had this before we had our swim.'

'And got cramp, eh?'

'Maybe, but at least I would have had a lane to myself. *Headlamps* of garlic.'

Neil leaned sideways and down, then sat up again with a yelp. Bernard said, 'What's the matter?' Neil said, 'Splinter'. Bernard gave a smiling wince of fellow-feeling and returned to his colour supplement, slightly smeared as it was with garlic butter. He licked the last of the butter off his fingers, enjoying his last tastes of it. When he looked up, there was still pain on Neil's face, and he was still inspecting his hand. 'Is it a bad one?'

'It's in a bad place, anyway.' The splinter had run under the nail of his left index finger. Neil held the hand out to him. The splinter seemed to have gone all the way to the back of the nail. Most splinters are like small spears; this one was like a small spade, as Bernard could see through the pale shield of Neil's fingernail before blood obscured it.

Bernard said, 'What were you doing, exactly?'

'Looking in my bag for the map. To see how far we are from the station. Only I didn't get as far as my bag. I must have got caught on the bottom of the table.'

Gingerly, Bernard patted the underside of the table, which was rougher even than the unpolished top. He thought for a moment. 'We need a pin.'

'Well, I haven't got one.' Neil was pressing down on the tip of his nail, to prevent any issue of blood, in a way that looked particularly painful.

Blood in general, and blood like Neil's in particular, had acquired a demonic status over the few previous years. Before that time, blood seemed largely a symbolic substance, and people's attitudes towards it signs of something else. Being a blood donor involved only a symbolic courage, and squeamishness about blood was an odd though perhaps significant little cowardice. Now blood had taken back its seriousness as a stuff. Bernard spent needless thought worrying about what would happen if a drop of blood landed on the table, as if the customers had the habit of running their tongues along the lacerating wood. They would indeed need to be pretty quick off the mark anyway, to have any hope of putting themselves at risk.

'Could have been worse, eh?' Neil said. 'I could have had a nosebleed.'

'I'll see if there's someone here with a pin,' Bernard said. The grandmother of the establishment was in a kitchen full of steam and the smell of burnt toast. Bernard tried to explain his need for a pin, but succeeded only in flustering her. He glimpsed, meanwhile, a bottle of bleach on a shelf by the sink, which a sense of responsibility to the public would oblige him to use if Neil shed his blood at all widely.

The young girl slipped in through the swing door and watched with a neutral interest. Bernard found himself missing that intermediate generation of staff, the competent mother-daughter who would make everything all right.

The grandmother produced at first some tiny forks with wooden handles, designed for the convenient handling of corn on the cob, and then a safety pin, which Bernard carried in sombre triumph back to Neil in the eating area.

Neil was still pressing his nail down, and had managed to prevent any real leakage. 'We'd better not do it here,' Bernard said. 'Put people off their food.' In fact the few people in the café were stubbornly focused on their plates and Sunday papers, but Neil followed Bernard obediently back to the kitchen.

Now for a change Neil pulled up the end of the nail, with a shiver of pain, and Bernard used the safety-pin, trying to skewer the splinter and draw it out. The field hospital established in her kitchen seemed to distress the grandmother more, if anything, than impromptu surgery would have upset her customers. She kept fluttering up to them from the stove, and saying, 'Are you sure you shouldn't go to the hospital?'

'We'll get the splinter out first,' said Bernard, speaking with false confidence, 'then we might get the hospital to take a look.' He tried to peer under the rim of the nail, hoping to see the contour of the splinter again. By working the safety-pin gingerly from side to side, he was able to snag the thin stem of the splinter. Neil's hand gave a little jerk as the pin started to pull on the embedded fragment. Bernard tried to move his hand as slowly and smoothly as possible. Neil gave another involuntary pull, and the narrow part of the splinter broke off, leaving the rest of it lodged in the quick.

Bernard pulled out a chair for Neil to sit down, and told the grandmother what she had been telling him for some time. 'I think we'd better go to the hospital. Is it near? Walking distance? Do you have a car?' He thought driving them to hospital was the least she could do to atone for the dangerous roughness of her table, but she shook her head in answer to the question about a car. He was surprised when she took her coat from the back of the kitchen door and put it on. 'We're not on the phone here,' she explained. 'I'll ring from my daughter's.'

'Does she live in Brighton?' Bernard asked, aiming at a joke.

She didn't smile. 'Just round the corner. I'll be back in a minute.' She murmured something to the girl, before she left, about being in charge.

The girl, all the same, chose to stay in the kitchen rather than attend to her customers. By and large they were patient Sunday customers, but every now and then a little self-righteous queue built up, and she would have to venture out to serve them.

Bernard's worries had transferred from spilled blood, no longer a risk now that Neil's clotting agents had started to work, to the safety-pin. He shouldn't leave it without some attempt at disinfection. He could pour a little bleach over it, before the girl came back in. Or might Neil be offended? Then again, if he had been a smoker, he could have lit up, and held the match flame under the safety-pin just for a few seconds, before blowing it out.

The girl came back in, and Bernard abandoned any plan of eliminating contamination on the premises. Her grandmother – if they were in fact more than professionally connected – came back the next minute. She hung up her coat and offered to make tea, on the house. Bernard only regretted that they had paid when they had ordered, and so had no opportunity of expressing emotion by withholding payment. Neil wanted to be ready for the taxi when it arrived, so they sat in the eating area, at the table next to the door.

There was no sign of the taxi. 'If this was America,' Bernard said, 'they'd be so afraid of being sued they'd treat us a lot better than this. We'd have a chauffeur to the hospital, I dare say.'

'If this was New Zealand,' Neil said, 'they'd polish the tables in the first place.' He had wrapped a paper napkin round the finger.

Again Bernard tried for the light note. 'Not much point in going to a veggie restaurant, eh, if the furniture goes and bites you.'

His impatience got the better of him and he stepped out on to the pavement to greet the taxi when it arrived. There were infuriating numbers of taxis rushing past already, but none of them so much as slowed down. They all seemed to have their signs illuminated, and Bernard tried frantically to flag them down, feeling that this emergency justified the breaking of his promise to the taxi that was on its way.

The taxis ignored him anyway, but not from solidarity. It became clear that Brighton was not a town where taxis could be hailed. They had to be ordered, and if they had an illuminated sign on top, that was to say 'I am a taxi,' not 'I will take you where you want to go.'

After several frustrating minutes, Bernard went back into The Pantry. He swept into the kitchen and announced that it was now twenty-five minutes since the taxi was called, not consulting his watch in case the true figure was less impressive. He bullied the grandmother until she offered to phone again, reaching once more for her coat on the back of the door. Bernard caught sight of the safety-pin on the table and picked it up, murmuring hollowly that he'd better take it along in case there was more he could do on the way to the hospital. As the grandmother left, he took a seat next to Neil near the door.

'How's it feel?'

'Not bad.'

'Hurt a lot?'

'Not much.'

Bernard hadn't seen him often enough in situations of ordinary adversity to know whether the stiff upper lip was a reflex or a performance. Then the grandmother knocked on the window next to them, and pointed at a cab that had drawn up at the kerb.

The taxi-driver needed some convincing that he was picking up the right party. Bernard began to feel that a telephone call was not enough to secure a taxi in Brighton; you needed a letter from the mayor. But once the driver was satisfied that he had got hold of the right people, he drove them rapidly and without conversation to the hospital, which was a little out of town to the east. As they passed, Bernard recognized the street that Rogues was in.

The hospital was shabby and far from new. An old lady was having difficulty in opening the door as she left; automatic doors were clearly a thing of the future in this part of the world. The casualty department was full of glum waiting people. Bernard pressed a button at the reception counter, which was unmanned, and a receptionist appeared after a few moments. Neil advanced his finger towards her, and she said, 'That looks nasty.' She took his details and told them to take a seat.

After a while, a nurse came timidly down the line of seats, calling a version of Neil's awkward Yugoslav name. Her despairing intonation suggested she spent most of the day calling out names that their owners regarded as parodies of the real thing. She took a look at Neil's hand, and said it looked nasty. Bernard was impressed by this prompt response into thinking that the health service was not quite as clapped-out as it seemed, until the nurse told them it would be at least an hour and a half before they were seen to.

Neil smoothly settled down to writing a letter to his parents in New Zealand. He expressed to Bernard his relief that it wasn't his writing hand that was affected. Bernard tried to settle with a book (there wasn't the desk-space necessary for marking) but found himself unable. He looked round at the rows of silent, passive people waiting to be attended to. After the hotel and the disco, both trying hard to pretend not to be bourgeois homes, it should have been refreshing that the hospital made no attempt to be anything but what it was.

He stood up, and asked the receptionist where he could find a toilet. Across the corridor, she told him, with a slightly furtive intonation that was explained when Bernard realized they were staff toilets, not in theory open to the laity. On his way back from using them – they seemed no more sophisticated than the usual ones, and demanded no extra skills – he spotted a hot-drinks dispenser. This too was labelled Staff Use Only. One of the items it offered was hot chocolate, so Bernard searched through his pockets for change. A pair of shoes strode through the corridor, and stopped behind him in a way he felt was intended to pass a message. They had the acoustic properties unique to white lace-ups worn by a trained person. For an absurd moment he thought he was going to burst into tears. He straightened up, and stopped the search in his pockets, which had so far yielded only copper coins and the safety-pin – in the closed position, mercifully – that he had planned to dispose of so responsibly. He trailed defeated back to the seat next to Neil's.

Neil's letter was reaching its closing stages, with the phrase 'Bernard says hello'. Neil passed the biro across to him and he wrote, embarrassed, 'hello', wishing either that he could embellish this message a fraction with something more personal, or that he could be excused from contributing at all. Out of the corner of his eye he could see that Neil was writing *Bernard says hello* in brackets after his word of greeting. It seemed like a schoolboy's letter home, but he had to admit that Neil currently held the monopoly on adult calm. It was Bernard who had the schoolboy restlessness.

He had intended to wait at least until Neil had finished his letter, but found himself asking prematurely 'Are you going to tell them?'

Neil didn't need the meaning of the question clarified. 'I don't know,' he said. Normally he was scrupulous about disclosing his antibody status, with the result that he was still waiting, after four months, for a dentist's appointment. If when Neil's appointment arrived – and it was still likely to be several months off – any work was necessary, Bernard knew that the dentist would use a low-speed drill to make sure he didn't volatilize any saliva, which might then be inhaled. Perhaps that was why, Bernard thought, it was taking so long for Neil's turn to come round. He could imagine the dentist spending hours on every filling with his hammer and chisel, murmuring behind his mask that people got these things out of proportion, when a few simple procedures were enough to eliminate any risk.

Bernard said, 'It shouldn't make any difference, should it, whether you tell them or not?

'But Brighton is a provincial town, eh?'

'A provincial town full of gay men, mind you. You're going to have to make up your own mind.' He hoped it didn't sound as if he were washing his hands of the matter. His private preference was for telling them – whoever 'they' turned out to be – but he didn't want to make Neil feel like a danger to health, quietly being quarantined.

'I doubt if it matters anyway.'

Towards the end of the stated time, another nurse, who turned out to be a doctor, paid a visit. She kept her hands in the pockets of her white coat, while Neil dutifully held out the finger. She peered through her glasses at it, then looked over the top of them and said, 'Come with me, please.' Neil followed her, and Bernard included himself in the expedition. They went to a room full of little cubicles.

The doctor, though only about Bernard's age, had a feathery growth of hair on her upper lip, which looked oddly touching in spite of its incongruousness. It was like an adolescent's moustache, a shy fanfare of hormones. She kept her hands in her pockets so long that Bernard expected them to be warty, or at least covered in hair, but when she did at last bring them into the open, and touched Neil's finger, they were sightly and even shapely. She put them back in her pockets immediately, in what was clearly the defining posture of her profession. Then she said, 'It's fairly clean, but I may have to cut the nail.' This at least made a change from calling it nasty. 'How long since you had a tetanus injection?'

'Years.'

'Two years?'

'Ten years.'

'You'll be needing one of them, then,' she said. Neil looked uncomfortable. 'And I have to move you again, I'm afraid, to where I keep the long-nosed tweezers. Don't worry,' she said, perhaps seeing Neil's expression. 'I'll give you an anaesthetic. Follow me, please. Your friend can come too.'

They followed her along the corridor to Minor Surgery, where Neil and Bernard had to take their shoes off. As he took off the ragged Winter Boots, Neil said, 'Perhaps someone will steal them, eh? With any luck.' Then he turned to the doctor, and said 'I'm antibody-positive, you know.' Bernard assumed that Neil was urged to frankness by the doctor's willingness to have Bernard along. A relaxed worldliness could be deduced from that. 'I see. That's unfortunate,' the doctor said, frowning as she washed her hands.

'In what way?' said Bernard truculently, assuming that she would now make difficulties about operating on Neil.

'My dear man, you hardly need me to tell you that. It's unfortunate because it makes life so very difficult.' She coaxed Neil on to the operating table.

Bernard's anger still had some momentum to it. 'I think anybody who doesn't work with people who are antibody-positive should be sacked on the spot, not because they're prejudiced but because they must be incompetent to be taking any risks.' He paused for breath.

'Funny you should say that,' said the doctor, and then when Bernard was preparing to ask, 'Why so?', 'That's just what I think myself.'

She helped Neil to push his finger through a sort of stiff cowl of material, so that it was singled out for surgery. Deprived of its fellows it looked almost amputated, even before the doctor had unpacked the case where she kept her long-nosed tweezers.

Sheepishly, Bernard fished the safety-pin out of his pocket and strolled over to a vivid yellow box labelled Contaminated Sharps. He dropped it into the hole in the top, feeling a bit ridiculous but reminding himself that it was, after all, contaminated and it was, after all, sharp. The doctor was unwrapping instruments, individually wrapped in gauze, from a sterilized tin box. Bernard noticed that although she was already wearing surgical gloves, she put on another pair from inside the box. 'Is that necessary?' he asked, with a slight turn of his earlier truculence.

'It's routine,' she said. 'Rubber gloves don't stay sterile for ever, you know. I could have taken the first pair off, but this seemed more sensible. Now shut up,' she said, without heat. 'But you can hold the patient's hand if you like.'

She began to unpack her long-nosed tweezers. Neil turned his head resolutely away, and Bernard locked glances with him. They stayed like that for a little while, like people trying competitively not to blink, then Bernard started flicking sideways glances at the fingernail. The doctor said, 'I'm putting the local in now.' Bernard could see her sliding two needles, one after the other, into the top of the finger. Neil blinked a few times rapidly in succession, and Bernard could feel his hand-grip tightening in spite of itself.

After some probing, the doctor said, 'No, this won't work, I'm going to have to cut the nail.'

'Cut as little as possible, eh?' said Neil, 'I've got a full-head bleach to do tomorrow morning at 10.30.'

The doctor gave a little laugh. She seemed to find this ambition amusing. 'We'll sort something out with the nurse, see if we can't get you a light-weight dressing of some sort.'

Bernard stopped taking his sideways glances, having no wish to see Neil's nail being cut. The two locked glances again, like pieces of heroic statuary. In a moment, the doctor said, 'All done.'

Bernard did the talking. 'How much have you cut?'

'The tiniest sliver. Take a look.'

Bernard kept his eyes where they were. 'Will you be able to reach the splinter?'

'I already have. All done, I told you. Take a look.' She was holding out the stub of the splinter in the mouth of her long-nosed tweezers.

Bernard could feel Neil relaxing against him. He tensed up again when the doctor said, 'Nurse will give you a tetanus injection.' She took off all her rubber gloves, scrubbed up, shook hands pleasantly and left.

Before doing any injections, the nurse fitted Neil with a light-weight dressing, as promised, and told him to go to a casualty department in London in a few days if he needed another. Bernard put his arms round Neil's neck while the injection was done. It occurred to him how stupid he was not to have done it earlier. A local anaesthetic involved having a needle stuck in you just as much as an inoculation did, but somehow the word 'local' made it sound trivial, something you shouldn't need to be helped through. A tetanus jab gave cowardice a wider scope, and Bernard took advantage of it.

Down the corridor there was a telephone which did not, for a wonder, bear the message Staff Use Only. Bernard used it to call a taxi, while Neil climbed awkwardly into his jacket.

It was already fully dark, although not as late by his watch as Bernard had expected. Neither of them knew the times of trains, but they went straight to the station, prepared to take their chances.

'How's it feel now?' Bernard asked.

'Not too bad. Throbs a bit. They say it'll be worse tonight when the local wears off. I may need a sleeping tablet, but we got off pretty lightly, eh?'

Bernard had to agree. They had got off lightly. He had underestimated the amount of practice the hospital would have had with this whole new world of risk and stigma. But he still felt damaged, and found it hard to be cheerful for Neil's benefit.

There was a London-bound train waiting in the station, already very full. There were only isolated seats free, so once again Neil and Bernard sat apart, though visible to each other.

Bernard was grateful for their separation. He needed time to recover independently, always assuming the damage was reversible. The train filled up still more before it pulled out of the station, so that there were people standing, who intermittently broke his view of Neil. From what he could see, Neil had his eyes closed, was asleep or meditating.

The train was a slow one, and stopped at every station it saw. Work on the track diverted it, and at least once it stopped – to judge by the absence of lights – in open country. Near Bernard there stood a woman dressed for a party, complete with bunch of flowers, and a harried mother, come to that, but Bernard felt no inclination to give up his seat. He felt he had a claim on it that outranked theirs. He was still in shock, apparently, though nothing had happened directly to him.

Something had happened to him all the same. He knew that love starts off inspired and ends up merely competent. He didn't resent that. That was bargained for. But he hadn't foreseen, in all his mental preparation, that the passage could be so drastically foreshortened. A tiled corridor filled with doctors and nurses opened off every room he would ever share with Neil. He had always known it was there, but today the door to it had briefly been opened.

He thought with nostalgia of the time when people had got so exercised about who loved who, and how much. Now it was simply a question of what character of love would be demanded of him, and how soon. It was as if he had been pierced in a tender place which he had though adequately defended, by a second splinter, not visible. The word *sick*, even the word *death*, had no power to match the fact of hospital. As with the first splinter, he had managed to break off the protruding part, but not to remove it. It gnawed at the nail-bed.

THE BRAKE

Sex brought him a number of things, all of them more useful than pleasure. His first memory was sexual, and not only that but it had a significant element of endlessness, of continuous quest, as was pointed out to him in later days by a psychiatrist with whom he had an on-again, off-again but not altogether unfulfilling affair.

In the memory, he was in a swimming pool with some of his father's army friends, and he was diving between their legs. They stood with their legs apart, laughing, and he dived through the underwater arches they made. Once or twice he tried to hold his breath and keep swimming, so as to swim through a second arch without surfacing, but the excitement was too much for him and he had to come up for air. His mouth making bubbles, he bumped upwards against the keystone of the arch. When he broke the surface at last, coughing and waterlogged, the laughter was louder than ever. As soon as he got his breath back he dived again.

For his eighteenth birthday, his father gave him a copy of *Battle Cry* by Leon Uris, saying it would teach him everything he needed to know about being a man. But when, the day after his eighteenth birthday, he announced his intention of joining the army, his father wouldn't hear of it. Even his mother wasn't so set against it, but his father was angry in his dismissal of the plan. That was his father all over, spelling out in detail what would win his approval, man to man, and then shooting him down in flames when he tried to put it into practice.

111

It didn't take much thought – and this was long before he met the psychiatrist – to work out that his first memory couldn't possibly be his first, or anything like. It was actually embarrassing, when he tried to establish which of his father's postings brought with it the privilege of a swimming pool, to realize how much older he must have been than he instinctively thought; and still he couldn't take the label 'first' off the memory of diving through the arches, seeing in close-up the muscly flesh goosebumped under its scattering of hair. Logic could strip the memory of its claims to age, but could do nothing to lessen its force. In that sense it kept first place among his memories.

With very little effort he could summon up a memory that must be earlier, and had its own sort of formative power. As a child, he was ready and willing to play with any toys that he was given, or that his playmates owned, even the educational ones, but there was one toy – toy was too small a word really – that he couldn't bear to share, and with which he established an almost erotic relationship. It was a construction set, but unlike Lego or Bayko its materials were grown-up; scaled-down of course, but still very much the real thing. Lego was pleasant to fiddle with, and he enjoyed making the nipples on top of one block snappingly engage with the hollow underside of another. But the houses it made were clumsy and uniform. Bayko was even worse. You had to start by sticking rods vertically in the baseboard, to the shape of the house you were building, and then you slid panels of bricks grooved at each edge down between the rods. You didn't build the roof, you just popped it on like a hat when you'd done everything else. And then all you got for your work was a house like the one his family lived in at the time, with a red tiled roof and one futile bay window.

In any case, he'd seen a house that looked a lot like theirs being built. It was on the way to school, and he passed it every day. He looked closely every time he passed, but there was never any sign of vertical rods. He thought Bayko was probably a cheat, but he wanted to be sure. He dragged behind his mother when the workmen were coming close to the roof level, just in case they put the rods in at the last minute, down through the bricks, to make them stronger. But he never saw any sign of them.

Contemporary Brickplayer was different. All it was was a baseboard and a box of tiny bricks of a dark pinky grey, and a packet of mortar mixture that you made up with water. You didn't have to plan anything and the pieces didn't need to fit together at particular angles. The only limit to your constructions was the binding power of the mortar, and there was no arguing with that. But you could cantilever things out until your building slowly, voluptuously, prised itself apart.

Often he would put a brick in his mouth as he started to play, as if the sour tablet was a sweet, not the crunchy sort of sweet or the chewy sort of sweet, but a sweet like butterscotch that you just moved around your mouth, sucking and sucking, until it faded away. Except that the bricks from Contemporary Brickplayer never faded away. Each new part of his mouth, as he shifted the brick, drew out its inexhaustible flavour of baked clay.

He would build and build until he had used up all the bricks, mixing more mortar when he needed it. And then when there really were no more bricks in the box, and none that had fallen out where he could find them, he would take the brick out of his mouth and add it regretfully to the complex structure on the baseboard. Because of its long immersion in saliva, it had a different colour from the others and stuck less well.

Demolishing the building was almost more fun than building it in the first place. All you needed was warm water, which dissolved the mortar, so he persuaded his mother to let him do it in the bath. He would sit in the hot water and simply hug his building. Everything would slide together in his arms. Then after a few minutes in the water the bricks would be clean and separate again, ready to be used. If his mother was watching, he would let the water drain away, pack away the bricks, and then have a bath on his own. If she wasn't, he liked to let the mortar-rich water dry on his skin in crusty patches.

Contemporary Brickplayer gave him a temporary second skin of greyish powder, which he shed on the sheets, much to his mother's irritation, but sex gave him a second name, one that didn't wear out but eventually replaced the first one for most purposes.

If his father had been more enthusiastic about his joining the military, he might have been able to put off, perhaps for years, tentative steps in a different direction. After that rejection, it took him a long time to understand his father's motives, and what was really expected of him.

There was a life that the army would have saved him from, a life that would save him from the army. He found himself a few months later on the brink of visiting a gay bar, the only one in the town where he lived. He stayed on that brink for a remarkably long time. He passed the pub a number of times, and went defeated home. The entrance was down a flight of steps, and he looked longingly down them as he passed.

When he did go down those steps at last, the image that accompanied him was not the image of his parents, whether angry, shocked or horribly understanding. It was the image of his two little sisters, six and eight years younger than himself, though if he had really run into them it would have been easy to pretend he was just visiting another pub. His sisters' feeling for him was not far short of adoration. In the image that he carried downstairs with him, they were clinging on to each other and weeping in bafflement.

Not that he got any further than the bottom of the stairs that time. As he paused there at the bottom before pushing the door open, he could hear a complex noise of layered conversation that was nevertheless the silence between two records on the juke box. This complex noise excited him. It must contain a voice that would speak to him. But as he was about to push the door open, the next record came on. Its first word was 'Stop!', followed after a dramatic pause by the words 'In The Name of Love'. Startled, he turned and ran up the stairs, and went home.

The next time he tried, the Supremes were off-duty on the juke box and he was able to break through the imaginary cordon of weeping sisters. On his first visit, there was no voice that would speak to him, perhaps because he stood very still and kept his eyes fixed firmly on his beer glass.

On later visits, he was talked to, and he talked grudgingly back. He was full of suspicion of the men who owned these voices. He was unwilling to tell them his real name. His parents were well known in the area, so there was some dim sense to this precaution, though his parents were not so well known as to make it worth anyone's while to hang around gay bars on the off-chance of ensnaring their next of kin. There was no rational reason, in any case, for withholding his first name as he did. The name was Gregory, which was hardly distinctive enough to betray him. To each person he spoke to, in the weeks following his first visit, he gave a different Christian name, as if by this discretion he could avoid having the successive burly boys who sat on the same stool and ordered the same timid drink identified as a single customer – a customer who was fast becoming a regular.

He could have been a David, he could have been a Walter. He had used those names in conversations that he had taken great care should not lead anywhere. His withholding of himself, in fact, was so long-lasting that his parents, if the object had been women and not men – and if they had known about it – might well have worried about him, thinking him underpowered or otherwise troubled.

But he was Roger when he took the fatal step of giving a man his telephone number. By dictating a handful of numerals he dragged himself from sexual pre-history. He was horrified even while he did it, but it never occurred to him to falsify a digit. The logical consequence, of course, was that a man would phone his parents' house, wanting Gregory but asking for Roger. The next night he hovered by the phone, ready to snatch it up, irritated that his parents seemed to be exchanging secret smiles at his behaviour. The call came the following day. Even a year or two later he would have been able to anticipate such a phone call almost to the minute, but when it came he was lying on his bed, relieved and regretting relief.

The man on the phone was confident that his call had been hoped for; he kept the suspicious woman who answered talking for a little while, long enough for Gregory to reach the phone red-faced with the idea of arousal. He became Roger as he reached for the instrument. In time, only the people in the house at the moment when he grasped the receiver, his parents and his sisters, continued to call him Greg.

His schoolmates had used the word 'roger' in a sexual sense, but it never occurred to him that this meaning might have a wider currency. He thought it was purely a school word, like a teacher's nickname. When, later on, he first realized that the sexual sense of his name had escaped its school context and was at large, when someone showed it to him in print in a dictionary, he experienced a bolt of shame, perhaps the very bolt that had been missing from the moment of losing his virginity. He had named himself after a piece of taboo slang.

Later, with some mental effort, he constructed a different rationale for the name. 'Gregory' actually contained 'Roger', albeit back to front. All he had done was set it free from its confines, reading his name against the grain of his parents' intentions. In fact 'Roger', in the moment he had chosen it to present to an attractive stranger, and before it acquired the power to change his life, had seemed to him to have a vaguely military association. It was the crisp, telegraphic, masculine way of saying, I understand. I obey. That the military association still had glamour testified to the continuing influence of his father.

No shame derived from his initiation into sex, but a desperate embarrassment hedged it about. Before leaving the house on his assignation, he had left on his bedside table an envelope, with an inscription instructing that it should be opened if he didn't return that night. He imagined he had no preconceptions about what was about to happen, but at the same time he couldn't visualize anything but returning home. The sex he had with himself led on to sleep, but he couldn't imagine the tense business of traffic with others having the same drowsy consequences. At most he was collecting the keys of the new house of adult sexuality. He wasn't moving in.

Inside the envelope was his partner's phone number, and strict instructions that his parents should not call the number, but pass it on to the police and let them investigate. In later life it amazed him, not that he had had so little trust in his first lover – or in his parents for that matter – but that he had had so much in the police.

In fact, he woke up to the smell of bacon. He pulled on his clothes in a fever, and rushed out of the bedroom, almost colliding with his host, who was carrying a breakfast tray.

'Got to go,' he muttered, and ran out of the house.

When he got home, there was no need even to go upstairs. The kitchen held only the fluster of breakfast-time, with no undercurrents. The meal was in full swing, though he couldn't help noticing that marmalade, here, stayed in the jar it was bought in, while on the tray he had run past a little earlier he had seen a glass dish containing a dainty mound of orange, and a fluted spoon like a miniature shovel. He said something about staying over with a friend, and his sisters immediately started asking when they would be allowed to stay the night with their friends. If his parents detected a particular satisfaction in his manner that morning, they probably decided that Gregory had become a man at last, and only hoped he had been careful. In fact, Roger was thinking how strange it was that you could take your life in your hands, and still wake up to a cooked breakfast.

He saw the man for whom he was Roger a few times, and through him was introduced to a small provincial circle. In later life, he forgot them wholesale as people, and remembered them only as the sources of particular catch-phrases that arrived in his mind, if not actually on his tongue, at long but never predictable intervals. Who was it would murmur when flustered, 'Not a pot washed nor a sausage pricked, and all these Spanish captains in the town'? Who was it sang softly as he shaved, 'How much is that doggie in the mirror?' Who was it used the phrase 'doing the cooking', which seemed at first so casually domestic ('Who does the cooking?', 'I'll bet he does the cooking') to describe a sexual role? There was one man he would remember whenever he heard the word 'hard-on', who gave it the fastidious plural 'hards-on', like someone correcting 'court-martials', to 'courts-martial'.

He liked them, and was grateful to them, but everybody already knew he didn't belong there. He could feel their valuation of him reluctantly rising, though they were also puzzled by him. He wasn't sexually aggressive, but he had none of the pliability of personality they valued in someone his age.

Staring coolly at himself in the mirror, he had decided that the blue of his eyes was his only physical asset (in fact his eyes were much more attractive when he wasn't using them to stare coolly). So he decided to wear nothing but blue jeans, and a narrow range of shirts, all of them incorporating blue as an important element, to point up his only physical asset. In later years, he wondered if his life would have been different if he had had, say, brown eyes. Would he have worn only brown velvet trousers, for instance? But his life would have been different if he had had brown eyes anyway. At least, after his single fashion decision, he was never diverted into dressiness, and his choice of uniform was historically fortunate, if not actually prophetic.

Meanwhile, his other fantasy, the one that started in the bath, had also come out of the water, and taken feeble amphibian steps on land. He was slow to realize that there was a profession that corresponded to the sensations he had experienced in the bath with the bricks. It was only when he saw, on television, film of Frank Lloyd Wright in old age scampering spryly over the Guggenheim Museum while it was being built, that he saw how it was possible to leave the bath, and go on playing for a long lifetime as if you were still there. 'Architect' and 'architecture' became words that took on any amount of glamour – the excitement that was meant to attach to 'marrying and settling down' as well as to 'satisfying career'.

There wasn't much he could find out about Wright at short notice, and none of it was necessarily true; but it was all promising. Wright had started off building windmills for his uncles. He had affairs with his clients' wives. You could hire him to build you a house, but that didn't give you the right to change the furniture around.

He had feared that when he first sat in front of a drawing board all the excitement would drain away, but instead it seemed to concentrate on the point of his pencil. He came to enjoy the drawing as much as he had ever hoped to enjoy a finished building. He had a particular soft spot for axonometrics, where the workings of a building, the secrets of its surfaces, were laid out as if from above and to the side: the point of view of a nosy helicopter, or a low-flying god.

In his early architectural drawings, even those submitted for examination, the buildings seemed to float in a depthless pink space, and there might be an effigy of Frank Lloyd Wright on a pediment, engaged in some complicated transaction with a group of boys and dogs.

It was architecture, and his pursuit of it, that brought him to London, but once he was there it wasn't architecture that took up his attention. He began to find that he had a strongly sexual charm, that he could make men find him attractive more or less by wanting them to. He was suspicious of this charm, and used it as little as possible. Rather later, when he got a credit card, he used that too, as little as possible, and for the same reason: not because his credit was limited, but because it seemed not to be. His credit limit on the card was extended every time he exceeded it, and it seemed to him that the settling of an account so long deferred could only be devastating, when the final sum was called in.

At first, he found gay life in London baffling, congested and chaotic, but then he had the same first impression of London driving. It wasn't long before he was threading his way through the streets and squares with confidence, and with pride in his knowledge, the mental maps he had built up.

He was lucky enough to arrive in a sexual capital at a time when a thick neck was considered a major asset, and a thick waist a minor defect, in some settings even an aphrodisiac. He fitted the metropolitan model of attractiveness far better than he had ever fitted the provincial. Ten years before, he would have been an anomaly even in London.

He made no modifications to his style of dress. At first, he went to a barber's where his hair was trimmed with clippers to a No. 1 on the sides and a No. 3 on top. Later, when more pretentious establishments, actual salons, offered similar cuts, now become fashionable, he transferred his custom. The atmosphere as such didn't do anything for him, but he loved to have his head massaged by a junior's stiff fingers while he was being shampooed. He went almost into a trance, loving this impersonal caress. Any too sensual or tender move in bed had the opposite effect, making him tense and suspicious.

He stayed clean-shaven even when gay fashion moved on to facial hair. He grew a beard just once, and kept it only long enough to receive his first compliment on its fullness, before he shaved it off.

The sharp focus that city life brought to his sexuality had brought with it disillusions as well as enchantments. He was more or less at ease with a fair repertoire of sexual acts. He no longer prepared himself – it embarrassed him to think about it now, cursing his provincial beginnings – for oral sex, or 'giving someone a blow job', by ranging on the bedside table two glasses, one empty and one filled with water.

He had come to a better understanding of himself, in certain specialized departments. He had assumed for a long time, on the evidence of what nude magazines he was able to obtain, that he was mildly undersized genitally. He was slow to gather from his sexual partners that there was something satisfactory about his equipment, and slower yet to twig that its satisfactoriness lay in disproportion. His penis ('cock') was a healthy average, while his testes ('balls') were unusually large.

But there was bad news too. As a sexual mechanism he functioned smoothly on his own, but he was never able to come with anybody there. He could perform only in rehearsal. In his early sexual career, he was able to fool himself that release would come for him when he found more compatible partners, but here he was, established in a setting that put a high value on him, and only confirmed in dysfunction.

He tackled the problem, with considerable enterprise, on three simultaneous fronts. In the first place, he started to chase heterosexuals. The theory here was that since for him the chase was everything, the conquest nothing, he could only gain by spinning things out. There was no play, after all, in reeling in fish that wanted to be caught, so he would learn to cast more widely.

He soon made the dismaying discovery that even straights could be landed. He was always forthright about his desires, and never made the mistake of going in for that David-and-Jonathan rubbish. Straight conversational skills lagged a long way behind gay, he was under no illusions about that, but he was willing to make sacrifices. The trouble was that all too often the opposition collapsed. He would just be setting up an enjoyable pattern of drinks, long phone calls and expeditions to the cinema, setbacks and concessions, when the specimen chosen for his unavailability would raise his beautiful, elusive face – he always went for conventional good looks, on the principle that lookers would be more used to admiration, and better at resisting it – and murmur the dreaded words, 'You've won. You know you've won. You can do anything you like.'

He was always going too far, and getting away with it, that was the trouble. He would be sitting on a sofa looking over an architectural book, the sort that seemed naturally to spread over four knees, and without preparation he would lean down and slowly take off his shoes. He would say softly, 'If I take off my shoes, that doesn't mean anything. But if I take off my socks,' starting to do so, 'that means I'm staying the night.' He would draw out the sock-striptease as long as he could, waiting for an interruption and a protest he imagined as inevitable. Then he would look up, and see instead a pair of eyes shining with more than their usual glitter, and an Adam's apple bobbing nervously under the hang of a classic jaw.

Coarse-fishing of this sort was all very well, but he seemed to spend an undue amount of time trying to throw these prize catches back, so that he could start again, separated by a goodly length of line from his thrashing prey. At least until the setback of their surrender he had their unattainable images to rehearse with. This was a different sort of sport, but still he thought of it as playing himself rather than playing *with* himself: playing himself like a fish, on both ends of the line at the same time, reeling himself in and then letting himself run, playing himself until he was exhausted and dangling, then letting himself off the hook, to slip back into the water.

There was another way out of his erotic cul-de-sac. Being the passive partner in anal intercourse ('getting fucked') was a problem-solving activity to someone in his circumstances. It was respectable for the person taking this role not to ejaculate: orgasm was as often as not only the signal that a sexual event was over, that some exchange had been consummated, and being penetrated was good enough evidence of that.

Since he was socially aggressive, and free of the mannerisms which made some poor people seem like victims of their sexuality rather than exponents of it, there seemed often to be an extra fillip given to his partner by his willingness to receive advances of this sort. He was quite happy to grant them their triumph, for the benefits he derived from it.

Inevitably, though, as he came to think, his body thwarted him, by growing a cyst in its, in his, back passage. Surgery didn't dampen his ardour, but certainly diverted it to other channels. The habit of sex stayed with him: he picked someone up the day after he left hospital, on his first tottery walk to the supermarket. For a long time, he remembered returning to bed in the middle of the night, from a session at stool which had made him weep with pain, and looking down on the peaceful sleeping face of this stranger – until he had to laugh instead, at the momentum of his habits, and the fringe benefits they continued to bring him, whether he wanted them or not.

His third line of attack took up the slack. Simply put, it involved refusing no advance whatever, on the offchance that he might stumble, even at this late date, on what really turned him on. In practice, he found that his willingness had limits that were beyond his power to negotiate. Having his hands handcuffed, tied or confined in any way, was unendurable; it gave him the precise physical sensations of drowning. Most other things he tried.

He picked people up or was picked up by them, at all hours and in all settings. Once, taking his mother to Sadler's Wells (his sisters had both married young and had a son each, so she had time on her hands), he linked eyes with a Mediterranean-looking stranger over cups of sour coffee in the Lilian Baylis Room, and had a piece of paper bearing the stranger's name and telephone number slipped into his hand, with secret-agent slickness, as he queued with his mother to resume their seats after the interval.

So too he found himself on one occasion lying on thick carpet in a luxurious flat, with a cashmere scarf tied loosely over his eyes by way of a blindfold, while his host applied something, something feathery, to his scrotum. The scarf felt wonderful against his face; it returned his breath to him, slightly warmed and lightly scented. He imagined the end of it wafting up and down with his breathing, rolling and unrolling, like a snorer's beard in a Disney cartoon. He thought he could even cope with bondage if it was done with cashmere. Cashmere bondage. Was there such a thing? What a nelly thing to be thinking. His host, who had an actorish voice, was perhaps an actor whose income was earned doing voice-overs for advertisements, said, 'This will sting, of course.' He lay there, trying to match the voice to a particular product. Ice cream? Holidays? 'Why should it do that?' he asked lazily. Just then, signals from his scrotum arrived at the brain. 'Well, nettles do, you know.' *'Nettles?'* He squirmed, but the sensations when they reached him were only as sharp as curries are, to a palate unused to spices. 'It has to be the young leaves, of course,' the voice went on, 'the earlier in the season the better.' The voice became sad. 'The season is terribly short.' The cashmere soothed as if it had been turned into a dock leaf, even as the nettles prickled him, and his scrotum took on an amorous glow.

His host's voice came from higher up, almost as if he had used the little set of library steps and was consulting the big dictionary on the top shelf. 'There's even a verb, to urticate. To thrash with nettles. Well, thrashing is too strong a word. What do you think? How would you describe it?'

As time went by, he developed a new ground rule: sex must always happen at his place, not anyone else's. Since by now he rented a small flat in Earls Court, and frequented pubs in easy reach of it, this was not a very restrictive stipulation. He decorated the interior in olive and grey, with accents of pastel, to general admiration.

The flat was small enough for tidiness to be forced on him. Its only glory was an outsized bath, both long and deep, which he could share in comfort with anyone of less than grotesque dimensions. He was doing so one day, and scrubbing the muddy back in front of him, which belonged to a rugby-playing geologist, when a voice from the general area of the taps said languorously, 'Until you've been well fucked in a hot spring, you haven't lived.' He went on to describe a field trip he had taken with his lover, during which they had sneaked down a ladder into a bubbling cave of hot mud. Roger went on scrubbing mechanically – the water took on a grey-brown tinge from the mud – but this lustful fervour awoke no echo. The conversation chimed with his two obsessions, the men in the pool and the bricks in the bath, and that was why he remembered it. But he always pursued them separately. The only links were verbal: the word *erection*, and the word *built*, always his adjective of preference for men he found sexually attractive.

There were, here and there, dissenting voices to the life he was evolving for himself. One lover lost his temper when Roger left a party they had gone to together, without telling him. Roger, unusually for him, had taken a few puffs of a joint, and felt suddenly sleepy. His escort was deep in conversation, and he hadn't wanted to interrupt, so he went home. He had only been there five minutes when the phone rang, and there was the lover, ranting. The dope that had softened Roger had only made him ratty. 'You know what you are?' he shouted, when Roger had explained his leaving, 'you're a control freak. Would it have been so terrible if you'd fallen asleep on the sofa? I'd have woken you. I know what it is, you're afraid of losing control. Tell me I'm wrong. You can't bear to let go, can you?' He sounded as if he was going to say something else.

'And another thing . . .' There was always another thing with this one. 'Do you know how oppressive it is being in that flat with you? You've tried to imprint your personality on that place so hard I'm surprised you haven't written your name on the walls just to be sure. Look, I like you, I'd even like the flat if you weren't there. But with you there, it's horrible. It's like . . . it's like being in the cinema and having someone read you the book of the film at the same time. Don't you see?' This was presumably a bid for the status of psychologist, and the staking of a deeper claim in Roger's life. But that was the moment when the lover took on the prefix *ex-*. Roger hung up.

Other people who were less than taken with his way of life at least had professionalism to back up their distaste. The doctor to whom he took his first case of gonorrhoea said, 'Listen.' Roger always said that in the 1970s he had gonorrhoea fifty times, clearly a Homeric figure. But he also always said he had seen *Some Like It Hot* twenty-five times in that period, so if you assume a constant ratio (that he contracted gonorrhoea twice for every time he saw *Some Like It Hot*), that is still quite a population of gonococci. Still quite a record of mucopurulence. Quite a little pile of pills. 'Listen,' said the doctor, 'you can burn the candle at one end. You can have a good time with your . . . cock,' (he said the word as if a penis was in itself a morbid growth) 'or you can eat too much, drink too much, smoke a lot, take drugs. But you can't do both.' Roger knew the doctor was beyond the range of his sexual charm. He could tell a closet case when he saw one. 'You need to put the brake on. If you don't, something else will. Lungs. Liver.'

He could only manage to feel guilty about the smoking. For a time he kept a record of smoking in his diary, so that the habit would become conscious, and so breakable. He would make vertical marks for the first four of every five cigarettes and a horizontal one for the fifth, to make a little gate. The plan was to fence off the habit, in due course, altogether. But the result was not to cut down his consumption of cigarettes. All he did was to incorporate into the bad habit a gesture of ritual repentance, which made the habit itself more durable. Some days his consumption actually increased, when his design sense made him smoke more cigarettes to complete a little gate towards the end of the day, puffing his way towards symmetry.

Sometimes he got the impression that he needed to defend his appetites even to gay friends. They seemed to need their share of explanations. He thought it wasn't the amount of activity as such, though perhaps it was that too; but it was really the variety that offended them, compulsive search without compulsive object. If he had responded only to boyish blonds or to older men, they could have excused the number of boyish blonds, the number of greying ex-athletes. If he had restricted himself to one-night stands or doomed passions that too would have been helpful.

He left his friends to their puzzlement, but privately he explained things to himself. He wasn't to blame if his needs were greater than other people's, if he was less efficient at converting sexual experience, into whatever sex became once converted. He remembered a magazine article about a toddler who dismayed his parents by dipping his food into a bowl of salt at every meal. They worried so much that eventually he was admitted to hospital, just for observation. After a few days, he died, and it turned out afterwards that his body had a severely impaired ability to absorb salt. The kid had compensated instinctively, and the bland hospital diet had killed him. It all went to show, Roger thought, that sometimes you had to shut out what other people said, and listen to your body. He was good at that. If his friends chose to live on a hospital diet all their lives, that didn't bother him. He would eat just as much salt as his system demanded.

This would have been a stronger argument if he hadn't had a sweet tooth as well as a salt thirst. At least his craving for sugar was seasonal rather than constant, but that actually made it more dangerous. Sometimes in autumn, tea and coffee with his usual dosage of sugar began to taste very sickly, and sweet foods lost all of their charm for him. It was an effort to keep on eating them. But if he gave up sugar, as his body seemed to want to do at this point of the year, other things changed too. His temperament quietened down, and he started looking for a lover – the only absolute requirement was good circulation, warm feet for cold nights – to nest with. He would be fond and even tender for the winter months. But then all it would take was three doughnuts in April and he would be off, crackling with aggressiveness, stepping out of the partnership as if it had never existed. The lover he left would not be much consoled to learn that it was not him personally that was being abandoned, since it was not him personally that had been chosen. The lover would be mortified, if anything, to find he had collaborated with an instinct not so much of romanticism as of hibernation.

Roger didn't want to go through that again with anybody, and in any case he did no work at all during those snuggling winters. So he laid down, in September, in October, a good mulch of ice cream, pastry, chocolate, until he drove the yawns out of his bloodstream. His body would finally come to its senses and cut itself, unprompted, another slice of cake. Then he knew he would be spared another winter without work.

His private life was complex and contradictory: professionally, Complexity and Contradiction became his architectural watchwords, after he discovered Robert Venturi's Museum of Modern Art monograph on the subject. This, and later Venturi's *Learning from Las Vegas* – which like most architectural books was physically too large to cruise with, while *Complexity* could fit a pocket with a little bending – became his bibles, the best sort of bibles since they set out to multiply heresy. He continued to admire Wright, but extended his susceptibilities. He looked with favour on historical references, irregular curves, erosions, the creative use of interstitial space. He broadened his tolerance for eccentricity. He loved, for instance, Peter Eisenman's House V, with its upside-down dummy staircase formally balancing the functional one – so useful at moments of reversed gravity. He enjoyed too the slim pillar in the bedroom, whose sole purpose was preventing the residents from moving their beds together; by doing so they would lose the dawn view he had prepared for them through a slit window. That, Roger thought, was the right way to treat a client. Even better than running off with the client's wife, make it hard for *him* to have an affair with her. Make sure he's awake to see plenty of dawns.

He was in love with the profession, but he hung back from a career. Technical drawing paid his bills, or at least the interest on his credit card. He reminded himself that Louis Kahn hadn't built anything until he was well past forty, and *he* hadn't done too badly (and had died in debt).

There had always been a strong element of frustration in his love affair with architecture. As a student, he had responded well to criticism, that is, he had listened politely while people made their comments (and not everybody liked his designs, ever) and then, when the critiquing session was over and everyone had gone, he would destroy his models (not everybody liked his designs, but *everybody* liked his models). Then came a phase when most people, almost everybody really, said they liked the designs, and still he destroyed the models, kicking them across the room in his rage at something or somebody.

He started teaching a little evening class, supposedly in Architectural Appreciation, but he soon changed that. At the first meeting of the class he announced that the course he was actually offering was A History of Horizontal Access. He wrote those words on a blackboard. There was a moment of profound shock in the room, and the sound of little dreams being punctured: dreams of taking civilized walks in a great city, making sophisticated comments on the buildings, and then finding somewhere to eat sandwiches. Then he explained that gallery access, which organizes the circulation of a residential building horizontally by way of balconies rather than vertically with internal staircases, had a particular beginning: with Gloucester New Gaol, the first purpose-built prison in Britain (1780). Gallery access was now the hallmark of council estates, and he proposed to show that the past and the present of gallery access were more than casually linked.

One person failed to reappear at subsequent classes, apparently unable to deal with the removal from the course of its element of the genteel. The others became more and more absorbed. For the last class he took them to Southwark and showed them the site of the Old King's Bench prison, which was familiar to them from contemporary prints. On the site was a council estate that closely followed the old prison in layout and contour. Roger then read to them a list of the facilities available in a prison like King's Bench (taprooms, cobblers, pie shops) and defied them to name a council estate that offered so much. These ideas were very much in the air, of course, and he made no secret of the fact from the class; he provided a full reading list. But he enjoyed the effect that he had on his students, and the identity they reflected back at him, even if it wasn't quite the identity he aspired to.

As regards his prospects of a successful career, his attitude was, rather surprisingly, like his father's, of puzzled waiting. It took him some time to realize that his father had been eighteen when he was born, that he had been a forethought as some children are afterthoughts. No wonder his father waited impatiently for him to be tied down, for him to choose a cage a little bigger than his father's – progress demanded that much – but not a lot bigger. He was almost tempted to remain uncommitted for ever, out of spite, but he had an impatience of his own.

The main problem was that he couldn't decide whether he was going to have a very long career, or one so short that it was hardly worth starting. It seemed to him that there was no intermediate possibility. In his late twenties he had a premonitory dream, except that since he never remembered his dreams it must count as a premonition proper. In the premonition, which was extremely vivid in some respects, or rather had an aura of vividness without giving anything away as detail, he was in a car with another person when it crashed. One of them died, aged thirty, and the other one lived to be over a hundred. But the dream didn't specify which of them was which.

As he approached thirty, he took more rather than fewer risks, on the principle that he certainly wasn't going to die before that age. Before his thirtieth birthday he made a will, and destroyed it on the day of his thirty-first. In the intervening year he had been defiantly faithful to driving, but he couldn't pretend not to be glad when those twelve months were over.

In the aftermath of thirty, with the sense of a reprieve that was an almost infinite extension of life, he visited, finally, America. His preferred architects had consistently been Americans; but he had also been hearing of America for years as the gay heaven on earth. An American in The Boltons had told him that in San Francisco there was virtually a gay city within the city. 'Oh, you mean like Harrods,' he had said, and the American had gone on to explain. Americans seemed to like jokes to be clearly signalled.

'No, it's like a gay district, a gay district where you can get anything you want.'

'It still sounds a lot like Harrods. Did you know that the telegraphic address of Harrods is *Everything, London*?' The American went on looking puzzled. Americans seemed to see camp as an on/off switch, so that something was either campy or it wasn't, whereas he felt that true camp, high English camp, worked like a rheostat, providing endless gradations of frivolity. Perhaps camp was something that set in fifty years after an empire, in which case America would have to wait a while till the beginning of the next century or so.

'By the way, do you have nettles in America?'

'Nettles?'

'A stinging plant.'

'I guess not. Poison ivy, poison oak, poison sumac . . .'

'But no nettles. Pity. You're missing something. But even here the season is terribly short.'

America opened his eyes just the same. It was partly the amazement, for an architect from a soggy but stolid climate, of landing in California and finding that the buildings which weren't up to earthquake safety standards had signs on them telling you so. And there wasn't a damp-proof course for hundreds and hundreds of miles. That seemed to be the nature of the place: there could be disasters, but never disadvantages.

Leafing through a gay magazine at a bookstall, he saw that some of the personal ads incorporated stylized symbols, one of a classical column, scrolled and fluted, one of the Eiffel Tower. Then he noticed that some of the symbols were standing upright, others lying down. For a moment he thought these advertisers were expressing a preference for classical or modern architecture. It took him a few moments more to realize that these symbols represented countries (Greece, France), while each country in turn represented a port of entry to the body.

The men did their share of bewitching. On his first night in San Francisco, a man directed breath on to the ice in his glass so that it bounced up to refresh Roger's face, after they had danced. The cooling mist that rose from the glass was like a version in domestic miniature of San Francisco's chilly fog.

In American cities at that time, you weren't 'lovers' with someone, you were 'keeping company' with them. You weren't 'gay', you were 'for men', though whether the preposition was meant to be two-faced – meaning 'in favour of', or else 'to be used by' – he could never quite work out.

There were other shifts of language. It struck him forcibly over those first weeks that it was never bad form in America to call a man 'stud' if you had forgotten his name since your last meeting, or while he was buying drinks, or while you visited the lavatory; and that was quite a relief to someone who wasn't so very good at remembering names. In London, calling someone 'stud' would be a cue for incredulous laughter.

But it was the quality of American promises that most pleased him. They referred only to self-belief in the present, to the pleasure given at the time by a commitment. They had no bearing in the future. He might start talking to a man at The Stud on Folsom Street – which had a surprisingly mixed crowd, despite the heavy-duty name – and they could have a long conversation about the dismalness of promiscuity, the importance of growing up and making adult choices, before taking each other to bed. And they could meet there again the next day, by accident, and have the same sort of conversation as before, without needing to apologize for the way their eyes ranged the room. In London, the realities of such a second meeting would be the same, but as a social experience it would be almost unendurable. Here there was a healthy mixture of the rhetoric of warmth and trust, and the fact of a mutual discarding.

Culturally, the city had much to offer. He never forgot the first time he visited a restaurant called Welcome Home on the Castro. A cowboy strode lazily up to him and murmured not some gruff warning about the breakfast bar not being big enough for the two of them, but 'Good morning, honey.' He turned out to be Roger's waiter, and was soon telling him that the special was a sour cream and jelly omelette, with hash browns, and very good.

He found the whole display ridiculous, but he had to admit it had never seemed out of place when it was a woman delivering the routine. Retrospective guilt made him, for a few weeks, a more generous tipper to waiters in general. He would stubbornly plonk down bills while his companions referred to those serving them as 'waitron' and 'waitrix', according to gender, as if they were androids of slightly differing models.

In Britain, he had tipped modestly. But then, in Britain, if you wanted breakfast when they weren't serving it, they made you feel wrong for wanting it. Here, at Church Street Station, he could order corned beef hash with two fried eggs, over light, at any time of day or night. Even more glorious was the accepted habit of eating out at one restaurant, then moving on to another for dessert. He could slide straight from corned beef hash to the rich pudding at the Café San Marco.

He watched Cukor's *The Women* at the Castro movie house, amazed. There wasn't a man on screen, and hardly a woman in the audience. In the film, Norma Shearer's mother told her that men were shallow, that men could only see themselves in someone else's eyes, that when they were bored with themselves they just changed the eyes they saw themselves in, so the best thing for her to do was to buy some new clothes, get a new hairdo, redecorate and wait till her man came back. The men in the audience, with their new clothes, their recent haircuts (and some of them only going to the movies while the paint dried in their apartments anyway), erupted in affirmation. Roger might have expected something of the sort when Scarlett O'Hara vowed never to be poor or hungry again, but he was startled by this mixture of resourcefulness and a communal masochism, self pity and rah-rah cheerleading.

Americans might have lapses like these, but they were free of other defects. In London it often happened that his partner would express an unhealthy interest in satisfying him. Suddenly playful, his partner might ask, 'What about you? It's your turn now.' Roger would smile lazily and say, 'Your pleasure is all the pleasure I need,' or 'Gay sex is all foreplay, don't you think?' In extreme cases he would retaliate with an onslaught of erotic distractions, nibblings of the ear and inner thigh, disguising his terror of patience as gratitude for it. Sometimes he had even pushed his breathing to an artificial peak, then given a series of low incredulous sighs. This was in its own way a consummation and a release, and he didn't associate it with a phrase that recurred in the more abrasive comedy programmes, faking orgasm. He was in the wanted place, and need not apologize for the route he had taken to get there. For practical reasons, the manoeuvre was only possible when the surfaces were already slippery, so he manufactured an interest in sensual massage, and kept a jar of hand cream by the bed.

In America, his partners were easily satisfied with tokens of climax, though they would sometimes send a hand down admiringly and say, 'I can't believe it. You're still hard.'

He resisted the temptation to consummate his relationship with America by buying T-shirts from All American Boy or Hot Flash. Instead, from an authentic cowboy (Oklahoma, no less),

he acquired the authentic affirmative 'uh-huh' – Basic American-
ism – and the trickier negative '*huh*-uh' – Advanced American-
ism. He bought an authentic Schott leather police jacket, a brown
one, not a pretentious black one. He had spent too much time in
the past informing enthusiasts of the material that what they
bought with their many pounds, labelled REAL HIDE, was a
veneer of skin blasted with dye and covered with a layer of
plastic. His new jacket was exempt from such sniping. All the
pragmatic romance of America was summed up for him by the tag
sewn into its lining, with cleaning instructions: FOR BEST
RESULTS BRING OR MAIL TO Leathercraft Process, 620 W. 13th
Street – NY, NY 10018. Tel. 212–555–8980.

From talking to American architecture students he had also
acquired a new idea of his profession. The unfamiliar word they
used was *charrette*, a noun they also used as a verb. A charrette
was an all-night session of work, and they seemed to feel they
were missing something if they didn't pull a charrette ('pull' was
the correct verb, if you weren't actually saying 'charretting')
every week or so. The word was explained to him as meaning
'little cart' in French: at one time students had to put their work in
a cart which would drive off at a pre-ordained time. They could
run after the cart if need be, and throw their work in, but if their
work didn't reach the cart there could be no excuses. From the
explanation as well as the word itself, charretting should be a
European rather than American tradition, but his informant
argued strongly for its status as American. Certainly Roger had
never heard the word in Britain. The equivalent British words, he
remembered, were *gnoming* or *grinding*; they were always words
of penance and failure. In London, gnoming or grinding was a
symptom of a disordered timetable or an erratic temperament. In
America, charretting was a fact of life, made palatable by the
imminence of worldly success, and the availability of speed of
various kinds.

He had always felt himself to be different in kind from his
contemporaries, more driven, less interested in ambling into a
niche. In future, when there was work to be done, he would pull

a charrette and glory in it, proud that he was incapable of doing the minimum. So what if his technical drawings, for instance, were absurdly over-specified, offered a foolish surplus of elegance and finesse? In due course, his commissions would stretch him. Till then, he would have to stretch himself. He made some wildly ambitious large-scale fantasy drawings that took up where Archigram, in its great days, had left off, or like some Sant' Elia steeped in popular culture.

Back in London, he made two major changes in his life. One was to be grown-up at last, and join a proper architectural firm. He made approaches to one firm only, specified the maximum number of hours he was willing to work, even the minimum size of office he was prepared to consider. He made it clear that no inducements would lure him into a suit. He indicated that these conditions were not negotiable, and sat back in his chair during the interview well pleased with himself.

He walked out of the office numb, and when it finally sank in that they had accepted him he burst into tears. He sat down on the kerb, and hunched his grief down to the bumper level of the cars parked on either side of him.

He also took a lover. He didn't set out to, but then he'd always been told that that was the way it happened. It was always the least likely person, as in a classic detective story. Larry wasn't the least likely person, exactly, but he wasn't far off: a quiet accountant with a bushy moustache and a taste for domesticity. It wasn't this that first gave Roger the idea of being lovers with him, but a sexual peculiarity. While most men, in Roger's experience, had the equivalent in facial contortion, pelvic movement and swearing, of a ten-second countdown to orgasm, Larry had a hundred-second countdown, which he reproduced exactly on every occasion. The third time they went to bed together, with the help of a judicious sniff of poppers (from the first bottle he had ever bought), Roger was able to ejaculate almost at the same time as Larry did. All he had to do was imagine he was on his own and masturbate as usual, synchronizing himself with Larry's providentially predictable countdown.

Roger was by now very good at starting a sexual relationship, and very good at ending one, usually in swift succession. He knew almost nothing of the bits in between, but he thought he should try to explore them with Larry. Now that he had finally achieved the hub of a sexual relationship, the spokes should follow as a matter of course. He had tried the other method of building up to sex, as if it was the keystone that would keep everything else in place, and that hadn't worked. Now he would start with the keystone and work downwards, see what happened.

What happened was nothing, except that Larry became very attached. For once, getting free, Roger felt a real guilt, since for once he had encouraged someone to expect things from him, things that turned out not to be in his gift.

For the first time in his life he was earning properly, but he still had manifold debts to clear, and he didn't have a lot to spare. He took as much time off as he could get away with – the part of him that thrived on failure hoping to be fired for his cheek and intransigence – and travelled more widely in America.

He spent one Christmas in San Francisco, where disco carols played in the bars and artificial snow fluttered down from the ceiling at a pre-arranged signal. The effect was of something so unlike Christmas as almost to be worth celebrating. He also heard Michael Graves lecture, in a building that made no promises about what it would do in an earthquake. Graves showed slides of his two favourite buildings: the Chrysler building in New York, and a small museum in London that Roger, to his shame, had never visited.

On internal flights in the US he always took advantage of the coin-operated insurance machines that paid out huge sums for pennies to the beneficiary of your choice, in the event of your death in a plane crash. He found it a good way of exorcizing his faint flutter of fear; he was too British to be able to take flying altogether for granted. But he also enjoyed looking through his address book for a suitable beneficiary. Some entries disqualified themselves by consisting only of a Christian name, or only a telephone number without an address. But he would start at one end of his address book, or the other, or in the middle, or at a favourite letter, and riffle through until he found an entry that was sufficiently full but rang no bells whatever. Then he wrote it down on the form. The trouble was not that people were promiscuous, he thought, but that they were promiscuous only with their bodies.

In New Orleans, he liked the way the men reserved masculinity only for the heaviest cruising. They would catch someone's eye while they were gossiping with friends, and would walk across the bar to him, shedding one set of mannerisms and assuming another, so that the person who arrived at the point of attraction was quite different from the one who had set out for it.

He liked to walk along Bourbon Street, loving the clarity of its division. On one side of a definite line, the street was clearly straight, on the other side it was just as clearly gay. Standing there on the divide, it was impossible not to notice that straight sex was sold, and gay sex given away.

He favoured a bar called the Café Lafite in Exile, and a twenty-four-hour restaurant called The Bunkhouse. During the days he would repair to a leftover hippie establishment called Till Waiting Fills, where the curtains were never opened and dim table lamps were the only sources of light. There he could get a pot of Earl Grey tea made with a teaball, so he could pull the leaves out of infusion after a little while, and make the pot last for hours.

In all the cities he visited, there were gay baths, establishments where he could have gone to have sex without a word's needing to be exchanged. It would have been perfectly polite in such a place to explain to a partner that he had just ejaculated, so freeing himself from expectations of performance. In Britain, after all, he had used a similar ruse, using a phrase adapted from the adverts for a credit card, 'wanking takes the wanting out of waiting', to account for his supposed depletion. But he never tried such places. If he had thought this was a moral qualm, inherited from childhood, there would have been a particular joy in overturning it. It wasn't moral. But just because he couldn't build sex into his life in the approved manner, didn't mean that he could build it out.

In Houston he went to the Y, whose gym contained equipment that was new to him. He quite liked the atmosphere of some such places, their hum of sexual thwarting. In San Francisco the gyms were excessively social, and the staff always voluble with worry that they wouldn't have enough drugs for the weekend. No tension built up in such an atmosphere, and he stopped going. Even the nude gym he visited, very Athenian except for the million-dollar sneakers, palled after a time.

He had overcome British prejudices, and was sometimes willing to be told what to do by an instructor. What he had never been able to stand were the self-appointed pals who stood over him at the bench press, and cheered him on, murmuring, 'Just five more reps, guy, three, four. All the way. Five, now just one more. One more for me.' They seemed not to notice that the veins that stood out on his neck and forehead were not swollen by the repetitions, but by their gruff litany of *No gain without pain*.

'Reps' for repetitions, 'lats' for latissimus dorsi, 'pecs' for pectorals. Blood that normally went towards finishing words seemed to be redirected to rebuild muscle tissue. Except that nobody referred to the body's largest muscle as the glute ('Hey man, great glutes'). Nobody referred to them at all, though he noticed people had eyes for little else.

The piece of equipment with which he was unfamiliar involved a pair of bars that rested on your shoulders. You bent your legs and braced yourself against the machine, which pressed down on you at regular intervals. The idea seemed to be to give you a fairly intense upper-leg work-out, without the risks of free weights.

Already Roger had seen one man faint while using this machine, but all he thought was, *shouldn't work out if you're not in shape*. This seemed to him afterwards a thought that could have come from any brain in that gym. It had none of his hallmarks. He stepped up to the machine and did as he had seen others do. It didn't occur to him to read the instructions written on the machine, some of which were in red.

He passed out. Not only that, but when he came to – it was only a few seconds later – his hair was drenched with blood. He had burst a small vessel in his scalp. As the instructor helped him up, he took Roger's hand and ran his finger with patronizing slowness across the red sentences, which warned of the importance of synchronizing your breathing with the machine, and emphasized its unsuitability for the unfit.

In New York he went to bars at the foot of Christopher Street that had no names written on their outsides, and more decorous bars in mid-town. He could always be sure of a bed for the night, and he could more or less rely on being bought dinner when funds were low. But he could never quite afford to forget which was all-you-can-eat clams night at HoJos. At a mid-town bar he met a gallery owner with whom he would have had his usual foreshortened affair, if the gallery owner hadn't mentioned, during one of their first conversations, that he ate regularly at The Four Seasons. That sentence became the pivot round which their relationship swung. Bob, the gallery owner, wasn't slow to realize he had power, though he wasn't sure what sort of power he had. But he knew enough to promise lunch at The Four Seasons, maybe tomorrow. He knew the *maître d'*, and could always fix things at short notice. Maybe tomorrow; or maybe the day after that. When they finally got there, with Roger wearing a Bill Blass shirt which Bob had bought him for the occasion, and which cost almost as much as lunch for one at The Four Seasons, they both realized they would not be seeing each other again. It seemed silly to Roger not to take off and hand back his borrowed tie as soon as the meal was over, but he didn't. He put it in the mail that afternoon. And even then he couldn't help thinking with a kind of pride: how many people can say they've sold their bodies for a chance of seeing a Philip Johnson interior?

Back in London he had what felt even at the time like an Indian summer of sexual self-esteem. This was thanks in part to a new sit-up technique that he was taught by a young man with a notably firm mid-section. Roger had been doing inclined sit-ups on a tummy board, with weights amounting to about thirty pounds grasped in front of his neck. He now learned that this was the worst possible way to treat his body. He should do sit-ups unweighted and on the level, knees bent and heels off the ground. He should put his hands on the floor behind his head, and swing forward, hold a pose as far forward as possible and then slowly lower himself back down, feeling the tension in his stomach throughout. He was so interested in what the young man had to teach that he was disappointed when he finished his demonstration and slid into bed. He was used by now to foreplay being the beginning of the end.

He did his reformed sit-ups assiduously, but in truth he was carrying too much weight for the exercise to modify his shape more than a fraction. But his old method of sit-ups had in fact been giving him back pain, and being free of it put much of the smoothness and pleasure back into his walking, and that was no small improvement.

In gyms in America he had seen men of towering virility use moisturizers, and for a trial period he dared to do so himself, even going so far as little pots of a more concentrated extract, specially formulated for the problem area under the eyes. All these products migrated in due course from the basin-side to the medicine cabinet, and then to the bin.

Even without moisturizer he had a sort of leftover attractive-ness. Once, long after he fitted any definitions of beauty, however eccentric, he was driving frantically round town running errands. He was all booked to go away on holiday later that day. A police car overtook him. He was running late so he speeded up, thinking he was safe from the police as long as he stayed in their slipstream. But the police car must have tucked itself away where he failed to see it, because suddenly there it was behind him, siren screaming, signalling him to stop. The driver said, 'Do you have any idea what speed you were doing, sir?' Roger said, with all the seriousness he could muster, 'The truth of the matter is, I saw you a little while back and I thought you were a good-looking man. I couldn't think of any other way of getting your attention. Will you have dinner with me tonight?' If he'd known how to bat his eyelashes, he would probably have done it then, and ruined everything. As it was, there was a terrible silence. Suddenly Roger thought, *Oh God, don't let him say yes*, mainly because he was booked on a flight that afternoon, but also because the policeman was not in fact his idea of a good-looking man. Luckily the policeman blushed, put away his notebook without a word and got back into the car.

He began to make significant progress professionally. The first actual work he did, inevitably, was a series of conversions. He got used to wives saying they needed more space, and husbands saying they couldn't do without their studies, even though (as their wives pointed out) they'd done no work there for years. He wondered how long it would be before he did work that wasn't a form of counselling, offering architectural solutions to marital problems and shoring up emotions with bricks and mortar. But at least he started doing some proper teaching in drawing and design, not just the baby evening classes.

He flirted outrageously with his more attractive male students. Eventually they formed a deputation, awkward in their cords and cricket sweaters, not to complain of sexual harassment but to say they were on to him. They knew, they said, that he wasn't really gay, that he was just trying to catch them out. But he really needn't bother. However big an act he put on, he wouldn't trick them into a single anti-gay comment. Some of their best friends, in fact, were gay, and they knew better.

That in its way was the high point. Already in America he had heard rumours and read reports of a new sexually transmitted illness, little flickers of hysteria, and subconsciously he braced himself for more of the same in Britain. It took longer than he expected, but when it came he got more than he bargained for. Early on, when the publicity was only moderate, sowing in hatred what would later be reaped in terror, he came across a bulky questionnaire in a gay bookshop where he had gone shopping for bad-taste greeting cards. Thick as it was, he welcomed it. He bought himself a coffee and sat down to complete it. At last someone was doing something, was doing a little fact-finding.

The questionnaire was completely baffling. Almost the first question asked him to rate himself as 'active' or 'passive' on a scale of 1 to 7. It offered no definitions of active or passive. For a moment he thought it must refer to sexual practices, but no, there were detailed questions about these later on. It must mean something else. If it had offered some framework, however silly – if it had asked him, say, if his chest hair touched the ground – he would have filled it in somehow. As it was, he left it blank.

The other questions were no improvement. One asked him 'How much of the time do you get more than 50 per cent of your contacts from (a) bars, (b) clubs, (c) public toilets, (d) parks, (e) . . .' He was willing to spill all the beans he could, but the questions stubbornly refused to make sense.

The question about sexual practices wanted to know if he indulged in Lindinism, which could only mean, he thought, having sex while doing the Lindy, a popular dance craze of the 1940s. Some time later he realized that this must be a misprint for Undinism.

An entire page invited him to rate his relationships as 'faithful', 'fairly faithful', 'not faithful' and 'don't know', from the point of view of each participant. A postscript told him to put the letter C against one of these relationships if it was continuing. The C seemed like a gold star for good work, and it seemed to him that it was possible, in spite of what teacher implied, to earn more than one.

He scrawled his objections, methodological, sexological and just plain logical, all over the form, and felt more frustrated than when he had started. It took him almost an hour. If he had considered himself personally at risk, he would have projected his anger further than the sheaf of mimeographed paper on his lap. But he had got used to the promise his premonition made him, that he would live longer, almost, than he wanted to.

All the same, he couldn't deny that the world was changing.

For months, people seemed to talk a great deal about buses. Roger heard more discussion of buses during this period than he had heard in the ten previous years. Again and again he heard people saying 'But I could be run over by a bus tomorrow,' as a way of rejecting unwelcome advice to be careful. 'I could live like a saint and still be run over by a bus.'

For a time before there was even a rough model of the illness's operation, gay men in London expressed their fear, which still occupied only a corner of their lives, as an aversion to Americans. Roger was in a bar off Oxford Street one night when a young and very handsome American came in, announcing himself as such by a lilac sweatshirt covered with little sprinting lambdas and the slogan 'FrontRunners, NY', even before he made the mistake of tipping the barman. People shrank back visibly; in dress and in posture he was saying, 'Hi! I come from a town where people get very sick and no one knows how or why! Let's talk!' Roger sent his eyes in a slow half-circle across the bar: everywhere were jeans, check shirts, cowboy boots, running shoes, Robert Redford and Marlon Brando imitators. It was like a bar full of anti-Semites with sidelocks and yarmulkas.

He gave the young American a few words of advice. 'If you want people to talk to you, wear that sweatshirt inside out and put your hand out for your change when you buy a drink. And say you're from Montreal.' But when he described the incident to a friend, expecting to be backed up in his condemnation of irrational behaviour, the friend just said he had never liked Americans, so he wasn't giving anything up by not sleeping with them. He spoke as if the virus – it had to be a virus, didn't it? Didn't everything point to that? – would be refused a visa by the authorities when it applied for one, and that would be that.

He was forced to examine his own defences. Only at this late stage did it occur to him that his premonition had not yet been confirmed by anything in the world. No car crash had happened, after all. He experienced a wash of panic, the sort reserved for Greek heroes when the ambiguity in the oracle turns and bites them. It only lasted a second before he got a grip on himself. Then he forced himself to be reasonable. The premonition only told him he would be one of two people in the car crash, one of whom would die at thirty – not necessarily in the car crash. The other would live to be over a hundred, so all that was certain was that he was the long-lived one. The car crash could happen at any time.

For a while he was reluctant to give anyone a lift in his car who might be thirty or under, or to accept a lift from anyone in that category. But he felt a fool asking people their ages, one thing that had never mattered to him, so he stopped. He thought he was being egotistical anyway. If he deserved a premonition, after all, so did the other chap, the one who wouldn't live so long. Let him have a premonition of his own.

His fears subsided. The next time he had a feeling of premonition it wasn't a true premonition at all, not a warning but the leading edge of the catastrophe itself. He was sitting at his drawing table, pulling a charrette, working on a project for a competition, the first one that he felt his design solutions – in particular an elegant circulation – gave him a chance of winning. He glanced across at the motto taped to the wall, just about the only quotation he had any time for: *All Those That Love Not Tobacco and Boyes are Fules*. The Elizabethan spelling gave it a satisfactorily delinquent air.

Then he looked down at his coffee-cup, which held a syrupy sediment, his drawing pens, the ashtray, which he had emptied at some stage but which needed emptying again, and the wrapper of a packet of Pro-Plus (not, he seemed to remember, his first of the night) that he had apparently finished, without quite meaning to. Then abruptly the objects seemed to change their relationships with each other, as if subjected to a complex camera movement, in a way that he would have considered artful in a film but which was downright ominous in real life. If this was a film, he thought, then it was the credit sequence of a low-budget detective thriller, which would be completed by a body slumping lifeless to the floor. He held his breath. His ears popped, as if he was in a plane just taking off.

His mind now contained the words, *This is it. This is the brake.* He wasn't conscious of thinking this thought as such, but he understood that his reference was to what the doctor had said at the special clinic all those years ago. Perhaps as a result, the sensation, when it came, was the sensation of a cable binding tight against a drum, a moving part slammed into stillness.

There was an afterwards, and in the afterwards he was able to walk unsteadily to the phone. At the hospital they kept him in for a couple of days, for tests, but they didn't exactly seem worried about him. They told him that he had probably had a mild heart attack. Subsequent investigations indicated that he had a faulty valve. It was likely to be an inherited defect, aggravated by a life-style that omitted almost nothing that was hostile to health.

The doctors seemed to him absurdly young, and their suggested surgical intervention literally childish, since it involved inflating a miniature balloon inside a blood vessel to free it from obstruction. They assured him it was a minor procedure. When it was done they pronounced themselves satisfied with him (except of course for the life-style). After the event, it was his turn to be childish: he learned there was an even more modern surgical technique, involving lasers rather than balloons, and he was piqued to have missed out on it. Was there some complication he had failed to produce, which would have secured for him the top surgeon and the snazziest hardware?

He was profoundly changed by the event in a handful of ways. The doctors gave him a great deal of information, some of which made no impression and some of which struck deep. He might have expected that a potentially mortal episode like the one he had experienced would bring him closer to his parents, or at least make him reconsider his relationship with them. But those bonds were no more or less elastic than before. He did reconsider one set of relationships, but not that one. It struck deep, out of what the doctors said, that the genetic defect he had inherited was likely to have been shared with his nephews. (It may be that his sisters were, or could be, similarly affected, but if he was told so, that was part of the information that made no impression.)

He took an interest in the boys for the first time. For the first time he felt that he had had a hand in their making, even if he had brought to their christenings not a bouquet but a blight. They became for him potentially tragic children, children with whom he shared a fate, instead of being a mild amusement, a mild distraction, a mild reproach. He became more attentive as an uncle, though also less indulgent, since he now steered them resolutely away from the junk food that was his major previous association in their minds.

The doctors told him that providing he changed his ways in almost every respect, there was no reason why he shouldn't live to be a hundred. In a sense it was what he had been waiting to hear for a long time. But just because he had been waiting to hear it, it didn't follow that he would have paid any attention to these strangers, if they hadn't been talking with the full authority of his body. His reliable body. They drew up a schedule for him, by which he was allowed to hold on to some vices longer than others. He was expected to tackle his diet, for instance, before he needed to do anything about his cigarette habit. The unhealthiness of his sex life was never mentioned, as if it had already stopped being an issue.

The designs that he had been working on at the time of his attack were finished, had really been finished for some time. A less driven personality would have submitted them already, but he had been unable to hand them in before the last entry date. That date now approached, and he submitted them.

His firm gave him time off. They didn't pay him or anything, but he still arranged a trip to the States (going into debt was a vice he planned to have long after he gave up smoking, even). This time he chose Chicago as his destination. He had never bothered with the city before; it had only the most moderate reputation as a sexual playground. But it contained an extraordinary variety of early modern architecture, notably by the Sullivan who had been Lloyd Wright's inspiration, mentor and employer. It was only after he had left Chicago that he realized he hadn't gone to a single bar.

He never got used to a healthy diet, skimmed milk and denatured cheeses, bran cereals and coffee that had had its reason for living extracted at the same time as the caffeine. But he made his accommodation. In the end, he found it easier to give up men than to give up the taste, even the smell, of fried bacon.

SUMMER LIGHTNING

You always were fair-skinned, Olive, and giving yourself to the sun wasn't something you set about lightly. We went well prepared on our trip to Aberlady Bay. You had your plastic bottle of tanning milk, with a high factor of sunscreen, and your sunhat; I carried the big new Thermos of blue-and-white plastic, whose workings we didn't altogether understand. Each of us, of course, brought a P. G. Wodehouse paperback along. Yours was *Summer Lightning*.

You were a great admirer of Wodehouse, though I know it pained your sentimental side that he had so few good things to say about aunts. The aunt-nephew relationship in Wodehouse is not a tender bond, and there were times when you found his exploration of its darker aspects oppressive. So I learnt to take a hint, and if you said your Wodehouse was getting a bit aunt-heavy, we'd do a swap, and hope that in my Wodehouse the master was being less severe about the relationship that gave us our connection.

There are two ways of pronouncing the name Wodehouse, as Wood- or as Woad-. I think it says something about our relationship that although we said the name of our hero differently, we pretended not to notice this little parting of the ways. Neither of us tried to prove the other wrong. Possibly it didn't occur to either of us that we might not be right.

It was a beautiful early summer's day, with a faint breeze, but as clear as if clouds had been outlawed or abolished. If we'd been offered a fiver for every cloud we saw before lunchtime, we'd still have had to dig into our pockets for the full cost of our holiday. When you first looked out of the window of our bed-and-breakfast room in Edinburgh, you said it was like the morning after a garden party.

On such a lovely day, we would have liked to take along cold drinks, but our B&B didn't run to the necessary ice. So we used the available amenities to the full, brewing tea with the electric kettle and teabags in our room. We transferred the tea to our Thermos, once we had grasped its basic principle, which seemed to involve thermal pads rather than a vacuum. You had to put boiling water in it for ten minutes, before you filled it with something that needed keeping hot.

We drove out of Edinburgh by way of Portobello and Cockenzie, stopping off at an Italian-run parlour in Musselburgh for what turned out to be some of the world's better ice-cream. Aberlady isn't far. The car radio played one of your favourite songs on the way, 'The Lady is a Tramp', and you sang along for a bit, as if you just wanted to point up the excellence of the lyric, the way people do who don't know whether to be proud or ashamed of their singing voices. You explained that one line in particular haunted you: *'Hate California, it's cold and it's damp . . .'* It haunted you because you could find no sense in it.

We parked the car by a golf course, at the point that looked on the map to be nearest to the beach we wanted. The beaches we want are far from the roads, pretty much by definition, but even by our standards this was a bit of a trek. You promised me that in Scotland there's no such thing as a law of trespass, and I decided to take your word for it. I don't know whether the golf course was technically part of the nature reserve, but certainly there were birds about, singing away when not actually visible, as well as the usual dogged golfers. We passed by them in silence, awed by the equipment and the dedication, above all by the tremendous space that golf opens up, which just hangs there waiting to be filled by something sensible.

By what felt to be the nineteenth hole of fathers standing

behind their sons and instructing them in matters of grip and swing, but was probably only the fifth or sixth, you were tired and thirsty. We stopped at a convenient bench, by a water-fountain put up in memory of a local resident. I was all for us staying there until you were fully recovered, but you were back on your feet after only a couple of minutes, and we pressed on past the golf course. The nature reserve contained some sort of sewage plant, but once we were beyond that we could smell the sea. As we climbed the dunes we could catch glimpses of a fine sandy beach, and of tightly curling waves. We could also see people standing on top of choice dunes, shading their eyes and peering around, as if they were on top of crow's-nests and not overgrown sandhills. They stepped back from the dunes, formed little groups, and then went back on lookout. They seemed to have borrowed from the nature reserve the watchfulness proper to endangered species.

It didn't take us long to find a dune of our own, one with a dip near its summit which gave us a minimum of privacy without shutting us off from a view of the water. You gave me one of your crinkliest smiles, and you spoke the formula that I've grown so used to: 'Well now, shall we turn this into a naturist event?' And of course I said yes.

How I cringed when I first heard it, the phrase that sounds to me now like Welcome Home! I was sitting in your kitchen, where I had always been so much at my ease, wearing the first grown-up suit I had ever owned. I knew about your new way of life, and I think I even guessed that the couple opposite me at the tea-table were implicated in it. But I was completely unprepared for your summons to nakedness.

I didn't do very well that first time. I had taken my jacket off already, but that was because I was in your kitchen and off my guard. While everyone else undressed without fuss, I loosened the knot of my tie – my fat early-seventies tie – and I undid the top button of my shirt, but that was as far as I could get. In those days the nearest I could come to the natural was the 'casual', a condition of permanent underlying tension that I wasn't yet willing to release. Being then at a particular peak of self-consciousness, I wasn't prepared even to take my shoes and socks off. I thought I would die if I did. I suppose my reflexive set of values still referred to my mother at that stage – and hers referred to the Royal Family. When I didn't think I had anything as subjective as an opinion at all, all I was doing was reproducing my mother's view of the world.

You were gentle with my refusal. I didn't even realize you were making an exception. Later on, I could see that you were normally strict about the conduct of naturist events, knowing that the clothed pose a threat to the naked, as well as the naked to the clothed. You must have sensed that my refusal was only the leading edge of acceptance, and that I wouldn't refuse you a second time. I refused only as a horse refuses, at an unfamiliar fence that is well within its power to jump.

All the time that I was trying to be Prince Charles, of course, he was trying to be more like a normal person, and was absolutely longing to be asked to take his shoes and socks off. But we didn't know that back then.

On my second brush with social nakedness, I came much closer. You were having a barbecue, in that little back yard of yours, and you needed my help. For a wild moment I thought that this too might be a naturist event (the fence round your yard was tall enough to make that possible), but I put the idea out of my mind. And of course you were dressed when I arrived, chopping vegetables in your kitchen for a dip, while the charcoal settled to a steady glow in the yard outside. But before your first batch of guests turned up, you undressed, and you persuaded me too from my clothes.

After the first ring came at your front door, when I could hear the amazingly matter-of-fact noise of the newcomers undressing in the hall, I retreated from my nakedness. I appointed myself cook, a job that in the case of barbecues has no qualifications except willingness, by picking up the big laminated apron from its hook on the back of your kitchen door. By the time you and your party came into the kitchen, I had safely tied its strings round my waist, and had pounced on a big fork and a pair of tongs to give colour to my impersonation. Trembling with tension, I led the way into the yard, and squirted some unnecessary lighter fluid on to the briquettes in the barbecue. A gust of flame leapt up through the grile.

Thanks to the apron, I was labelled a cook and not a person with his own reasons for attending. But there were also elements of martyrdom in the role I played. The design of the apron was much enlarged from the label of a matchbox; I bore the legend 'ENGLAND'S GLORY', and the additional phrases 'Finnish Made' and 'Avge Contents 48'. Behind the apron I felt like a match myself. My head was blazing with metaphysical heat and excitement. I was also exposed, where the apron didn't protect me, to heat from the barbecue on my face and shoulders, and to spitting protests from the meat that I was watching over.

I was closer to nakedness in a social setting than I had been since – I suppose – my christening; but I was set apart by my costume from the true nakedness of my companions. They were in a state of nature, while I looked as if I was stranded half-way through a routine of striptease, my apron an item of would-be allure. Even where we were identical we were marked by differences, so that my buttocks, framed by the apron-edges and dramatized by the apron-strings round my waist, were mysteriously barer than theirs.

As the meat in front of me spat and darkened, the burgers shrinking and the sausages becoming gnarled, I was caught between the shame of being clothed and the shame of going naked. But surrounded by these various flames, something inside me melted and gave way; some final resistance was driven off. When I put on my clothes again at the end of the evening, I remained a naturist beneath them.

I knew there would be trouble when I got home, but my mother gave me only the regulation frosty reception, just as if I'd been out late with a girl. There was none of the extra chill I expected for associating with her so suspect sister. I had thought her anger would at least recognize the magnitude of the change the evening had worked in me. She couldn't have changed my decision, I don't think, but she could have had the satisfaction of greeting what was a turning point in her life, as well as in mine, with emotion on an appropriate scale. But then she was never one, proud as she was of her hard-headedness, to see things as they are.

We weren't like that on our side of the family, were we, Olive? Though if there was 'our side' – me and you – there must have been 'their side' too, and our opponents (I don't say our enemies) never managed to act in concert. My mother and your Joan had the same ideas about what was important, but they could never abide each other. Whenever they were in the same room together, even when your Joan was quite young, there was a great surge of recognition and denial. It was as if each of them was at the same time a cat and a person who hated cats. There was a sustained feline hissing just below the threshold of audibility, and if it was a social occasion people would look down at their drinks, expecting the ice in their glasses to have suddenly melted.

In the long run, your Joan was far more trouble than my mother. At first she bided her time, being too young to translate into action the adult-sized will that had been evident since her cradle days. But she must also have been laying her plans, for what turned out to be a long campaign.

There's a word that naturists use, a term of abuse for everything they despise in the clothed world. You disliked that word, and would never use it of anyone, let alone of your Joan; I'm afraid that doesn't stop it from applying. But then you were a tender naturist, Olive, a naturist without rancour. I salute you. You built up no new defences to make up for the ones you had cast off. Sunhat and sunscreen; that was all. You asked for little, and you managed on a lot less. In my innocence, I thought that all naturists had the same goodness of heart you had, the same robust freshness. I had to learn for myself that there are meannesses of mind and spirit not lodged in folds of clothing or stowed away in pockets. I had to learn that a person can be naked and still be wrapped in bitterness.

The word is 'textile'. The word of abuse. A textile is someone who doesn't exist except as a succession of costumes, and I'm afraid your Joan was a textile through and through. She could certainly wear clothes. She could groom like nobody's business, but that was all she could do, and she couldn't groom the whole world to her liking.

She didn't have a lot to object to, I would have thought. Naturist activity in your house was confined to a maximum of two nights a week. On those nights she was under no pressure to stay in. Joan was always a looker, and there was no question of her being short of escorts. Most young women would actually quite appreciate some more or less compulsory nights out, and I suppose even Joan wasn't unwilling. But still she did her best to spoil things. She would come home maddeningly early, flaunting her chastity as if to show up her mother's goings-on (I don't think she ever understood the prudish side of naturism). I imagine her rushing home the moment the credits rolled on the big film, dragging her date behind her, just so she could put a damper on things.

I remember in particular Joan's Grace Kelly phase. Icy fifties glamour certainly suited her style of beauty, I have to admit that, and I suppose she deserves credit for contriving such a unified look from meagre resources – she haunted charity shops, and she made things herself when she had to. I'm even sure that the magazines she read were promoting just such a look of luscious unavailability. But there was still something perverse about the sheer number of unnecessary items she managed to wear. I seem to remember sashes, shawls, gloves and any number of hats. Your Joan would enter, brazenly covered up, a room from which bodily embarrassment had only recently, and always provision-ally, been seen off. She would shake hands all round, sometimes even extending a hand to me, with a raise of her exquisitely plucked eyebrows. She would accept a small drink, sip it demurely but leave it unfinished, shake hands one more time and retire to her room.

I think the only other person who has ever worn gloves and touched me naked has been a doctor. Perhaps that was the key to Joan's power. But she wasn't interested in making anything better. She left a bruise in the evening that took some time to heal.

I imagine her in her room, listening to the social noises below. I imagine her, come to that, outside the front door, saying goodnight to whichever boy it was at the time. Perhaps the magazines she read were advocating Grace Kelly morals (the screen morals, of course, when there's doubt) as well as the costumes. In which case, how odd for her to be crying up the enigma of her body, with a naturist event in full swing just the other side of the door.

But you and I know there was more to it than that. Understanding people is a perfectly valid alternative to liking them, though I'm not sure you ever thought so. But one way or another, it's something we should have discussed. Your Joan was shattered when her father left you, and of course she was very young. I think she was like the traumatized witness to an accident, who confuses the sequence of two impacts. Your husband left you, and a little after that you became a naturist. I think in Joan's mind a primitive scene was constructed, in which it was actually your taking off your clothes that drove him away. So perhaps if she could will you back into your clothes, manipulate you back into your clothes, shame you back into your clothes, her father would come back too, and the whole ensemble of her life would start to match again.

Naturism gave you a new life, Olive. Naturism gave you a new wardrobe, you who had never been a standard size, being built (as you said) for comfort and not for speed. In naturism, as you were fond of remarking, there are only standard sizes. But you were also doing your own bit of superstitious thinking, not so differently from Joan.

*

Your husband left you, and you never willingly mentioned his name again. You became a naturist, which was something you said you'd always wanted to do. I'm sure it was. But there was a special symbolism involved. When your husband left you, you didn't retreat from the sexual world; you advanced away from it. You entered a nunnery of flesh, a nunnery without habits. And it was as if by the simplification you achieved in your life, you were trying to send the message that getting rid of your husband had been the first part of the same process. You claimed control retrospectively, as if you had shed that man as you now shed your clothes, and the history that clung to them like cigarette smoke at a party.

I never told you my interpretation of your naturism. It would have seemed ungrateful, after everything you had done for me – and everything that naturism had done for me, for that matter. I'm sure you would have been as indulgent of me as you always were. But that wasn't really the way we shared things anyway. We shared holidays, we shared expeditions. We shared things the way we shared the apple we ate in our dune at Aberlady Bay. You took it out of your bag and bit calmly into it, your eyes screwed up against the glare. I asked if I could have the core, you said there wasn't going to be one, and then you handed me a stem still amply, even voluptuously, covered with fruit-flesh.

The beach was certainly a beauty spot, once we'd got the whiff from the sewage plant on the nature reserve out of our nostrils, and provided we half-closed our eyes to avoid seeing Cockenzie power station on the skyline.

I found a piece of driftwood roughly the size of a bedhead in our dune, and wedged it upright in the sand where it would give you some shade once the sun lost a little height.

I wanted a swim, and perhaps you did too, but you had taken too much trouble applying your sunscreen to want to wash it off so soon. You waved me off down the beach, picked up *Summer Lightning*, and lay down on your big towel. The access was steep from our dune to the beach, so I slid down it rather than walked down.

There was a swimmer just leaving the water as I trotted down the beach. 'How warm is it?' I asked, and he shook his head to get the water out of his eyes, before he answered 'About 70 degrees.' I was about to voice my pleasure at this news when I realized his teeth were chattering, and that I wasn't in for any sort of warm swim after all.

I don't know whether the tide was going out or coming in, but as I touched my toes to the freezing shallows I realized that there must be a submerged sand bar a little way out, since the waves came to the point of breaking, and then re-formed. It was as if they had second thoughts, until they were pressed to it a second time, about their moment of foaming disclosure.

I had second thoughts, too, about my swim. I had just reached the point that the body recognizes as the point of no return, with ice-cold water inches below my groin, when I found myself, thanks to the sand bar, walking uphill again.

The experience of walking into a cold sea is one of the few in which the genitals – I imagine for both sexes – seem authentically to be at the centre of the universe. Swimming naked makes that moment less bleak: even the most hardened textile can only feel betrayed by a costume that protects the parts from cold and wet for the smallest illusory instant, and then keeps them in contact with cold and wet even after leaving the water.

I found myself walking uphill again. I had to recommit myself to the long slow slope towards immersion. Standing on that sand bar, I turned towards the beach. I lifted an arm to wave, before I had properly located our spot in the dunes, and then I saw you, standing with both arms raised above your head. Just then a wave took me by surprise, a little higher than I expected so that I rose by reflex on tiptoe, and I almost lost my balance. I turned round again to anticipate any further surprises, and set off away from the false deep and towards the true one.

I've given much thought to those waves since then, to my wave from the sandbank, to what I took to be your wave from the dunes, and yes, to the wave that caught me by surprise and led me to turn my back on you. I encourage myself to be grateful that we parted with what seemed at the time to be a communicative gesture.

I stayed in the water only long enough to duck my head under the surface and take a few token strokes towards the shore. I might not have done even that much if I hadn't been conscious of you watching – as I thought – and of the need, even with the most intimate audience, to meet minimum standards of hardiness.

The water drained promptly from my left ear, but lingered in my right, so I had the irritating sensation, which no amount of finger-wiggling or head-shaking could dislodge, that while the rest of me was in the open air that one ear was enclosed in a small echoing box. Only when I was standing on the wet sand by the shoreline did I look up to the sand-dunes where you were.

Everything was wrong. Your sunhat had fallen off, and though you were still on your towel, your head was downhill from your feet, and you were lying on your front. You never lay like that. I'd offered to rub sunscreen into your back often enough, but you were shy of that contact, oddly so in view of our closeness, and preferred to bear the filtered weight of the sun only on skin that you could efficiently anoint yourself.

I ran. I ran from wet sand on to dry, and from the flat beach to the foothills of the dunes. Then I tried to run up the dune but scrambled instead, stumbled and scrambled. The sand resisted me like the sand in bad dreams, but even if what I had to climb had been a smooth staircase I think I would have felt the same terrible sensation: making no headway, but dreading to arrive. It was an absolutely generic experience of fear, with nothing distinctive about it, nothing that corresponded to the particularity of my love for you.

When I reached you, it didn't take me long to understand that you had yielded to the superior nakedness of death. At that moment, when I expected tears, I heard instead the dismal popping of the membrane of water in my ear being released, and the sound of my own breathing, suddenly further away.

There were other people in the dunes, but they had respected our territorial claim and fallen back a little, though from the sea I had caught glimpses of them on lookout duty. Standing by you, I could see no one, and I had to run back and forth in the long grass for some time before I found someone – who leapt to his feet and started backwards when I invaded his patch of dune. He turned out to be a tourist, and he couldn't help me find a phone. Finally I turned up someone who knew where the nearest phone was, and was even willing to make the call for me. He pulled on his shorts and ran off, warning me that it would be a good long time before anyone came.

I went back and squatted by your side. The sun still had plenty of elevation and power. I know nothing about the posthumous effect of sunlight on flesh; it's not something that interests me in a general way. But it did bother me to see the sun beating down on the unprotected backs of your legs. You would always wince in sympathy when we saw men with flayed shoulders, or girls with sunburned shins and pale calves.

Every few minutes I would hear someone padding into our dune, out of sympathy or maybe just curiosity. I took to humming at those times, humming being the simplest way of conveying without rudeness that I had no immediate needs. After a while people stopped making approaches.

Then I realized that I did have a need after all. Salt from my swim was still on my lips, and I was thirsty. I put it off until I could think of nothing else, and then I picked up our Thermos and unscrewed the lid. But then the tea we had made that morning was so fresh and steaming that I didn't have the heart to drink it. So instead I poured it away. I don't know what gave me the idea, but I walked round you as I did the pouring – I suppose the idea was to surround you with a magic circle of tea. The air was hot and the sand was very dry, so the tea started to evaporate almost immediately, but for the time being it left an emphatic track, edged with splashes, in the sand.

After that it seemed perfectly natural, though I realized at the same time that it was a peculiar inspiration, to take your plastic bottle of tanning milk and squirt that too in a circle around you, this time in the other direction, pointing the nozzle at the middle of the damp track I'd made already. My shoulders and the back of my neck were getting sore from the sun, but it seemed important not to benefit from any protection that you were denied. The bottle made increasingly intimate noises through its nozzle as I came to the end of the tanning milk.

I sat back on my heels for a moment to think. I was looking at the Thermos, so deep, so broad at the neck. It was still damp inside, so I took a handful of sand and dropped it in. The sand stuck to the curved bottom and the sides of the Thermos, as I should have known it would, so I didn't try to empty it out. Instead I poured more handfuls of sand in. Then I took your P. G. Wodehouse and laid it gently on the bed of sand in the Thermos. I added sand until it was fully buried, and then I put in the empty bottle of your tanning milk. I filled the Thermos to the top with sand, and screwed the lid on. The lid squeaked and rasped as I screwed it home, from sand caught up in the thread.

I sat back on my heels to think again. Then I placed the Thermos by your head, just outside the fading circle of tea and tanning milk, and put your sunhat on it.

I sat back and looked at what I had done. There was something baleful about the Thermos with the hat on which I hadn't anticipated, but which placed it in the tradition of grave-ornaments, things intended to watch over the dead and given a small charge of imaginative power for the task. But there was also something Egyptian about what I had done – it was partly the sand that made me think so. But I must also have been thinking when I was putting *Summer Lightning* and the bottle of tanning milk in the Thermos that these were things you might need on your journey. The same applies, I suppose, to the sunhat and the Thermos itself. Anyway, that seemed like an Egyptian thought. It was as if I had an aunt who was a Pharaoh.

Then my head cleared and I realized what you would want me to do. What I had done with your things let me express my emotions, but there was something remaining to be done that would express you. I took the edge of your towel – luckily you weren't lying with your full weight on it – and pulled steadily until it came free. Then I used the piece of driftwood, which I had intended as a sunshade, as a clumsy spade instead, and I dug a clumsy hole to bury the towel in. I did this not because it was soiled and I was ashamed of its soiling, but because I didn't want the police to cover you up, to tidy you away as if you had done something wrong by dying.

I kept looking round as I was digging, but people were still being tactful and keeping out of sight. I put our clothes, mine as well as yours, and your bag, in the hole along with the towel, and for the same reasons. It struck me afresh how absurdly sensible your taste in clothes was, when you didn't think clothes, deep down, were sensible at all. I used the piece of driftwood to smooth over the mound I had made, and laid it on top to cover my workings.

It took me a long time, and I had sand under my nails by the time I had finished, but I was satisfied. I still had a long wait before the emergency services arrived. When people from the beach did from time to time pop across to our dune to ask if I was all right – they seemed to leave the dunes on either side empty, as if for reasons of quarantine – I noticed they were wearing their costumes, out of respect. I was keeping mine off, of course, for the same reason. I think there was also a worry in people's minds about whether they had a legal right to be naked, or whether someone had once, way back, misunderstood 'nature reserve' as 'naturist beach'. They weren't going to take any risks, not with the police expected any minute.

I knew that the police, when they arrived, would have body bags or stretchers of some description. I knew I wouldn't be able to defend you for very long. I didn't, I admit, anticipate that the East Lothian police, when their Range Rover appeared at the top of our dune, lights flashing and wheels spinning, would have a maroon-coloured coffin ready in the back, of a plastic that looked like metal. But I was still determined, at that stage, to resist them.

Long before they arrived, the humming I had adopted to keep

people at a distance had turned into a peculiar message in its own right. My lips started to move, though I kept my voice right down. But I found that the tune I had chosen, without thinking, to hum was the one you liked so much on the radio that morning – 'The Lady is a Tramp' – and I found that stupid words of my own were replacing the originals, replacing even the line that had haunted you with its nonsense:

> *Lucky Olive Cooper! She died in the sun*
> *And of her clothing, the po-lice found none*
> *Lucky Olive Cooper! She died on the beach*
> *That's why my aunt is out of reach.*

ℛEMISSION

Yoghurt. Yoghurt taught me something yesterday. I was eating a yoghurt, not one I'd bought, something one of the lovers picked up for me, a really creamy one with a crust of fat, not at all my usual style of yoghurt. Maybe it was the creaminess, or maybe it was the absurd clashing of the fruits (apricot and mango, of all combinations), but I could really taste it; first thing I've really tasted in months. The fruit was only there in shreds, but there was enough juice in those shreds, juice or sugar or something, electricity for all I know, to give my mouth the feel of something vivid. And I thought – first thinking I've done in months, too, I dare say – I thought, illness is a failure, that's obvious. You don't have to be well to know that. But what is it a failure of? And at that moment, the answer seemed to be: imagination. It seemed to me then, reeling as I was from the impact of the fruit in the yoghurt, that with a little effort, with a little imagination, I could taste anything, take pleasure in anything.

The yoghurt didn't stay down, of course; it wasn't such a new beginning as all that. But what it had to teach me it taught me on the way down; on the way up it had nothing to say. And even that was a lesson of sorts. It was no more unpleasant to vomit that yoghurt than it was to throw up my usual watery potlet. Its curds were no viler as they rose in my throat. I suppose I've been following a policy of appeasement with my stomach, and that's always a mistake. I've been behaving as if my insides were just being temperamental, and if I could find some perfectly inoffensive food for them, they would do the decent thing and hang on to it. And it just isn't so. I might as well eat what has a chance of giving me pleasure. My stomach will lob it up indifferently.

At the end of all that, after I had vomited, I was – I imagine – just fractionally weaker than when I had started. I had used some energy (vomiting is hard physical work) and I hadn't managed to get any nourishment. Trying to break down the yoghurt had been, as it turned out, a costly waste of gastric juice. But in spite of that, I had had three distinct phases of pleasure. One, the taste of the yoghurt itself. Two, the long, incredulous moment when it seemed that it would stay down. Three, the euphoria, after it came up, of having expelled poison, of knowing it wouldn't be fizzing in my guts for the rest of the day. Set against that the single phase of unpleasantness when it was actually coming up and in some strange way it seemed that I was ahead on the day's transactions. That's when I thought of making this tape.

It's only a cheap little secretarial Sony, this machine, but it's got everything I need. The controls are very simple; you don't even have to look at them. When things get bad, I can curl up with it under the bedclothes, a muttering foetus that can't get comfortable. [   ] If I get a coughing fit, I can edit it out, like that, by using the pause button. I've just got the two tapes, so I can change them over very easily, with the minimum of fumbling around.

There's the shits-and-vomits tape, which I'll use when I'm making the same old complaints, when I'm sicking up the same old record of bodily disasters. I'm never going to play it back. I'll just record on top of it, same old rant anyway. It's not for listening to, just for getting out of my system.

This tape is different. I've written the word *remission* on the spine of the cassette, and that's what I mean to concentrate on, every little quantum particle of forgiveness I can find in my body or my circumstances. I'll play it back eventually, but I'll wait as long as I can, so that I have a real hoard of positive moments to refresh myself with.

It's a bit odd, using the same channel to get rid of some

experiences and intensify others. But I don't have to look further than my underpants to remember a similar arrangement.

And if there's a medical breakthrough soon, very soon – in the next twenty minutes, say – then I may not have to go back to the shits-and-vomits tape at all, just steam on with my remission. But I'll still go on thinking *remission*, however long it lasts: I'll never say *cure*. I can't be doing with that word. It makes everything impossible. It's a real obstacle to getting on with things.

What else fits the requirements for the remission tape? *The video*. Sleep is sweeter than it ever was, and I resent time wasted on anything else. But my video has taken all the angst out of insomnia. I sleep quite a lot in the day, so I'm likely to wake up in the middle of the night, quite suddenly, as if there was someone flashing a torch an inch from my eyes. Television will have packed up hours before, the sleepy-head announcer yawning after the late film (it's past midnight, imagine!), wishing all the other sleepy-heads out there good-night. There's a programme on before close-down that has the nerve to call itself *Night Thoughts*. It's on at different times depending on the schedule, but always before one. *Night Thoughts* indeed! Can you beat it? The tube trains are hardly tucked up in their sheds for the night, and there's a lot of thinking to be done before morning, unless you have a video.

I bought the video quite a while ago, and it was one of those bits of self-indulgence that turn out to be good resolutions in disguise (having said that, I can't think of any others). I thought I'd turn into an addict, and I certainly taped a lot of programmes, but I never got round to watching them. I'd just buy more tapes as they got filled up. I never got into the habit of labelling the cassettes, so now I never know what I'm watching. I watch episodes of *Hill Street Blues* from two different series, and the only way I can tell them apart is by seeing whether Henry Goldbloom has a moustache or not. Promotions and romances don't help me much with the chronology, but with Henry's moustache I know where I am. I always did like moustaches. On top of that, Henry Goldbloom is forever talking suicides down from their high places, reasoning with them through his megaphone of good intentions, and I suppose that's bound to strike some sort of chord.

The great thing about the video, of course, is that I can play things as fast or as slowly as I want. The other night I watched an old episode of *The Avengers*, in which John Steed was meant to dispose of a bomb by lobbing it into the bell of a euphonium. The detonation made the euphonium uncoil, like one of those irritating party-blowers. Except that the actor was too clumsy, or too drunk, to throw the bomb properly, and it rolled under a chair. The euphonium blew up all the same, of course, but if you rewind the video and play the sequence again you can see that it had no reason to. I found the whole thing extravagantly amusing, the other night, and I played it again and again, perhaps because it was one of the few things I'd come across in some time that was in no way a metaphor of my present condition.

That can't be right. Surely I can do better than that. With the explosion, all the instrument's brass knitting unravels. What remains on the carpet is revealed as an intestine, tarnished and smoking. Good. Do better. What *The Avengers* was telling me, in an episode made around the time of my puberty, is that euphoniums end up unrolled and in ruins, even if they don't take a bomb in the bell. That's just what happens, with euphoniums. Good thought. Hang on to that.

Change the subject. *The lovers.* I have two lovers at the moment. *Lovers* is the wrong word, but then it always is. All I can say is, these two do everything for me a lover could do, and that's pretty amazing. We treat each other as if we had a history of sex, but that isn't the intimacy that binds us. I've had half-lovers before, even three-quarters lovers, once or twice, but these two are somehow fully loving towards me, and that's worth putting down on this privileged spool of tape (chrome dioxide for a longer life).[

]*Dead parents.* Anyone whose doctors are not cheerful should try as a first step not to have parents alive. I'm not being unduly oriental here; it's not that I think it's disrespectful in some way to turn in while your parents are still around and about. But I'm sure it confuses things. There's a touch of the bailiff about parents, I've always thought, as if they were waiting for you to fall behind with the payments on your life, so they could repossess it. What a terrible thing to say.

I'm not always so cynical, but I try. Anyway, I'm sure it makes it worse, having your parents around. Not my problem. Having your parents die is unpleasant in its own right of course, and not only in the expected ways. Example: my father had this terrible rightness about him. From his hospital bed he corrected the doctors' pronunciation and finished their sentences for them. I always hated that. It makes me think, now, how robust he was in his dying, how reliable his vitality was right up to the moment that it fell away from him. But the point is that while he was alive, I didn't realize that I have a scarcely less terrible rightness myself, though everyone I've known must have noticed it. I finish people's sentences for them too – I just interrupt them later on in their flow – so I've always fooled myself I'm a good listener. And compared to my Dad, I *am* a good listener, but the people I've shut up over the years didn't know that.

The lovers are going to get a bit of a shock, when I get some strength back and start bossing them about. I think they deserve an entry of their own, while their patience has yet to be tested, while my character is still blurred by my powerlessness.

The lovers. I had a lover, of a sort, when I was diagnosed, but I soon got rid of him. I'd already placed a small ad which defined me as a Lonely Heart, which was my way of serving notice to myself that I was going to serve notice on him, and then I was diagnosed. I thought at once, that settles it (that was my first thought), I've got to get rid of him, and I did. He thought his health made him necessary to me, and I had hell's own job convincing him it made him even more of a nuisance than he was before, more of a menace, more of a pest. I couldn't carry him and illness too.

So when the magazine forwarded the replies to my ad, everything had changed, and they were replying to someone who didn't exist any more. There were only two replies, perhaps because I was never the world's most beautiful man, and my advert wasn't exactly raging with self-esteem. But I thought they deserved an explanation, and I arranged to meet them, both of them together so I didn't need to repeat myself.

By treating these strangers well after behaving so badly to someone who thought he was close to me, I think I was exercising in some final way the prerogatives of vigour. That's how I've worked it out since then. It was a choosing spree, and now my choices are made.

All the same: it wasn't as easy as I thought. I felt a terrible lurch when I started talking, and I had something like an anxiety attack. Perhaps it was simply grief for the person who had placed the ad and wasn't around any more. It's hard to be sure what it is you're having when you know your body is scheduled to fail you piecemeal – and your mind doesn't have a lot to look forward to, come to that – and you experience a sensation of intense heat and horror. Whether it was only an anxiety attack or what, I wasn't able to stay as long as I'd meant to, and I stumbled out while the drinks were still half finished. And a couple of hours later they phoned, the two of them, to ask how I was, and to say they'd like to help me in any way they could, if I'd let them.

If I try, knowing them as well as I do now, I can probably reconstruct the conversation that led up to their phone call. But I don't care to analyse something that has become so necessary to me. I answered. They offered. I accepted. We've developed some useful routines.

Diagnosis broke me up, the way a plough breaks earth, and all the recent growth, rooted so lightly, was pulled right up. But I was left all ready for seeding. When they phoned – it was Rory actually holding the phone and doing the talking – I remember I said, 'Let's get one thing straight. I have never depended on the kindness of strangers.' Then I had to break it to them that what I was saying was Yes.

The lovers. Leo and Rory, my lovers, my lions. They pay their visits separately; I know they meet up at least once a week to arrange their timetables. They used to visit in the day, but now they know that day isn't really the time they're most useful. They used to be great soup-merchants, the pair of them, but they soon got sick of eating their own soups. Now Rory helps me pay my bills on time, which is much more important. Leo has a car, and Rory doesn't, so it's Leo who stays the night, assuming he's free, when I have a clinic appointment in the morning. If it's Rory keeping me company, we take a taxi.

The taxi costs money, of course, but I prefer Rory's company at the clinic. Leo gets very tense, and I more or less have to look after him. Rory is different. I've been particularly unwell for a few weeks, and the hospital wanted a stool sample. That's not easy when your stools move at a hundred miles an hour, like mine do at the moment. With a straight face they gave me a little pot with a screw top, as if what they wanted collecting was a butterfly and not a bowel movement. Rory wasn't with me that day. Anyway, I tried. Day after day I'd go to the lavatory with my little pot, but I was never quick enough. It was as frustrating as my train-spotting days as a boy, when I would stand by the main line in the early morning mist as the express thundered by, trying to read the number on the engine. Anyway, I got my sample at last, and took it along. After a week, I went back for the results, and they told me the sample had leaked and couldn't be used for analysis. They hadn't phoned me, of course, to say so. Didn't want to depress me, I dare say. So they gave me another pot and sent me back home again, to wait for the express.

These grumbles shouldn't be on this tape at all – they're classic shits-and-vomits stuff – but it all leads up to Rory and why he's good to have around. When I'd got my second sample to the hospital and they'd analysed it at last, the doctor prescribed Dioralyte, which she said I have to take every time I have a loose bowel motion. She added, 'It comes in three flavours, avoid the pineapple,' and I could catch Rory's eye and know that he was feeling the same tickle of amusement at her phrasing. The doctor pinched the skin of my arm to see how dehydrated I was, and we both watched the little swag of raised flesh she left, which took a good long time to fade. If they'd told me about Dioralyte earlier on, of course, I wouldn't be dehydrated in the first place, but you can get it from the chemist even without a prescription, so it's not the sort of thing that holds a highly trained person's attention.

Or she can be explaining about *cryptospiridion*, the guest in my gut, and be saying, 'It produces nausea in the upper tract and diarrhoea in the lower, you see, because the whole intestine is implicated.' I can look at Rory and know he's thinking what I'm thinking: *Implicated? It's up to its bloody neck*. Leo would just sit there squirming, willing her to change the subject and talk about something nice.

I wish I'd had Rory with me when the doctor – the first doctor – asked me his three little questions. Did I receive anal intercourse? On occasion I did. He made a note. Had I visited Central Africa? On occasion I had. He made another note. Had I received blood there, by any chance? I seemed to remember something of the sort, when I was weak and confused from hepatitis. As I came out with the last of my answers, I could see the doctor's lips framing a word that looked like 'Bingo', and it would have been handy having Rory's eyes there for mine to meet.

Not that Rory's perfect. When we first heard about *crypto*, he and I, when she first mentioned the name, he blurted out, 'Oh dear, that's a stubborn one, isn't it?' I couldn't resist saying, 'Thanks a bunch, that's all I need,' just to see him flinch, though it really doesn't make any difference to me. In fact I'm glad he knows what he's about, if he does, so I don't have to worry about him the way I worry about Leo.

It's at night that Leo comes into his own, and not because he sleeps in the buff. He has a beguiling little body and all that, hairless and pale-skinned, but it's really only memory that tells me so. I let him sleep on the side of the bed away from the window, otherwise he thinks he won't sleep. It doesn't bother me which side of the bed I'm on, but with Rory I pretend I have a preference for lying away from the window. That way I know who it is that's staying over, even when I'm half asleep, just by our positions, just by feeling which side the warmth's coming from.

I couldn't really be in any doubt, anyway. Leo may wear no

night-clothes, but he keeps to his side of the bed, and he turns his back on me – slowly, quietly, as if I'll be offended – when he's going to sleep. Rory sleeps in a night-shirt, but all the same he hugs me and holds me to him, which is all very nice. Just as he's dropping off to sleep, he's been known to stroke my nipple absent-mindedly with his thumb, but my nipple, quite unlike itself, inverts instead of stiffening.

There can't be much doubt in their minds about who they're sleeping with, that's for sure. The guest in my gut, the gate-crasher in my gut, sends out smells beneath the duvet. And when I have my sweats, I can't think it's pleasant for them. The sheets spread my wetness pretty widely.

I cheat them both, I suppose, by sleeping so much in the day. But it makes such a difference having a lover installed and snoring if I'm not doing much sleeping at night. And Leo is perfect, regularly breathing, just the minimal presence I need. Leo's snoring is my night-light. Sleep works on him like a humane killer, stunning him before it bleeds the consciousness out of him. If he stays up too late, he slurs his words, and then starts to doze with his eyes open, and I expect he's replying to my conversation in his head, and doesn't realize he's making no sound.

In the morning it works the other way round. He opens his eyes when I bring him a cup of tea, but it's a minute or two before he can properly hold the cup. Till then he blinks, yawns, changes position, groans and scrabbles at his hair. I know he's embar-rassed that I bring him tea in the morning, but I'm solidly grateful that he sleeps so soundly, and I'll reward him in any way I can, even if it involves effort.

Rory is a much more partial sleeper, and when I get up he often joins me in front of the video. Or he'll go to the kitchen and mix up some Complan, with bananas and honey, the way I 'like' it, the way I can sometimes even tolerate it.

As he pads in, Rory asks me which series we're in, that is, are we escaping to 1982 or 1984? Does Henry Goldbloom have a moustache?

I tell him what year it is in the violently reassuring world of *Hill Street Blues*. Sometimes Rory seems to be doing a Henry Gold-bloom himself, but all it means is that he's skipped shaving for a day or two. He gets rid of the growth before it has a real prospect of changing the balance of his face. It's a shame, he's got a great thick growth of hair right up to his neck – what we used to call a poor man's cravat – so he actually looks a little odd clean-shaven.

It's wonderful of him to keep me company, I know, but I wish he'd go back to bed. Sometimes I put on a yawning routine, and we both go back to bed again, then I sneak out and go back to the video. It's not him I mind, it's the company he brings with him. If I can slide out of bed without waking him, I can get half an hour uninterrupted in front of the video. But when he gets up, and especially when he starts moving with a sort of muffled purpose-fulness round the kitchen, a gnawing and a churning wake up too. The gnawing is hunger and the churning is nausea, and wouldn't you know it, the gnawing is exactly in the middle of the churning, so there's no way I can get to it. So what with Rory and the Complan and the gnawing and the churning, it gets to be too much of a huddle round the video, and my view of the screen gets blocked off.

Lower levels of illness. I'm supposed to be have mellowed: that seems to be the general verdict. I don't believe a word of it, myself. What really happens is different. There's an awkward interval, when you're ill but not yet conditioned by illness. You're far enough down to be spending all your time below ground, but every now and then you come across shafts of something very like daylight. That makes you impatient and hard to deal with. Things get easier, for other people at least, when you don't have moments of real vitality to show up the false. By now it's second nature for me to follow the cues I get from Leo and from Rory, and not to hang around waiting for my own spontaneity. Only if that draining away of impulse is mellowing can I take credit for it.

The new, eroded me – but for form's sake we'll say *mellow* – the new mellow me has learned to put up with a lot of goodness from people lately. I had to get Rory to pay for this tape recorder, for one thing, and for everything I needed for quite a while. I could have given him cheques, of course; all it would have cost was a little embarrassment if I'd needed help writing them. But he didn't mind waiting for his money. I have this memory thing, you see. I have trouble remembering how to spell, particularly the last part of words for some reason. The words are all there, but I can't seem to spell them. That's what makes this recorder such a good idea. But it also means I can't remember the code number for my cashcard. I hadn't written it down, so I couldn't tell it to Rory. If I'd been up to it, I would have gone to the cashpoint myself, just to see if there was still some memory in my fingertips when I stood in front of the machine. As it was, Rory went for me. I told him he could take his revenge for every time the machine has been out of money on a Saturday night, or swallowed his card without provocation. I told him to mash the keys just as hard as he liked, all three times the machine gave him a chance of getting the number right. Then the card was swallowed up, and my bank sent me a replacement, and by the next post the new number for it. This time I gave the number to Rory to look after.

He's earned my patience. He tries to get me to lie down when I eat, as if that was going to help me hang on to my food, when all it means is more trouble being tidy when I throw up, but I forgive him for that. I know he means well even when he mixes me up some Dioralyte the moment I've had my *loose motion*, though I'm quite capable of throwing up the Dioralyte on the spot, before it's even properly gone down. My system likes to make clear that it discriminates against digestion impartially, from both ends of the process.

These days I keep my mouth shut when Rory talks about diabetes. His dad is diabetic, but so what? When Rory talks about it I get rather too clearly the feeling he's trying to teach me something. He tells me diabetes used to be a fatal illness, and that insulin is the crudest sort of treatment you could imagine: just a matter of smashing up bits of animals and injecting them into you, but that's enough to change everything. I want to say, wasn't there a film about the heartbreak of diabetes in that season

175

they had on the box, just recently, of socially concerned American dramas (made for TV, naturally)? I'm sure I taped some of those. Instead I listen to what Rory has to say about his father. Before too long I'll ask Rory if he thinks there might be something of the same sort coming my way, some sort of vinegar-and-brown-paper job, some way of jury-rigging the body, just to show him I've been listening.

Eroded as I am into mellowness, I've even learned to have mercy on Leo. We were in bed the other night, but for once he wasn't sleeping, for the very good reason that every time I lay down in bed I was having an attack of coughing. I tried sitting up in bed for a while, and then gradually sliding down to horizontal, but you can't fool a cough that way. I was trying it one more time just the same, when there was a knock on the door. It was very late, and we were both surprised. Leo put on a shirt and went to answer it. When he came back, he took off the shirt and got back into bed without explaining. I asked him who it was, and he said it was someone delivering pizza who'd got the wrong address.

'At this time of night?' I asked him.

'Yes.'

I didn't even know you could have pizza delivered around here.

'What address was he looking for?'

'Don't know.'

'Did he find where it was?'

'Don't know.' We lay there for a moment, and Leo turned slowly over in bed, away from me.

Suddenly I had the idea that what I wanted most in the world was pizza. A sudden flow of saliva even soothed my cough for a moment. I suppose it was partly because it was so late, my nausea was deeply asleep, and for a moment I had a clear view of my hunger. And then the pizza seemed so near, so ready on the other side of a door. So I said, 'Leo, this may sound silly, but could you go out and see if that pizza man is still around? If he is, tell him I'll take it off his hands. I'm not fussy about toppings. I'll even pay full whack.'

Leo dragged himself slowly out of bed, put on the shirt again, some trousers and some shoes, and stumbled across the room towards the door. Then he came back and sat on the bed. He told me then that he'd made it up about the pizza. When he'd opened the front door there was a man there in dressing-gown and slippers, holding out a bottle of Benylin, that heavy-duty cough stuff, and saying, without a lot of warmth, 'Try this.' Leo hadn't wanted to tell me. He put the Benylin somewhere where he was going to pick it up the next morning and take it away with him. He hadn't known what else to do.

Nor did I for a moment, and then I asked him to fetch me the bottle, I'd have a swig anyway, just to be friendly. The nausea was wide awake by then, so it didn't cost me a lot to be generous, just a little. Leo undressed again and fell asleep soon after that, and so did I, I think, though I woke up towards morning for a little practice hacking, which Leo slept through, and I hope everybody in the street did too.[

]*Salmon sperm!* What's the word? Milt. It's unbelievable! They just told me today. It turns out that milt is clever stuff. It has a Suppressing Effect. What it Suppresses is Replication. It's such clever stuff. And what that means is, salmon sperm is on my side. Milt loves me! And I love milt.

They're very dour about it. They say, don't build up your hopes too high. They never said that about fears. They never said don't build up your fears too high. And I'm not getting carried away. All I say is, milt loves me and I love milt! I don't even need to fellate the fish to get at it, though God knows I'd do it if I had to. They've synthesized it for me. They say, warning me, that it'll taste like metal. I say, you're wrong, it'll taste like Life. And they say, warning me, that I'll have to take it every four hours at first, day and night. And I say, nursing mothers have to put up with a lot more than that. I'll set the alarm for the middle of the night, and when it goes off I'll know what makes it worth while waking, there's no sleep so deep that I won't know. I'll know it's my Life waking me for its four o'clock feed.

They tell me it isn't a cure, as if I didn't know that. I tell them I know it could only be a poison, that's all doctors can ever give you, poison. You just have to hope that it hates you less than it hates what you've got. They tell me salmon sperm can attack your red cells, and your white cells come to that, so it might help to take some iron and vitamin B. I tell them I've always liked spinach. Oh, I've got all the answers. I just want to be able to put off the questions a bit.

Remission. Maybe I'll be able to move over to this tape for good. Shut away the shits-and-vomits tape in its little case and never need to pull it out again.[

]Remission. I had my remission.[

]I had my remission, and I didn't record it. I didn't even write anything down.[

]When I listen back to this tape, I hear myself explaining what I'm going to use it for, but I never do. I never do.[

]Some things I don't need help remembering. I remember getting the first prescription for my salmon sperm, and going along with it to the hospital pharmacy. Rory was with me that day, but he was shutting up for once. The new twist my case was taking seemed to have robbed him of his small talk. The Aussie I've always hated was on duty in the pharmacy, with his usual tan, only more so, and the stupid bleach-streaked hair, only more so. And of course the awful voice! When you're waiting your turn, eyes down or looking at the warnings on the walls for innocent things like whooping-cough, and he's bellowing instructions to the customers before you in the line, you can think he must have picked up an old copy of *Punch* from the table, and rolled it up to make his voice so deafening. Then when it's your turn you find it's even worse. He *roars* at me as he passes over the box of Dioralyte, 'Make up a sachet after every loose bowel movement,' and then tells me how many times a day I need to take my antibiotics, as if it wasn't written on the container. He seems to have a heroic notion of his job, as if he was still a life-guard back in Australia – though I think you need broad shoulders for that – striding across toasted sand and warning redheads not to sun-bathe. Then he pushes across the salmon sperm. I'd expected it to be a liquid, somehow, a heavy metallic liquid, what with its being so new and precious and rationed. I must have been thinking, too, of cod-liver oil. So I was disappointed for a moment when it was just ordinary capsules, like the time-release symptom-suppressors you take for a cold, except with a different paint-job, white with a thin blue belt at the middle. Then I was impressed all over again by the size of the bottle, it wasn't really big, but bigger than I'm used to, so it looked like a sweetie-jar in an old-fashioned corner shop. For a moment I thought, almost tearful with gratitude, *All that, for me?* £250 for a fortnight's treatment isn't peanuts, but why should I have been so surprised to be worth it? Then the Aussie booms out, 'You have to take these every four hours, day and night, do you understand? The best thing is to take 'em at four, and eight, and twelve. That way you only need to get up once in the night.'

And I thought, this idiot knows *nothing*; if I was sleeping eight hours a stretch I wouldn't be needing the salmon sperm, would I? I'd be holding down a job, wouldn't I, the way a paper-weight holds down a pile of prescription forms, the way you hold down yours. The week before, I'd just have let it wash over me, but this time it was as if the salmon sperm was giving me strength already, just by sitting there on the counter, so I said, 'Oh, I think I'll miss the four o'clock dose, get a full night's sleep.' I tried to make my voice campy. 'I'm not really an early morning person.' I could see Rory out of the corner of my eye, trying not to giggle.

But of course the Pharmacist From Bondi Beach looked really concerned, and he even lowered his voice, and he said, 'You really should, sir, it's important.'

If I'd had more than just the sight of the salmon sperm to give me strength, perhaps I'd have said something really crushing. But I couldn't think of anything anyway, so I just lowered my voice, all the way down to a whisper, and said, 'Just to please you then.'

There was no holding me. I nipped into the waiting room on my way out, flashed the nurse a big smile and asked, 'Would it be possible, do you think, to trace the kind person who brings along all those back numbers of opera magazines?' Then, just as she got launched on the sort of smile that says you've made someone's day, I said, 'Because I'd really like to push him off a small cliff. That would make my day.'

I remember that day because I had only had a premonition of health. I was still outside the world of the well, that world which I understand so little of now.

I have to reconstruct those weeks, those (admit it) months, from what they left behind, like a pathologist reconstructing a dead person's last meal. I remember looking at my first capsule, with a tiny animal printed on it in blue, like the little lions that used to be stamped on eggs, and what I took to be the word WELCOME in tiny letters. I remember thinking with real fervour, *Welcome yourself*, before I saw that the L in the word was double.

I know I became impatient with Leo and Rory almost instantly. They seemed so petty and nannyish, so ignorant of the real business of life. They nagged me to take my salmon sperm, as if it was something I'd forget just to be annoying. In fact I became very good at waking up seconds before the alarm went off for the three o'clock and seven o'clock feeds – I just had to be different, didn't I? – as if there really was a baby in the room, screaming. It should have struck me as funny when Leo struggled out of sleep at ten past seven one morning and started shaking me, convinced that I'd missed the seven o'clock feed and probably the three o'clock too, which of course he'd also snored through. It should have seemed funny, but it didn't. I suppose it was hard for them. They had suited themselves to me by an effort of will: it must have seemed ungrateful on my part to discharge myself – and so suddenly – from the intensive care I had demanded from them. But that didn't stop me from thinking what my mother used to say, poor bitch, of a piece of furniture that no longer pleased her: I'd rather have your space than your company.

Something peculiar must have happened. I stopped being feverish all the time, in that low-level way that becomes your new normal after a few months. But I entered another kind of fever; I was in a fever of health. That must be the explanation. I know I took a lot of trouble to repeat, in my new health, experiences that I'd had in sickness. That must be a very sophisticated pleasure.

I know, for instance, that in my sickness I had made a trip to Highgate Ponds. I needed to be driven, by Leo of course, and I needed to take a little rest at the unofficial gay sun-bathing area before I tottered down to the nudists' compound.

Leo and I laid out our towels on the concrete. I'd brought along a blanket and a pillow (which Leo was carrying, of course) for a little extra padding, but at least I laid the towel on top. I wasn't ashamed to strip off, though of course I was worried in case I had to run for the dingy lavatory, under the eyes of the ghastly crew by the weight-bench. But shame didn't get a look in. As far as I was concerned, this was strictly between me and the sun. I wasn't going to be done out of our date just because I could hardly walk.

I was surprised to see that Leo was shy, and kept a pair of swimming trunks on. I wanted to tempt him out of them, so I could at least look at the label and see whether they were bought from C&A or the British Home Stores.

After a while I struggled into a swimsuit myself, and walked weakly through to the pond. I was hoping that I would feel strong enough for a dip at least, which was a pretty bizarre hope. Perhaps I thought that, all other sources of energy having failed, I would turn out to be solar-powered. I lay down on the diving-board. I had been there about ten seconds, feeling the wind on me almost warm, and watching the people sprawled on the raft in the middle of the pond, when a man came out of a hut and shouted at me that sun-bathing was not allowed in the swimming area.

The trip I made in my health, I seem to think, was very different. I took bus after bus to get there, by myself. I strode past the sun-bathing area, and straight into the compound, though this time I was reluctant to take off my underwear. By then I had a little roll of tummy fat which I was very proud of, and which showed to best effect above the waistline of a pair of underpants, and I wasn't in any hurry to have it vanish the moment I took my briefs off and lay down. I expect I was waiting for someone to call out, 'Wonderful! I can't see your ribs. Well done!'

Before the sun had properly got to work I was standing up again and pulling my swimming trunks up. I went out into the swimming area, but I wasn't quite brave enough for the diving-board. The water looked cloudy, but I knew it was supposed to be pure and clean, equally free of pollution and disinfectant. I let myself down an iron ladder that had a lot of weed attached to it. The ladder wasn't full-length, as I had assumed, it stopped only a little below the surface, so I slipped into the coldest water I have ever touched. My body gasped and went on gasping. The water was unexpectedly deep, too, considering it was so near the edge of the pond. I set out to swim to the raft, which supported what looked like the same group of sun-worshippers as last time, but I found myself swimming instead in a tight circle back to where I started. I wanted to strike out for that floating island of health, but my body wasn't having it. My feet had no memory of the ladder, and scrabbled for purchase where the rungs were imagin-ary. Then I remembered, and felt for the actual bottom of the actual ladder, and managed to pull myself out.

I slumped on the jetty to recover. Not even the most officious attendant, seeing me there flat out and wheezing could imagine I was having a sun-bathe on the sly, but the men on the raft set up a round of ironic applause that I could hear even through the numbness of my ears.

I wasn't going to give up. I didn't hang around until my skin had dried off and my trunks felt cold and clammy. I went back down the ladder and swam out through the cold. The water got warmer after a while, or else it stayed cold and I got used to it. The raft was only fifty feet or so away, but that was quite far enough. I could feel the special uneasiness of swimming in water of unknown depth. As I got near the raft, all I could see above the edge of it was the soles of someone's feet, those odd sort of feet with the second toe longer than the big one.

The ladder by the raft was even shorter than the one on the

jetty. In my memory, it has only two rungs. I know I had to pull myself up with what felt like the last of my strength. But when I looked round at the raft, which rocked under my weight and wasn't as securely tethered as I'd expected, it was covered with shit. I don't mean that the men there were lying in it: they were too fastidious for that, with their uniform tans, as if they'd all chosen the same shade from a paint card. But there were substantial little turds scattered all over the raft. They were bigger than anything I've known a bird do, but I couldn't imagine what beast could have got there to lay them. I was tired out from my swim, but lying in shit was too recent a memory – from nights when I improvised a pair of incontinence pants out of an old Marks and Sparks bag – for me to be able to stay on the raft. I climbed down the rusty ladder, losing my footing one more time, and swam back to the jetty. It may be that my strength was failing towards the end, but I think the water near the jetty was the coldest of all.

I know I did all that. I even remember it all, in the sense that I still bear traces of those thoughts and sensations. I remember what my body felt in its health, what it touched, how it reacted. But I have no sense of how my body felt to itself. Health was just one more thing that happened to me, and I have kept nothing from it. The tape is blank for all those weeks and months.

And now I am back in my siege of fevers. What it feels like, as always, is shame, as if this raised temperature was nothing more than a hideous extended blush, which I could get rid of if I just did the right thing. I find myself wondering what it was I did wrong, what crime my body remembers with this heat of shame. They didn't lie to me about the salmon sperm. I knew it could nibble away at my cells. I knew there was a price to be paid for the job it did. I knew it wasn't a medicine so much as a protection racket; I just hoped we could get along. I took vitamins, I took iron, I took supplements. Was there one night when I passed up a dish of green vegetables, in my feverish health, snubbing all those B vitamins, and went out instead? There must have been. I know there were times when I was too bound up in the play I was watching to remember my feed. I'd glared in the dark at people whose watch alarms went off in the theatre for too many years to commit that crime myself. And there was the terrible day I lost my bottle of capsules. I had to dash across London, whimpering, for replacements. I'd lost six expensive days' worth. To make myself feel better I asked if anyone had lost their salmon sperm before me. But I was the first.

How can I put it, to make myself feel I have made heroic choices? Health for me is more than being not-yet-dead. It's not something you patrol; it's something you must forget to patrol or it's not any sort of health at all. That should do it. That sounds right. That must be why I didn't use this tape to hoard up bits of my health, so I could live off them at a later date.

And here I am with a body that's ashamed of itself, that's burning with remorse for something it did or didn't do, and with the word *surge* beating in my ears. They warned me what would happen when I came off the salmon sperm. A surge of virus. Virus replicating uninhibited. *Surge* is a word that sounds overwhelming even on the smallest scale, down on the cellular level. What chance do I have, against a *surge*?

Every time I went to hospital for some more salmon sperm, and they took blood, I must have known they were monitoring my levels. Fourteen. Twelve and a half. Eleven. Nine. It was more than a pit stop. And when I went below nine, and they started to give me transfusions, I knew what they were about. But I tried to think, closing my eyes when the prick came in my arm, and then the slowly growing ache in it, that I was giving blood rather than getting it, that from my overflowing health I was giving freely of my surplus. Nine and a half. Nine. Eight. I tried to think I was paying my taxes, when all the time my bloodstream was being heavily subsidized. On long car journeys as a child, I remember, to stop from feeling sick – from motion, from too many boiled sweets, from my father's Senior Service and my mother's Piccadilly – I would close my eyes and try to interpret the sensations in terms of movement backward, though I don't quite know why that was comforting. I could produce a surprisingly strong and consistent illusion until I opened my eyes at a bump in the road, or when my mother asked if I was asleep, and the world came crashing back at me.[

]The lovers are back. They can deal with me again. And I suppose that really means that I can deal with them. Rory has that handsome look in the face that means he's certain to shave in the morning, and Leo smells so strongly of soap he must wear a bar round his neck.[

]They've done something very tactful with the key. I'm not very steady on my feet just at the moment, and my neighbour has a spare set of keys. She's always been a hypochondriac, can't bear to be in the room with anyone who has a cold, so I suppose it's something of a miracle that she's not returned them, or that they don't reek of disinfectant. This I noticed today, and it qualifies for inclusion on this tape. That's what this tape is supposed to be for, isn't it? Sometimes my neighbour even leaves groceries outside the door. Anyway, when Rory last came by he let himself in, and explained that he had happened to run into my neighbour outside the house. Then *Leo* let himself in next time he paid a visit, and he looked all tense and startled, as if at any moment he might be called upon to lie. So my guess is they've made a policy decision not to make me walk any more than I have to. They must knock on my neighbour's door every time they come round. For all I know, they get her to leave the key under the mat when she goes out. I think they're waiting for me to twig and get angry, but they'll have to wait a little while longer. I'll either keep it to myself or let it hitch a ride on a real grievance. 'And another thing,' I'll say, 'about the keys . . .'[

]We've started taking baths together, the lovers and I. Rory lifts me into the tub very competently, which is so reassuring it's sinister, but at least he climbs right in with me, like no nurse in the world who wants to remain in employment. Suddenly I wonder if he answered my ad – poor idiot – to get his life moving again after grief, and has to keep his teeth clenched on his knowledge. So I'm more than usually grateful that he gets into the bath with me. He sits behind me with his knees bent, so I can rest my head on his chest, and he strokes me a little awkwardly with a sponge. It's a posture I like anyway, and now in particular I'm glad of it because it's not a position that encourages talking. We can't really see each other's faces. I think he closes his eyes in the steam, and from time to time he seems to drift off. He doesn't seem to mind that the water gets cold; perhaps he doesn't even feel it.

If there was just a little more water in the bath I'd be floating. As it is my head bumps softly against Rory's chest. Here and only here, in this limbo inside another, I remember my lover, the lover I disposed of so efficiently, dumping his body in an acid bath of resentment. What I remember isn't the friendship, which I resisted, or even the sex, which I wanted only when I wanted it, but the game we used to play when we were out together, the game he taught me and that he may even have invented, the sweetly innocent game he called *compelled*-to-fuck. One or other of us would say, 'If you were *compelled* to fuck a set number of people – under pain of death, mind . . .' (or later just, 'If you were *compelled* . . .'). Then the other would say, 'How many?' And the answer would be, 'One on this bus,' or 'Two before we leave the Food Hall,' or 'Three before the next traffic light.' Then he would say, 'Three? You'll be lucky. That one, at a pinch. Another one? No chance. All right, the thinner of these two bobbies, the less fat I mean. That's the lot. That's my last offer. One more? Do I really have to? Let it be the one with the tie, then. Cancel that. The other bobby. If I have to.' What I remember best is the grudging lust in all its variety that he could call up on his face, as he made his protesting selections.

Sooner or later I have to tell Rory that it's time for me to get out. I start shivering, even in the water, even against his skin. He doesn't risk trying to lift me out while he's wet and slippery, so he dries himself as quickly as he can and comes back for me with a hot towel. By now I'm really shivering. He helps me stand up and pulls the plug out. He wraps the towel round me and rubs away until at last a tingle passes to me from the towel. By then I'm likely to be exhausted, and once he even had a shot at carrying me to the bed. He was staggering by the time we got there, and he didn't so much lay me down as fall with me down on to the mattress.

Leo is different, of course. He has a hard time lifting me into the bath, so I hang on to the towel rail just in case – though I'm not sure I could support my weight for more than a second or two, if he lost his grip. He puts stuff in the bath so that it's full of nutty-smelling bubbles by the time I arrive in it, which relaxes me and relaxes him too, because he doesn't have to see me naked for more than a few moments. I'd rather he joined me in the bath – the edge of the tub is hard against my shoulders – but he likes to stay where he is. Still, he's becoming something of a pro as a back-scrubber, and that's something. At first he used a nail-brush, but one day he couldn't find it so he used my toothbrush instead, and we've never gone back to the nail-brush. He's even brought along a toothbrush which is specifically for scrubbing my back.

He starts on my left shoulder, pressing hard with the bristles, moving his wrist in tiny circles. It's extraordinary how – even the first time he did it, and much more so now – my skin anticipates the sideways progress of the brush as he moves it across my back, so that I develop a roving itch that is always just a fraction ahead of the scrubbing. When he has reached the outside edge of my right shoulderblade, he drops his hand an inch or so and scrubs steadily back to the left again. I try to concentrate all my attention on the itch, which moves ahead of the toothbrush all the way. It's as if there was a poem written on my back that I learned by heart in childhood. I have wholly forgotten it, but each word that I am prompted to remember sparks the memory of the next. I close my eyes. The travelling itch holds still, for once, at the extremity of my back, until the brush comes to scrub it out.[

I lose the ability to talk. My voice unravels, and speech drops away from me like the mouthpiece of an instrument I am suddenly unable to play, a medieval instrument that I don't even recognize as a possible source of music.

When I open my eyes again, they are both there, both the lovers. Leo and Rory. Imagination is the last thing to fail me. I see them lying side by side on their fronts, their arms around each other, their faces pushed into the pillows. They turn towards each other, and I see Rory trace a line with his finger down Leo's cheek. I can see a tear on Leo's skin by the tip of Rory's finger, but from my point of view I can't make out whether Rory is following its progress as it trickles, or drawing it out of Leo's eye with the gesture he makes. Rory leans over and kisses the tear where it has come to rest, and I flinch in spite of myself. Leo turns away from the kiss, so they are both on their sides now, facing the same way.

Rory sets up a gentle motion of the hips, which Leo's hips take up. A terrible rattle of protest and warning bursts from me, behind clenched teeth. Their hips are in rhythm now, and Rory's face is pressed against Leo's neck, just as it was against the pillow a few moments ago.

I turn my head away, and see the cardboard box that contains all my medicines in their varied containers. I see also the little pile of Leo's and Rory's clothes. Their two pairs of trousers have fallen in an oddly symmetrical pattern, forming a sort of star, and I can see among the keys attached to one belt-loop a new pale-silver copy of a familiar shape. I glance at the keys on the other trousers, to locate the twin of it. But I forgive my lovers their ability to comfort themselves and each other, and I forgive myself for bringing them together, as I cross the room as quietly as I can and open the door, as quietly as I can. Then I close the door after all, walk back across the room, not worrying any more about whether I make any noise, and sit back down on the edge of the bed.

BEARS IN MOURNING

When I think about it, it was terrible the way we behaved when Victor died. We behaved as if we were ashamed of him, or angry. It didn't show us at our best – we didn't cope at all well. We all knew Victor was 'ill', obviously, but none of us really took on board how bad things had got.

He was in the middle of our little group, our sect, but somehow he got lost all the same. I suppose each of us paid him some token attention – his conversation tended to go round in circles, particularly with the drink – and then left it to somebody else to do the real work, supporting him and talking him through the dark days. He was our brother Bear, but the fraternity didn't do well by him.

We Bears are a varied crowd. There's an organist, a social worker, a travel agent, an osteopath. That's not the full list, of course, that's off the top of my head. If it wasn't for membership of the Bear nation we would have nothing in common. Somehow we always thought that would be enough.

It's amazing that Victor was able to hold down his job for as long as he did but then he'd done it for a long time. He was working with friends, people who would make allowances. In any case there was a structure set up, and within limits it ran itself. Every few months Victor, or rather the company that employed him, put out the first issue of a magazine devoted to some sure-fire subject – French cookery, classic cars, sixties pop. When I say the first issue, I mean of course Parts One and Two, Part Two coming free.

It doesn't take long, with a half-way decent picture researcher, to get enough stuff from reference books to fill a few magazine pages. Tasters for future issues take care of the rest. Part Three never arrives, and maybe people wonder why not. Maybe they think, shame nobody bought Parts One and Two – it was such a good idea. Pity it didn't catch on.

I used to wonder what would have happened if one of Victor's magazines had really taken off, had sold and sold off the news-stands. Would there have come a time when Part Three became inevitable? I don't think so. I think Victor's employers would have carried on repackaging their little stack of ideas for ever. With a little redesign, they could put out the same Parts One and Two every two years or so. Which they did.

Victor was prime Bear, Bear absolute. I know I haven't explained just what a Bear is, and it's not an easy thing to define. There have always been tubby men, but I can't think they ever formed a little self-conscious tribe before. *Tubby* isn't even the right word, but at least it's better than *chubby*. *Chubby* is hopeless, and *chubby-chaser* is a joke category.

To be a Bear you need, let's see, two essential characteristics, a beard and a bit of flesh to spare, and preferably some body hair. But it's a more mysterious business than that. Some men will never be Bears however hairy they are, however much surplus weight they carry. They just look like hairy thin guys who've let themselves run to seed, thin men who could stand to lose a few pounds. A true Bear has a wholeness you can't miss – at least if you're looking for it. It's a great thing to watch a Bear become aware of himself. All his life he's been made to feel like a lump, and then he meets a person, and then a whole group, that thinks he's heaven on legs. On tree-trunk legs. He's been struggling all his life against his body, and suddenly it's perfect. There have been quite a few lapsed health-club memberships in our little circle, I can tell you.

One of them was mine. I remember the first time I was hugged by a Bear, as a Bear. We were Bear to Bear. I remember how his hand squeezed my tummy – *tummy*'s a childish word but the others are worse – and I realized I didn't need to hold it in. He wasn't looking for a washboard stomach, the sort you see in the magazines. He was happy with a washtub stomach like mine. He liked me just the way I was.

And Aids, Aids. Where does Aids come into this?

All of us were involved in the epidemic in some way, socially, politically, rattling collection buckets at benefit shows if nothing else. And of course we were all terrified of getting sick. But that's not what I'm getting at.

Aids is like the weather. It doesn't cause everything, but the things it doesn't cause it causes the causes of. So, yes, you'd think there'd be a link between a group of men who like their lovers to have a bit of meat on their bones, who like men with curves, and a disease that makes people shrivel away into a straight line up and down.

But I don't really think so. The Bear idea would have happened with or without Aids. The English language had a hand in it, by putting the words *bear* and *beard* so close to each other in the dictionary. Perhaps it's a sexual style that works differently in other languages. Has anyone in history ever really enjoyed beards, let alone based a little erotic religion around them? I suppose Victorians were the people in history most exposed to facial hair, and they weren't in much of a position to shop around or compare notes.

The beard is a mystery worn on the face. There are beards of silk and beards of wire, each with its charge of static, and it isn't easy to tell them apart without a nuzzle, or at least a touch of the hand.

We in our group are great observers of the way a beard shows up different pigments from the rest of the head hair. Ginger tints are common; less often, we see magical combinations of darkness and blondness. Beards age unpredictably, sometimes greying before the head hair, sometimes retaining a strong shade when all colour has drained from the scalp. The first frost may appear evenly across the beard, or locally in the sideboards, or on the chin, or at the corners of the mouth.

We in our group are tolerant of tufty beards, wispy beards, beards with asymmetrical holes. There are beards that Nature more or less insists on, to cover up her botches. Only a few bearers of the beard, we feel, positively bring it into disrepute, usually by reason of fancy razorwork. The beard to us is more than a sexual trigger, not far short of a sexual organ. Some of us even defend jazzman beards, goatees, beards that look like a few eyebrows stuck together. As a group, we particularly admire a beard that rides high on the cheeks, or one that runs down the neck unshaven.

Bears don't discriminate against age. It's just the other way about. We often say that someone is too young for his beard – he'll have to grow into it.

A man with a pure-white beard can expect as many looks of appreciation, still tinged with lust, as someone twenty, thirty years younger. There are many couples in our group, though few of them even try to be monogamous, and some of them are made up of figures who we might describe as Bear and Cub, Daddy Bear and Baby Bear – but even they don't take their roles very seriously. Neither of them tries too hard to play the grown-up.

It's as if in every generation of boy children there are a few who put their fingers in their ears during tellings of *Goldilocks*, filtering out the female elements in the story, until what they are left with is a fuzzy fable of furry sleepers, of rumpled beds and porridge.

Every happy period is a sort of childhood, and the last ten years have been a happy period for the Bears, in spite of everything.

So when I say that Victor was an absolute Bear, I mean that he had pale skin, heavy eyebrows and a startlingly dark beard, full but trimmed. No human hair is black, even Chinese or Japanese, and Raven Black hair dye is sold as a cruel joke to people who know no better, but Victor's came close. He was forty-two or three then, I suppose, and five foot eight, ideal Bear height. He pointed his feet out a bit, as if his tummy was a new thing and needed a new arrangement of posture to balance it.

We met in a bar. Under artificial light the drama of his colouring wasn't immediately obvious, and I mistook him for a German who had been rude to me in another bar a couple of months before. I suppose my body language expressed a pre-emptive rejection, which in the event Victor found attractive. After a while he came over to me and said, 'You win. You've stared me down. Let me buy you a drink.'

I went home with him in his old Rover to Bromley, an unexpectedly long journey and a suburban setting that didn't seem to fit with the man who took me there. Later I learned that this had been his childhood home. When his mother died, Victor had let go a West End flat so as to keep his father company. It was a doomed gesture, as things turned out – one of a series – because his father soon found some company of his own. The companion may in fact have dated back to the days before Victor's mother died.

It was late when we arrived at Bromley. I assumed we were alone in the house, in which case Victor's father was stopping out with his lady friend, but perhaps he was asleep in a bedroom I didn't see. If so, he slept soundly, and got up either before or after we did.

The bedroom was in chaos, but – not knowing Victor – it didn't occur to me to wonder whether it was an ebullient chaos or a despairing one. There was a big bulletin board on the mantle-piece, with photographs, letters and business cards pinned up on it, but there was still an overflow of paper and magazines. There was the inevitable shelf of Paddingtons, Poohs and koalas, and a single Snoopy to show breadth of mind.

Victor wanted first to be hugged and then fucked. He mentioned that this second desire was a rarity with him, and I could believe him. He was vague about the location of condoms. Eventually I found a single protective in a bedside drawer, of an unfamiliar brand (the writing on the packet seemed to be Dutch) and elderly appearance. I could find no lubricant that wouldn't dissolve it. I put it on anyway, to show willing, and lay down on top of Victor. I enjoyed the heat and mass of the man beneath me; I made only the most tentative pelvic movements, just vigorous enough to tear the dry condom. Then Victor remembered that he had some lubricant after all, under the bed.

Victor was apologetic about the confusion of our sexual transaction, but, looking back, I find it appropriate. He was both in and out of the world, even then, and he could summon up separately the elements of lovemaking – desire, caution, tenderness – but not string them together.

At some stage I noticed he was crying, and he went on for over an hour before he stopped. I hugged him some more, but I can't say that I took his distress very seriously. I didn't make anything of the fact that we didn't have a particularly good time in bed. Good sex isn't very Bear, somehow. I was already well used to awkwardness, lapses of concentration, sudden emotional outpourings. What could be more Bear than a fatherly man on a crying jag?

Bears are never far from tears, or wild laughter, come to that. I have seen Bears cry just as hard as Victor did that night, beards matted with their tears, and be cheered up by a bowl of cereal or a cartoon on television. But of course Victor only stopped crying when he fell asleep. The curtains were open, and it was already beginning to get light. I hate sleeping like that – this Bear likes his cave dark – but I didn't stay awake long enough to do anything about it.

That was my only intimate contact with Victor, but the Bear community continued to revolve in its eccentric orbit around him. Everybody I met seemed to know him, and I ended up keeping track of him without making any great effort. Victor's father died a few months after we met, which I think was the great event in Victor's life. After that he had a succession of room-mates at the house – Bears, inevitably. They didn't stay long. Victor was hard going by then, even for Bears. But while they stayed, and while he stayed coherent, Victor took a fatherly interest in them, and would try to fix them up with compatible Bruins. That's a nice characteristic – that's a good thing to remember.

I invited Victor to dinner once about that time, and he phoned me on the evening arranged to warn me he'd be late. He never arrived. From friends on the Bear grapevine I learned that this pattern was typical.

After Victor died, the room-mate at the time wanted everything of Victor's, everything that was even reminiscent of Victor, cleared away at once. He wasn't being heartless, he just couldn't cope with a dead man's presence being imprinted so strongly on the rooms. I went along to help out, but it wasn't as straightforward a job as we had thought when we started. Apparently neutral objects kept leaping into hurtful life.

It turned out that Victor used to offer himself as a photographic model for his magazines and their stablemates. Surprising that a man with low self-esteem should so much enjoy being photographed. But apparently he used to tease the company's photographic editor about the scarcity of bearded images in the media, and offered himself to make good the lack. So as we cleared the room we found that the slippered individual on the cover of a mid-seventies hi-fi magazine, head cocked while he stroked a spaniel and listened to a hulking array of quadrophonic speakers, was a mid-seventies Victor. The genial chef on another cover, stirring a golden sauce in a kitchen hung with gleaming copper pans, was also Victor. Victor was even a tasteful Adam on the cover of a pop-psychology mag, Parts One and Two, receiving a glossy apple from an Eve with scheming eyes. Finally all the traces of Victor's presence were gone, stuffed under beds or bundled into bin-bags.

The worst part of the visit, though, was that we found in a wastepaper basket something that was like the opposite of a suicide note. It was the note Victor would have left for his room-mate if he had managed to decide to go on living. 'Dear Bear,' it started, and it said, 'Sorry I've been so hard to be around lately, that's the last thing you need. Thanks for bearing it anyway (bad joke), and I think I've turned the corner. I'll leave the car tomorrow – no point in taking it – and I'll see you in the p.m. Don't chuck the *Guardian*, there may be some jobs in it. Love Victor.'

I had known that Victor was due to appear in court the next day for drunk driving (not his first offence), and was certain to lose his licence. I hadn't heard that he had also lost his job, over his general unreliability, I expect, though the pretext had to do with fiddling expenses, or paying somebody who was already on the staff to do piecework under another name.

Instead of turning up in court, and instead of leaving the note, which he crumpled up and threw in the wastepaper basket, Victor took the car and drove down to the country – Kent somewhere; I'm afraid I've blotted out the details. I think it was where his parents had met, or had their first date, or went on their honeymoon. It had a private significance, but I've forgotten exactly what. I imagine it was a beauty spot, and that he reached it in the early hours. He must have waited a bit, after he arrived, for the crumbling exhaust pipe of the old Rover to cool down from the journey. He wouldn't have wanted to burn his hands or melt the hose. Perhaps he waited again afterwards, before he restarted the engine.

He didn't leave a note, but he hardly needed to. For weeks he had been sitting around drinking and listening to a record – the first single he had bought for years, I dare say. It was called 'The Living Years' by Mike and the Mechanics, and by bad luck it was at Number One. For a few weeks it was impossible to avoid it on the radio. It was all about not telling your father you loved him while he was alive, and Victor played it over and over again. Mike of the Mechanics is one of the very few beards in pop music, but I don't think that had anything to do with it. Far too lanky to be a Bear.

Victor had a little bag of runes, a sort of Celtic I Ching, given him by an Irish Bear who used them to make every decision, and he would draw a rune from the bag every now and then when he was drinking. He seemed to draw the blank tile rather a lot, or so I heard, from the black suede drawstring bag. The drawstring bag of fate. The blank rune means death, according to the little booklet that comes with the set, but I hope he read a little further, and learned that it could also mean the absolute end of some-thing. The blank tile can actually be a positive sign: new beginning. Still, I don't expect it would have mattered what tile he drew, or what he thought it meant.

I don't expect it occurred to Victor to think of that old magazine cover, with a younger and hopeful-looking him patting a dog and listening with an expression of neutral pleasure to an unspecified music. But I find myself thinking, as I didn't when Victor's death was fresh, of the two images, the one of posed contentment, and the other of real-life squalor and misery – a middle-aged man letting a pretentious pop single contain and enlarge all his sense of failure.

Suicide rates go down in wartime. Isn't that a fascinating fact? Except that I can never work out what it means. Does it mean that people with a self-destructive streak volunteer for dangerous jobs or missions, so they don't need to go to the trouble of topping themselves – they're either killed or cured? Or does it mean that people forget to be self-obsessed when there's a genuine crisis out there in the world?

You'd think there'd be a lot of Aids-related suicides, but there aren't. It can't just be a matter of being British, not wanting to make a fuss, all that. There must be a few people who freak out when they're diagnosed HIV-positive out of a clear blue sky; they're the most likely to lay hands on themselves. But anyone who's already shown symptoms must at least have considered the possibility. Knowing the worst can even calm people down, in a certain sense.

It's different for people who are really sick. They're faced with a series of days only fractionally better or worse than the one before, and suicide is such an all-or-nothing business. It's really tricky deciding what individual trial finally tips a life over into being not worth the living, and then sticking to your decision. It's like a problem in algebra. What is x, such that x *plus* 1 is unbearable?

But how do the survivors feel if someone does commit suicide in the middle of a war? That was the problem for the Bears. That was what we were dropped in. We knew damn well that Victor wasn't physically sick. He couldn't have taken an HIV test without our knowing. It seemed to us that he'd just thrown away a body that any of our sick friends, any dwindling Bear, would have jumped at. OK, so Victor was short of puff, no great shakes when it came to running up stairs. There are plenty of skinny people who could have learned to put up with that.

We were angry. Didn't Victor know there was a war on? We Bears had given bouquets that had appeared at the graveside stripped of their messages. We had laboured to clean the bathrooms of the dead, so that their heirs found nothing so much as a stain to alarm them – and had had our names forgotten, however many times we were introduced. We had held our candles high at Trafalgar Square vigils, year after year, forming helpful compositional groups on cue for press photographs that never got published. And there was Victor, beautiful in his coffin, plump in his coffin, his poison-blued face hardly presenting a challenge to the undertaker's cosmetician.

Everywhere we look we see Aids. We can be driving along, not thinking of anything. We stop at the traffic lights and there's a cyclist waiting there too, foot flexed on the pedal, ready to shoot off first. The picture of health. Except that he's wearing a mask to filter the city air that makes us think of an oxygen mask, and there's a personal stereo fastened by a strap to his bicep that reminds us of a drip feed – as if he was taking music intravenously.

So how could Victor see anything but Aids? What gave him the right to follow his obsession with his father so far? Somehow while we were all busy he found the time to invent his own illness. Wasn't Aids good enough for him? We loved his flesh, but it was unnatural that he died with it unmelted. Dying fat is an obscenity, these days. You're not supposed to be able to take it with you.

These days I understand Victor a little better. His anti-suicide note has made me understand suicide in a way that no suicide note could ever do. His father dying made his failure final. When we eventually worked out the access code for his home computer, we found it was full of rambling journal entries saying so. But in another way he must have been relieved. With both his parents dead, he didn't need to resist the temptation of suicide any more, for their sake. With both of them gone, his loyalties weren't divided any more. He had no loyalty to life. He felt no patriotism for the mortal country.

I realize now that Victor's life only amounted to a little loop of track, like a child's first model-railway layout. There was only one set of points in the whole circuit, and every time Victor passed it he had to decide whether to commit himself to going round again. But even if he did, he knew that he'd be passing the points again soon. Sooner or later he was bound to make the other choice.

He didn't steer the way we do. He wasn't affected by our weather. His despair was a gyroscope. But any other time, we would have grieved for him.

I didn't go to the memorial service, though I know that one or two of the Bears did, along with a couple of colleagues from work. But all the Bears turned up to a funeral feast at the Bromley house. We had a sort of picnic, but there was an ugly feeling behind it all, a resentment we didn't quite come out with. Most of us got a little drunk, which didn't help. I remember wandering through the house, looking for signs of Victor, even though I had helped so recently to clear such things away. I found a photo of him in a drawer, and slipped it into a pocket. Then a little later, someone dragged out the bin-bags of Victor's papers and possessions, and a little after that we made a bonfire.

BABY CLUTCH

The half-dozen Walkmans that used to live on this ward, bought by a charity for the use of the patients, were walked off with in a matter of days. The next batch, if the charity decides to replace them, will have to be chained down, I expect, like books in a medieval library.

At least the television in my lover's room has a remote control; that's something. There used to be a remote for every room on the ward, but one or two have also gone walkies. Replacing them isn't a high medical priority, though perhaps it should be. Life on this ward can seem like one big game of musical chairs, as if death, being spoiled for choice, will come by preference to the person with no flowers by the bed, with no yoghurts stashed away in the communal fridge, the person whose TV has no remote control.

A television looms larger in a hospital room than it could ever do in someone's home. There are so few excuses not to watch it: visitors, coma. Once I came in and was shocked to see a nurse comforting my lover. She was bending over him with a tenderness that displaced me. My lover was sobbing and saying, 'Poor Damon.' It was a while before he could make himself understood. The nurse wasn't amused when she found out Damon was a young man on *Brookside* who'd just been killed.

She'd have been even less amused if she'd known it was the first episode of *Brookside* my lover had ever watched. He hadn't seen poor Damon alive. But I suppose it was the mother's grief having no actual content for him that let him share it so fully.

There's another television in the day-room, which even has a video recorder and a little shelf of tapes. The day-room also contains an eccentric library, *Ring of Bright Water* rubbing spines with a guide to non-nuclear defence and a fair selection of periodicals. My lover and I find ourselves listing the self-descriptions we find least beguiling in the small ads of the gay press.

'Antibody-negative,' is his first contribution. He resents the assumption that good health is as intrinsic to some people as blue eyes are to others, or the condition, so common on these pages, of being 'considered attractive'.

It's my turn. 'Straight-appearing.'

'Healthy,' is second on my lover's list.

'Discreet.' What kind of boast is that, after all?

'Healthy.' My lover can't seem to get over this little preoccupation of his, so I shut myself up, without even mentioning *non-camp, looks younger, genuine* or *first-time advertiser*.

Deep down I'm pleased by the silliness of the small ads, pleased to find any evidence that there are still trivial sides to gay life. More than anything, I want there to be disco bunnies out there somewhere, still. But I expect even the disco bunnies are stoic philosophers these days, if only in their free time. What used to be the verdict on men who loved men – something about being locked in the nursery, wasn't it? There's nothing like being locked in a hospice to make the nursery look good.

We are having a respite between waves of my lover's visitors. Less than half-joking, I suggest that one of the nurses on the ward should function as a secretary, to make appointments and space the visitors out, to avoid these log-jams of well-wishers. I resent the brutal etiquette of hospital visiting, which means that a new visitor tapping hesitantly at the door instantly shuts down our intimacy. I try to be tactful, do some shopping in the area or talk to one of the other patients, but I doubt if I manage to be nice about it. Making myself scarce only encourages the other visitors to stay, to cling like leeches. I find the whole business of dealing with the visitors exhausting, and I'm not even ill.

Gently, taking care not to scare off his good fortune, my lover tells me that he is the only patient now on the ward who would benefit from a secretarial service like the one I am proposing. The other inmates have, at the most, two guests at a time. The difference may be one of character (my lover is agreed to be lovable); it may also turn out that the other patients have come back here so many times they have lost the ability to reassure their visitors, after which point the visits tend to dry up.

This is my lover's first major stay in hospital. Transfusions for anaemia don't count, even when he is there overnight. Everybody I come across refers to transfusions in the cheeriest possible terms ('just in for a top-up, are you?' is the standard phrase) though everybody also knows that transfusions can't go on for ever. That's an example of something I've been noticing recently, of how easy it is for people to rise above the fates of third parties.

I'm generally impatient with the visitors, but I make exceptions. I'm always glad to see Armchair, for instance. My lover knows so many Davids and so many Peters he gives them nicknames to tell them apart. Armchair is a Peter; other Peters are Poodle and Ragamuffin.

Armchair is, as advertised, reassuring and cosy, all the more comfortable for having one or two springs broken. Armchair is a fine piece of supportive furniture. When he phones the hospital to leave a message, he doesn't bother any more with his proper name; he just says Armchair. A nurse will come into the room and say, 'Someone called Armchair asks if it's all right to visit,' or, 'Armchair sends his love,' with a faint gathering of the eyebrows, until she's used to these messages.

Armchair is actually, in his way, my lover's deputy lover, or I suppose I mean my deputy. They met a month or two ago, while I was away, and they've slept together once or twice, but it's clear enough that Armchair would like More. It isn't a physical thing between them, exactly – my lover isn't awash with libido at the moment – but Armchair would like my lover to spend nights with him on a more permanent basis. Armchair would like to be a regular fixture at bedtime.

I wouldn't mind. It's my lover who's withdrawn a bit. But Armchair assumes I'm the problem and seems to think he's taking a huge risk by putting his hand on my lover's leg. My lover's arms are sore from the VenFlow, the little porthole the doctors keep open there, and his legs have taken over from them as the major pattable and squeezable parts. My lover's blood beneath the porthole, as we know, is full of intercepted messages of healing and distress.

Armchair looks at me with a colossal reproach. But can he really want to sit where I sit? Where I sit is sometimes behind my lover on the bed, wedging him as best I can during a retching fit, so that he is cushioned against the pain of his pleurisy. I hold on to his shoulders, which offer a reasonable guarantee of not hurting him. My medical encyclopaedia tells me that the pleura are 'richly supplied with pain fibres.' My lover has worked this out all by himself.

My lover threatens to give Armchair the yo-heave-ho. I tell him to be gentle, not to dismiss these comforting needs, and not only because Armchair too is richly supplied with pain fibres. I have my own stake in Armchair and Armchair's devotion. If Armchair stops being a fixture, I'll have to think long and hard about my own arrangements and my tender habit of spending as much time away from my lover as I possibly can. I do everything possible to look after him, short of being reliably there.

Whatever it is that ties us to each other, my lover and I, he is much too sensible to tug on it and see, once and for all, how much strain it will take. Much better to stay in doubt.

When I told my lover – he wasn't in hospital at the time – that I was thinking of spending half the week in Cambridge for a few months, he didn't say anything. It took him a while even to ask exactly how far away Cambridge is by train, and he seemed perfectly content when I said an hour and a bit – as if it counted as normal variation, in a relationship, for one party to keep himself an hour and a bit away from the other. He didn't ask if I had some grand plan, like writing a textbook, which I think I mentioned once a while back as one of my ambitions. There's something very stubborn about his refusal to call my bluff.

He knows, of course, that part-timers don't have a lot of say in their timetables (part-timers least of all), so if I've managed to fit all my teaching this term into Monday, Tuesday and Wednesday, then I've been setting it up for months.

In Cambridge I stay in the flat of an actress friend who has a short-term contract with the RSC. She's staying with friends in London herself, and all she wants is for the place to be looked after. She warned me that she might come back for the odd weekend, but she hasn't shown up yet and I've stopped expecting her, stopped cleaning madly on a Friday and filling the fridge with fine things. So all I have to do is keep the place reasonably clean, water the plants and listen from time to time to her accounts on the phone of Barbican Depression and of understudy runs that the RSC potentates never stir themselves from the Seventh Floor to see. Her flat is very near the station, which keeps my guilt to a minimum. It's not as if I was holed up in Arbury or somewhere. I'm only an hour and a bit away.

What I do here, mainly, is take driving lessons. In anyone else, learning to drive – especially after thirty – would be a move so sensible no one would notice it. With me it's different. It's a sign of a secret disorder, a malady in its own right, but only I know that.

I've always set my face against learning to drive. I've used public transport as if I'd taken a pledge to do nothing else and have always been careful not to accept lifts unless I have to. You get superstitious about favours when you can't pay them back, not in kind. If someone who has offered me a lift stays on soft drinks, I find myself refusing alcohol as if that was a helpful contribution to the evening. It's probably just irritating. I dare say people think, if he likes his drink so little he'd make a handy chauffeur, why doesn't he get his bloody licence?

I seem to have based a fair bit of my character around not being a driver. Perhaps that's why I was so disorientated when I walked through the door of the driving school that first time. It felt like learning to swim, and this the deep end. But in all fairness, the air in there would give anyone's lungs pause. All the instructors smoke away at their desks when they're on phone-duty or doing paperwork, and there's a back room that's even smokier, with a sink and a dartboard and a little fridge, not to mention a tiny microwave and a miniature snooker table.

I must say I admire the way the driving school draws a new pupil smoothly into apprenticeship. I was given a time for a two-hour consultation with an instructor, who would suggest a test date. I was certainly impressed, and mainly with myself, the competent me they were hypothesizing so suavely. It'll take more than suavity to convince me that I'm viable as a driver, but I signed up for my session of consultation just the same, rabbit paralysed by the headlights, unable to disobey the order to climb into the driving seat.

Now that I'm familiar with the place, I can't help thinking that BSM stands for British School of Macho. There's only one woman in the place, who does paperwork the whole time and smiles at me with a forlorn sweetness. The rest of the staff, I imagine, conduct their job interviews in the pub, brusquely screening out non-drinkers, non-smokers, non-eaters of meat, non-players of pool, non-tellers of jokes. I imagine them rolling back with the candidate to the driving school after closing time for some cans of Special Brew, and I imagine them huddled outside the lavatory with their fingers to their lips, when he goes to relieve himself, listening for the clinching chuckle when he sees the HIGH FIRST TIME PASS RATE sign stuck up inside the lid. I imagine them giving each other the thumbs-up sign when they hear it. And only then, after the candidate emerges from the lavatory, do I imagine them asking, 'By the way . . . can you drive?'

But somehow Keith, my instructor, slipped through their net. He does all the manly things, but he isn't a man in their sense, not at all. He's not a bachelor, but he's not by a long way a family man either, and he moved out of a perfectly nice house to live in a field.

He's a pleasantly runty fellow, brought up in a Barnardo's Home, and he still has a boyish spryness although he's in his late forties. To get from the driving school to the car, or back again at the end of the lesson, he bolts across Bridge Street, whatever the traffic's like, nipping through the smallest gaps between vehicles.

We set off in the driving school's sturdy Metro. It's white but very dirty, so someone has been able to trace the words ALSO AVAILABLE IN WHITE in dust on the coachwork. The side mirrors are both cracked, and one is even crazed. I promise myself that I'll reward the car, if and when I finally pass, and not the examiner as is customary. I'll splash out on some replacement fixtures.

Towards Keith I have absurdly mixed feelings. I trust him blindly, and have for him the sort of disproportionately solid affection that goes with the analyst's couch more often than the steering-wheel. I admire his self-control. It's not that he doesn't get irritated – when I don't lose enough speed, for instance, approaching a roundabout – but he calms down right away. It's as if he was offering me an example, in terms of temperament, of the use of the gearbox, and how to lose momentum as efficiently as possible. When I stall, he says, 'Never mind, re-start,' without any hint that he's disappointed in me. As with any indulgent parental figure, I have an urge to test his patience to the limit, to make sure that he cares underneath it all.

Once the car ran out of petrol on Queens Road, but all I could think of when I lost power was that Keith had withdrawn his faith in me, and was overruling my accelerator with the brake on the passenger side. 'Are you braking?' I cried, and he said, 'No, I'm scratching my arse as a matter of fact,' before he realized I wasn't messing him about. We weren't far from the driving school, but he's so little of a walker that he insisted on staying put. We sat there, while his eyes flickered between the windscreen and his multiple mirrors, waiting for one of the other school cars to come by and give him a lift to the petrol station. No one came, and at last, with the light dying, we had to walk after all. But I was so pleased not to have made the mistake myself that I let slip a precious opportunity for mockery – which is pretty much Keith's natural language – and I didn't tease him at all. It was nice to be the one doing the forgiving.

Alongside the exaggerated trust I feel a sharp submerged resentment towards Keith and a desire to do something atrocious, like run someone over on a crossing, while he's taking responsibility for me. In reality, he would put the brake on in a second, but I imagine myself unfastening my seat-belt after the impact and walking away, never traced for some reason though the driving school has my details, and leaving Keith to deal with the consequences.

Sometimes he sets out to provoke me, as if he wanted to bring the crisis on. He murmurs, 'Closer, son, just a little closer, and you're mine,' when a child is playing too close to the road, and remarks on the economic advantage to parents of having a child wiped out sooner rather than later, before too much money has been spent on it. But I know this is just his style of cussedness, the same style that makes him answer 'no' in the back room of the driving school to the question, 'Got a light, Keith?' even when he's busy smoking away. It seems to be his solution, as a member of the artificial tribe of driving instructors, to the problem of how to be popular, without being despised for wanting to be liked.

Keith doesn't ask why I want to learn to drive. He takes it for granted, like everybody else, that I should, though in that case he should at least be curious about why it's taken me so long to get round to it. Even if he asked, I don't think I'd tell him my own theory on the subject: that it's to do with control, and also with risk. Anything that gives me the feeling of control is obviously going to come in handy at the moment, whether or not it's a sort of control that I have historically had any use for, but I think I'm also giving myself an education in risk. Being a pedestrian, being a passenger, isn't so very safe – and rattling around on a bicycle, as I do, isn't safe at all – but behind the wheel of a car you have a different relationship with the risks that you take.

I try not to keep secrets from my lover, but I don't talk a lot about what I do in Cambridge. I'm superstitious about that. I seem to think that if I talk to him more than vaguely about

Cambridge, the seal will be broken and I'll start talking about him to the people I meet in Cambridge. For the whole cock-eyed arrangement to work, I need to think of the railway line from London to Cambridge as an elaborate valve, which allows me to pass from one place to another but strips me each time of my mental luggage and preoccupations.

The ward is full of its own life, and I don't think my silence shows. The patients tend to keep their doors open, so as to make the most of whatever passes along the corridors. The staff don't tell you when someone has died, but at least if your door is open someone comes along and says, with an apologetic smile, 'Let's just close this for a moment.' I expect that other people do what I do and peek out of the window in the door, which has horizontal bars of frosting so that I can't be seen, with any luck. I try to work out, from how long it takes for the trolley to make its collection, who it is that's inside it.

I'm sure I'm not the only one making calculations, though it's not a subject that comes up a great deal in conversation at the regular Tuesday tea parties. Then the focus of attention tends to be the chocolate cake brought in every week by an ex-patient, the offering that is richest in symbolism as well as in calories, which somehow always gets finished. Even my lover puts in his few bites' worth.

There's just one man on the ward who's in a different category, a private patient who's recovering from a heart attack in a room that is costing his firm, or BUPA, £210 a day, not including the phone. He takes only short walks as yet, but sooner or later he'll come to the tea party or twig in some other way to what the problem is with everyone else in the ward. Once he asked my lover why he thought he had come down with this particularly nasty pneumonia. My lover just scratched his head, as if it had never occurred to him to wonder. But it's only a matter of time before the cardiac patient or his wife see two men holding hands. They'll be on that expensive telephone to BUPA right away, demanding to know why someone with a bad heart but otherwise good character has been sent to spend his convalescence in Sodom.

The day-room plays host to other events, as well as the tea parties. There are the art classes and the Wednesday morning discussion groups. Often there's someone over by the window on these occasions, making faces and emitting harsh sighs, but if so it's just a patient strapped into the emetic aqualung of pentamidine, grimacing with controlled disgust as he inhales through a mask filled with bitter gas. Sometimes it's even a discharged patient, coming back for a few lungfuls of fly-killer to keep the bugs at bay.

Through the open doors, at various times of the week, come the visitors who aren't quite friends. There's a manicurist, for one, who asks her clients, when she's finished, if they'd like a dab of nail polish. She quietens any protest by saying brightly, 'Some does and some doesn't, so I always ask.' The first time she offered her services to my lover, she'd broken her wrist and had her arm in a sling. She couldn't work, obviously, so what she was really offering was manicure counselling, rather than manicure as such. My lover said, to comfort her, 'I bite my nails anyway,' and she said, to comfort him, 'Well, you do it very well.'

An aromatherapist comes round from time to time to rub essential oils into people. She doesn't rub very hard, and my lover longs for a real massage, but it isn't easy telling her to be merciless. His pentamidine drip has brought his blood pressure right down, and it's easy to see how she might get the idea he should be handled with care – seeing he needs to be helped if he wants to go as far as the lavatory, which is three steps away. The aromatherapist takes away the pillows and blankets, and gets my lover to lie face down, with his feet where his head usually goes.

I get a shock every time I visit my lover after she has laid her too-gentle hands on him. It's as if there was some new symptom that could spin him bodily round, from end to end and top to bottom, casting him down passive and aromatic, his eyes half-closed, on the crumpled sheets.

In the evenings, there are volunteers manning the hot-drinks trolley. They're noticeably more generous with the tea and the coffee than the domestics who push the trolley during the day, who can make visitors feel about as welcome as bedsores. With the evening trolley-pushers, I don't have to pretend that it's my lover who wants the drink if it's me who does really, and we don't scruple to ask for two if we're in the mood. The evening staff don't look right through me if I sit up on the bed next to my lover in my usual slightly infantile posture, facing the other way down the bed and hugging his big feet. This is the arrangement we've evolved now that so much of him is sore that a hug calls for as much careful docking as a refuelling in deep space. For him to see my face has become proportionally more important, as our bodies have had their expressiveness so much restricted.

My lover's soreness is dying down; I can tell because the fidgeting has gone out of his feet. I ask, in an interviewer's tenderly wheedling voice, 'What strikes you most about the whole terrible situation?'

Obligingly he answers, 'It brings out the best in people. And the worst.'

'What, you mean the best *and* the worst?'

'Both. The two.'

He's getting drowsy from the drugs he's on, as the chemical invasions of his body get the better of the surgical ones.

There's a hesitant knock on the door, and when I say to come in, this evening's volunteer stands in the doorway and asks what we want in the way of tea and coffee. I see him flinch when he spots the bag of blood on its wheeled stand, and the tube going into my lover's arm. But I notice too a quickening of interest in my lover, in the few seconds before our volunteer leaves the room to get the drinks from the trolley. Even before my lover murmurs, 'Isn't he gorgeous?' I have realized that the volunteer is very much my lover's type. He bears a passing resemblance to Joy Adamson's husband in the film of *Born Free*, a furry-faced scoutmaster on safari.

But now the volunteer returns with the teas and keeps his eyes turned down from the blood-drip. My lover has noticed his aversion and asks kindly, 'Does the blood bother you?'

'A bit.'

'Just a bit?'

'A lot.' Finally he admits that he sometimes feels faint. My lover looks affectionately at the sump of blood suspended above his arm and drawls, from the drastic languor of his medication, 'Just think of it as a big plastic kidney.' The volunteer resists the cue to look at the blood-bag, with the result that he continues to look deeply into my lover's eyes.

My lover pats the side of the bed. 'Do you have a moment to sit down?' I move over so that my lover can move his legs out of the volunteer's way, but my lover leaves his legs where they are, so the volunteer must make contact or else perch on the very edge of the bed.

The volunteer sits quiet for a moment, then clears his throat. 'Do you mind if I ask you a question?' he asks.

'Feel free,' my lover says. 'You're the guest.'

'Well, you're having a transfusion, and what I can never work out is, what happens to the blood you have extra, when you get someone else's on top of your own?'

'Yes, I used to wonder about that,' admits my lover. 'What happens is, they put another tube in your big toe, and drain the old blood out of there.' He gives the sheet a tug to loosen it from the bottom of the bed. 'Do you want a look?'

For the moment, the volunteer wants to go on looking at my lover's face.

'Don't you think you should?' my lover goes on. 'Shouldn't you try to overcome this silly fear of yours, if you're going to do the sort of work you're doing? Wouldn't that be the responsible thing?'

Mesmerized, the volunteer looks down at my lover's foot under the sheet. My lover pulls the sheet away from his foot. The big toe is pink and normal-looking. My lover looks startled and says, 'Oh, *Christ*, it must have come out, *now* we're in trouble, can you see it anywhere?' The volunteer casts his eyes desperately this way and that.

For some time I have been sending my lover signals of mild reproach about the wind-up job that is giving him so much pleasure; finally he gives in to them. He drapes the sheet over his feet again and says, 'Actually, since you ask, I pee away the surplus.' He smiles at the volunteer, who smiles back, at first incredulously and then with wonder at my lover's healthy sense of mischief.

My lover asks him please to tuck in the sheet around his feet, since it seems to have come adrift.

When the volunteer has gone at last, my lover says again, 'Isn't he gorgeous?' He looks thoughtful. 'But he can't be gay. That's never a gay beard. It's too overgrown.'

'I'm afraid you're right.'

'And you saw those corduroys.'

'Cords are a bad sign. Still . . .'

My lover sighs. 'At least he's not mutton dressed as lamb. He's mutton all right. But he has definite mutton appeal.' It sounds like an advert for stock cubes. 'He just can't be gay, that's all.'

My lover has a fantasy about living in the country with a vet who drives a half-timbered Morris Traveller, and this stranger comes close enough to set it off. A half-timbered Morris Traveller is apparently a car which even animals recognize as the appropriate vehicle for a person who will take care of them, so that they quieten down, even if their injuries are severe – or so my lover says – when they hear its engine note, some time before the car comes into view.

There is something I recognize as authentic in this fantasy of my lover's. It has about it the whiff of self-oppression, which we are as quick to recognize in each other as other couples, I imagine, are at spotting egg-stains on ties or lipstick on collars. The imaginary vet is classified by fantasy as virile and caring, in a way no man could be who loved other men, while my lover enters the picture as a damaged animal, a creature who can't hope to be treated as an equal but who accepts subordinate status, the price of tenderness.

All the same, the volunteer pays a number of return visits. He goes on holiday to Malta for a week and phones the hospital twice, so that the cordless phone – a treat that testifies to the volunteer's special status – is delivered to my lover's room, its aerial extended and gleaming. My lover has exercised once again his knack for being loved. The volunteer out of *Born Free*, meanwhile, is awarded a mark of privilege, a nickname: the Vet. Now my conversations with my lover have an extra layer of mysteriousness to nurses who hear me asking him if he's seen the Vet today. The Vet turns out to be older than he looks, in his mid-forties, so that he could almost be my lover's father. There's certainly something fatherly about the Vet when he sits on the bed and plays absent-mindedly with the hairs on my lover's leg. Sitting there, he might indeed be a father, trying to put off explaining the facts of life to an adolescent son, or a public-school housemaster explaining the meaning of confirmation.

One day I give my lover a bath; feeling clean, after all, is the nearest that people on this ward can come to feeling well. My lover is dizzy and unsteady on his feet, so I use a wheelchair to carry him back along the corridor to his room. I return the wheelchair to the bathroom right away, like a good boy, and the Vet must have arrived just while I was down the corridor, because when I come back I see that the door is closed. I look through the window and see the Vet perched on the bed, conducting his usual earnest conversation with my lover's leg. So I kill time doing a tour of the ward.

I offer to buy the patient in the room next to my lover's some of the ice-lollies he sucks when his mouth flares up, but he's well supplied at the moment, and his thrush doesn't even seem too bad. In fact he's unusually perky altogether. It was his birthday last week, and his ex-lover continued the custom they'd had by bringing him one practical present (a toasted-sandwich-maker) and one pampering present: a big bottle of essence of violets from

Jermyn Street. I'm mean enough, by the way, to think that ex-lovers can afford to be generous when they visit; I look on them the way lifers in a prison must look on youngsters who are in for a short sharp shock.

The sandwich-maker was taken home, and the essence bottle was wrapped in a flannel and put by the basin, where a cleaner smashed it two days later. She burst into tears, and he told her not to worry about it, but in fact he wants to be reimbursed, and if the hospital doesn't have the relevant insurance he wants it taken out of the cleaner's wages. So now he's unpopular with the staff, but he's sticking to his guns. If dirty looks were radiotherapy he'd have lost a lot of hair by now, but the sense of defending a principle has given his health a definite boost.

When I return to my lover's room and peep through the window, the conversation shows no sign of stopping, so I leave them to it and go back to his neighbour's room, where the basin still smells like a florist's. There was something I glimpsed on the window sill a minute ago that puzzled me, and I summon up the nerve to ask about it.

It's a soft toy in the shape of a fat scheming cat, but a cat that seems to have two tiny hoops of wire fixed high on its stomach.

'That's my hospital Garfield,' explains the neighbour with a little embarrassment. 'I only use it in hospital.'

'No, I don't mean that,' I say, 'I mean, what are those?' I point at the little hoops.

He blushes outright and shyly opens his pyjama jacket. 'What you really mean is, what are these?'

His nipples have little inserted hoops of their own, and the hospital Garfield is indeed, as I thought incredulously at first glance, a soft toy with an erotic piercing.

My lover's neighbour nods at his customized toy. 'The nurses have this great sense of humour,' he says. 'They did that while I was out.'

I am slow to take in the information he is giving me. It is a few moments before I realize that by 'out' he means not just *socially unavailable* but *profoundly unconscious*.

I keep away from my lover as long as I plausibly can. Purely from a medical point of view, flirtation is likely to have a beneficial effect on his low blood pressure. A little teasing romance may actually make him stronger at the knees.

From my own point of view I feel not jealousy, but a definite tremor of worry. My lover's instinct for help is profound and I trust it. If he thinks I'm capable, then I am. But if he enlists the Vet, I lose confidence. It's not that I don't want to share the load. I'd love to. But if my lover is hedging his bets, then I suddenly fear that he has good reason. Perhaps he now realizes I will crack up or get ill myself. My equilibrium falters, and the glands of selfish worry, that I have been suppressing for the duration, flare up at once and all together.

On subsequent visits, the Vet consolidates his burly charisma in my lover's eyes by turning out to own the right cars. He doesn't drive a Morris Traveller as such – that would be a little bit spooky. But he does buy glamorous or gloriously dowdy cars cheap in auctions, and garages them with friends or in fields when they need a little more work than he can do, handy though he is. He drives an Alfa that costs him more in insurance every year than he paid in the first place. One of these days he knows that the police will pull him over and ask him ever so nicely not to wear it in public again. Waiting in various locations for a little more cash or an elusive spare part are a Bentley, an Aston Martin and a Wolseley.

My lover has a passion for fast and/or classic cars. Before I knew him he owned an MG – he put an old phone in it, in fact, the kind you crank, and used to mime conversations at traffic-lights in summer, with the top down. This was before the days of car phones, let alone the days of commercially made imitation car phones – which I think makes it all right.

I don't follow my lover's car conversations with the Vet. I don't begin to understand what makes one car boxy but lovable, and another one nippy but a little Japanese about the hips.

There must be something about cars that makes people use a different register, almost a different language. Keith, my instructor, uses a whole mysterious vocabulary of phrases, so that I had to learn to understand his language, if not actually to speak Instructor, before I could really begin learning to drive. He mutters, 'Baby clutch . . . *baby* clutch,' when he wants me to be subtle with my left foot, and, 'Double gas . . . TREBLE gas,' when he wants me to be brash with my right. When I'm fumbling between gears he prompts me ('then three . . . then two'), and when I've finally got it right and married speed to ratio, he says with mild put-on surprise, 'It works!' or else he gives a sort of jeer of approval ('Yeeeeah!'). If I don't need prompting for a minute or so, he'll murmur, 'Looking good' or, 'I'm almost impressed.' More often he gets me to slow down, with a warning 'Cool it,' or to speed up – for which he mutters, 'It's not happening' and makes gestures with his hands, sweeping them forwards.

I used to interpret the phrase and the gesture the wrong way, as if what Keith wanted was for the road to be taken away from in front of him, but I suppose that was just my old reluctance surfacing again in the lightest of disguises. I've got it worked out now and give the accelerator a squeeze. If I've been slow to understand him and to deliver the speed he requires, Keith gets more direct. The phrases for this are 'Let's piss off out of here' or 'Give it a bit of poke.'

If I take my time before changing up, he goes 'mmmm', with a sharp intonation that says what-are-you-waiting-for? If I'm not properly positioned in my lane, he makes a flick of the hand to guide me in the right direction. Often, when I've misjudged a manoeuvre or underestimated a hazard, he says, with a quiet satisfaction, '*Not* a good gear.' To remind me of the mirror he sometimes taps it with his forefinger or mutters – there seems no obvious reason for his choice of language – '*Spiegel*'.

I start to relax in the lesson at the point where Keith lights up his first cigarette. I'm sure he's got enough of a craving that he'd light up sooner or later, whatever sort of idiot I was being, but I become more competent knowing he's felt able to focus his attention on the cigarette packet and the matches for a few seconds. Unless of course it's my terrible driving that makes the comfort of a cigarette so hugely attractive.

Keith opens the window a crack and leans forward to adjust the heating. I take every move he makes as a looming comment on my driving, so I'm absurdly relieved when he's only making adjustments to the car's interior climate. Then Keith talks. It's as if he's trying to simulate the distractions of traffic, when we're on a clear road. There's nothing I find harder than giving talking a low priority; left to my instincts, I'd rather be attentive in the conversation than safe on the road. It's not that I get flustered when he's really trying to put me off my stride – like the time he asked, 'When you going to get married, then?' after he had warned me he was about to request an emergency stop, and before he actually smacked the dashboard to give me my cue. That question doesn't faze me, though I gather it's pretty much guaranteed to make the young men botch their manoeuvre. But I'm interested in Keith and what he has to say, and when he stops talking because there's tricky work ahead I can't wait to get the hazards behind me, whatever they are, and go back to what he's saying.

Sometimes Keith talks about nothing, anything, the daily papers, and how he's going to give up the *Sun* when they stop running their Bingo game – unless of course they announce another. He wrote a letter to the *Sun*'s Grouse of the Week column just recently, which they didn't print, complaining about a doctor in the news who'd overturned the car giving his daughter a driving lesson in the grounds of his house. It was taking a living away from driving instructors, that was Keith's Grouse, and served the doctor right, and what would *he* think if people started doing operations on each other in their kitchens?

Sometimes he talks about his history, about Barnardo's and the army and home-ownership.

'I had a lovely house in an acre, lovely car, two-car garage, garden with a rockery and floodlights – spent a grand on landscaping – fruit trees, currant bushes, but it wasn't what I wanted, none of it. I think I worked that out before I finished laying the rockery, but I still installed those bloody floodlights.'

He moved out from the house he shared with Sue and took up with Olga. Olga is the battered mobile home where he lives, parked in a muddy field a few miles out of town. She's a hulk, but he seems well set up there, in his way. We went out there once, on a lesson; I needed practice, apparently, manoeuvring in muddy conditions, and Keith certainly needed a Calor Gas container picked up and taken for refilling. We had a cup of tea in Olga while we were at it, though his eyes narrowed with distrust at the idea that anyone could drink it without sugar. He takes four spoonfuls and gives the tea-bag a good drubbing with the spoon, as if the point of the procedure was not to infuse a drink but actually to wash the tea-bag free of stains.

Laundry is one of the few services that he's not found a way of doing for himself. He does any telephoning he needs at the driving school, and even brings his electric razor in to work for re-charging with BSM current. He leaves the right change for milk and newspapers in Olga's mighty glove compartment and has them delivered right into her cab. But laundry is one thing that's beyond him and so he pops over to Sue's every week or so (and takes a bath while he's at it). He has a 'leg-over' while he's there, but to hear him talk about it, that leg-over isn't the linchpin of the arrangement. I imagine Sue in front of her mirror on one of the evenings Keith is expected – he doesn't always turn up, but he knows how to keep just enough on the right side of her that she doesn't come to find him, her horn sounding furiously all the way from the main road as her car crawls into the treacherous field where Olga sits. I imagine her powdering her face and wondering whether she should try some new perfume. She doesn't know it's Ariel that arouses Keith's senses, not Chanel.

I need a pee after my cup of tea. Keith shows me the lavatory, which is chemical and tucked away in a low cupboard. Keith can stand up in most parts of Olga, but there's nowhere that the roof's high enough to give my head clearance. To use the lavatory, I have to kneel and face forward. Keith gives me a little privacy by going to the cab, where he hasn't bothered to put up cork tiling. He presses a hand to the roof and says, 'Some mornings the condensation's unbelievable in here. It's like Niagara bastard Falls.'

Only when I'm finished with my rather awkward pee does he mention that personally, *personally*, speaking for himself, he finds it more convenient to piss in a bottle and then pour it away, though of course everybody's different, aren't they? There's a coffee jar, scrupulously clean and free of labels, tucked away at the side of the lavatory, which I suspect is his chosen bottle. I wish I'd spotted it earlier, though I doubt if I'd have had the nerve to use it.

Before we leave, Keith shows me his photo album. It's like anybody's photo album – anybody who wasn't thought worthy of a photograph before he joined the army, who built a raft in Malaya based on what people built in films when they were marooned, who had four children by two wives before there was ever a Sue, who kept sheep and chickens for a while in Devon – except that nothing's in order. It's the sort of album where each thick page has a thick sheet of Cellophane to hold the pictures down, no need of photo corners, and Keith seems to like keeping even the past provisional. Perhaps on non-bath evenings he amuses himself by rearranging the photographs, shuffling the blurred sheep and the precise soldiers, the blurred children. In every picture that shows Keith, he is pointing out of the frame, insisting that the real subject is out there somewhere, refusing to be the focus of the composition.

On the way back to town, he gets me to do some emergency stops. If it's at all possible, he synchronizes them with young women walking alone. He smacks the dashboard just before we pass. The woman usually glares at us as we stop dead right next to her and then she relaxes into a pitying half-smile when she sees it's only a learner driver. No real threat. Then her face goes half-way back to its original expression, when she sees that Keith is staring at her with a defiant hunger. At times like this, I am able to look at Keith outside the terms of our sealed-in little relationship, outside its flux of resentment and dependence, and he seems, I must admit, like a pretty ordinary little shit.

Even when I have passed my test and put Keith behind me, I can't imagine that I'll do a lot of driving. Public transport is enough to get me to the hospital, though I sometimes use my bicycle on a Sunday, partly for the exercise and partly to dramatize my errand, if I'm bringing something for my lover. On the bicycle I can feel like a courier whose package will make a difference to the person waiting for it.

My lover keeps the television on all the time, just turning up the sound when there's something he actually wants to watch. At the moment, a weatherman is standing in front of two maps of the country. I expect they represent the weather tonight and tomorrow. But the weatherman, if he wanted, could also show us the weather of our two healths. His vocabulary of symbols is meagre but it will stretch. My map will be full of smiling suns and light refreshing breezes, a fantasy of summer; my lover's map a nightmare winter, chock-a-block with gales and freezing showers. My lover looks without interest at the screen as it changes. Some of his calm is really exhaustion, but some of his calm is really calm. It helps that he's still in touch socially with the few people he exposed to risk. With a bravery that to me seems insane, they've all taken the test, and they all tested negative.

He keeps a list of his sexual partners, does my lover, though it's not so detailed he could use it to track people down if he'd lost touch. I only found out about it recently. It's at the back of his diary, but then I only found out about the diary recently. Suddenly there was this battered book on the bed, and my lover was saying, oh yes, he always used to keep a diary, he'd just got out of the habit. He'd just now come across it and was taking a look.

Even my lover had to admit, after a little reading, that his diary-keeping had never been regular; he wrote in his diary only when a relationship was on the rocks. It took tears to get the words flowing and then he would write what were in effect letters to his lovers, full of sombre accusations and depressive spite. He even read me a detailed account of my own selfishness. This was his version of a crisis of which I have no version, since I survived it by not noticing.

I asked if I could look at the diary, and he passed it across. At the back of the book there was a list of numbers and names, starting with '1. John in Toyota Corolla.' Number two was Mark, and number three was Mark and Ben. The list went into the low forties before it met a scrawl, twice underlined: '*Enough of this rubbish.*' The list-making impulse had started to falter even before then. Two numbers in the thirties were entered as 'What was the name?' and 'Macho Letdown'.

My lover gave me a beady look as I read his diary and asked, 'Are you the sort of person who reads people's diaries?'

I didn't know there was any other sort of person, but I avoided the question by holding the book up and waving it. 'The evidence against me is strong.'

'I mean, when the owner's not around?'

'Only if I can find it.' I've only made a couple of searches since then – as much to see if he was bothered enough to hide it as because I'm curious – and I haven't found it, so I suppose the answer to the question is, Yes, he was bothered enough.

The limitations on my lover's future make his past the more precious, and I find that I'm a bit bothered, after all, that I don't know where his diary is.

I bring my lover hot thick soups, in a big old-fashioned vacuum flask with a wide neck. Conventional soups bear the same relationship to my soup as the sun bears to those collapsed stars whose every speck outweighs it. An oxtail is a wispy thing compared to what I make of it with the strong rendering of my pressure cooker. My soups are concentrated expressions of the will to nourish.

But tonight my lover is not to be nourished. 'You know I hate innards,' he says, pushing the plate of soup away almost as soon as I've poured it.

I'm ashamed that I don't know my lover's preferences as well as I should, but I'm also offended and I protest. 'Oxtail isn't innards!'

'It's as good as.'

'Oxtail couldn't be further from innards. Be reasonable. If cows kept their tails on the inside how could they deal with flies?'

Even as I say this, I realize that talk of flies is among the poorer triggers of appetite. The ward is full of tiny insects, as it happens, sustained out of season by the warmth and the abundance of fruit.

Even unmolested, the fruit would look incongruous beside the stack of moulded cardboard vomit-bowls on my lover's bedside table. They look, with their broad rims turned down at one side, like jaunty little hats, as if they were there for use in a big dance production number. We've tried to bring them into our private world by referring to them as 'Berkeleys' or 'Astaires', but the name that has stuck, *vomit-hats*, leaves them uncomfortably real. These homely objects resist the final push into euphemism.

Our little tussle over the soup reminds me of how poorly matched we are in habits and appetites. We don't even have the same taste in bread. I like wholemeal, but his stomach can deal most easily with inflated plastic white, and naturally I give way to him. All the same, I'd have thought somebody could make a killing out of couples like us, by producing a hybrid loaf that combined the two, all the goodness and bran sucked out of each alternate slice and shunted into the next one.

In this way among others, we don't present a united front. Our teamwork seems ragged, while the illness we're fighting is ruthlessly co-ordinated. But then it's only recently, since he came into hospital in fact, that I have thought of him, truly, as my lover.

Before then I compared him in my mind – often very flatteringly, it's true – with other men past or possible. But now I compare him only with the world as it will be when he is subtracted from it, not with rival beds but with his bed, empty. That is what locks the phrase in place: my lover.

My lover and I never used pet names or endearments before his first visit to hospital, but how stupid it sounds when I say so. It's like saying *I never had much use for pot plants and cushions before I came to live in this condemned cell.* Except that the unstoppable progress of medical science has taken our condemned cell and turned it into a whole suite of condemned cells.

Our endearment system is based round the core-word *pie*, derived from the phrase *sweetie-pie* but given its independence in a whole series of verbal caresses. The turning-point in its history was my buying an Easter egg with the message piped on it, 'WITH LOVE TO MY SWEETIE PIE.' This was at a time when a raised patch on the roof of my lover's mouth had been diagnosed as a cancer, a separate sentence on his mouth that his tongue must read and remember every time it makes contact, and I wanted to go to meet him armed with more than a hug. It comforted me to watch the woman at Thorntons in Cambridge – where a free message in icing was a seasonal offer – at work on the egg with her expert nozzle of fondant and her smile of romantic voyeurism. The smile would have hardened on her lips like painted sugar if she knew she was decorating a sweet to take the bitterness out of a malignancy.

Pie was the word that stuck, the last part of the inscribed egg that my lover would have eaten, I'm sure, if he hadn't kept the whole thing intact, as a totem of chocolate. *Pie* stuck to a number of phrases, private ones at first and then sentences of ordinary conversation, by slip of tongue to start with and afterwards defiantly, mixing embarrassment and the refusal to be embarrassed. *Pie* functions as pet name (*dear one*), as interrogative (*are you awake?*), as exclamation (*how could you say such a thing!*).

So near have I approached to that which I vowed I would never use, the edged endearment of the grown-up, the *darling* of protest if not yet the *darling* of bitter reproach.

Pie is allied by assonance with *my* (*my Pie*), by alliteration with expressive adjectives: *poor Pie, precious Pie, pretty Pie*.

Occasionally it appears in phrases of estrangement, though its use acts as a guarantee that estrangement is reversible: *crusty Pie, poison Pie, piranha Pie.*

Written down and rationalized as an irrational number – π – it loses a little of its sugar. Transposed into fake Italian *mio Pio* – it acquires a register almost operatic. As a double diminutive – as *pielet* or *pilot* – it brings into play a fresh set of overtones.

Perhaps endearment, verbal sweetness so concentrated nothing else can survive, will prevent infection, the way honey does. Honey yanks the moisture out of bacteria with the violence of its osmosis. Honey has been found uncorrupt in the tombs of the Pharaohs, though it had been left there to be used, after all, to sweeten the darkness of the dead.

Who could have thought when the treasures were laid out in the vault that the bees' modest embalming would last so well, that their glandular syrup of flowers would turn out so nearly eternal?

My lover raises the remote control panel and turns the television off. Late at night, the nurses stop being so demanding, and even Armchair and the Vet can be relied on to stay away. My lover and I don't have to be so guarded in our behaviour.

This is the time we draft our imaginary letters to newspapers and public figures, our radical complaints and proposals. My lover wants to live long enough to be the only survivor of an air crash, so that he can say at the press conference, where he will have an arm in plaster – perhaps only a finger – 'You see? God doesn't hate me after all. Whatever *you* think.' In the meantime he will settle for composing imaginary letters to the papers, setting the record straight day by day.

Sometimes one or the other of us will shed some tears, but we haven't properly settled the agenda of our crying. We're both New Men, I suppose that's what it comes down to, so we have a lot of respect for tears and what they represent. Crying is a piece of expressive behaviour that needs no apology and isn't, absolutely isn't, a demand for attention. We pride ourselves on being able to ask for affection straight out, without needing to break down to do it. There's something a little crass about a hug as a response to tears. A hug can be an act of denial, even, and neither of us is going to make that mistake. We claim the right to cry uncomforted, letting the discharge do its work uninterrupted.

But in practice, I get so distressed by his tears, and he by mine, that we regress just as fast as we possibly can, and smother the expressiveness that we have so much respect for under a ton of hugs.

Endlessly we reformulate our feelings for each other. This is the same superstition that makes people put up bumper stickers – *Keep Your Distance, Baby on Board, I ♥ my π* – to make the roads safe and life go on for ever.

Fate is a dual-control Metro, that much I know, but I'm not clear about who's in which seat. It may be me, or it may be my lover, that squeezes the brake when we approach a bend too fast, or who pops the clutch in to prevent a stall. 'Baby clutch,' I can hear a familiar voice saying in my ear, '*baby*-baby clutch,' as we move off up the hill to where we must go.

The Changes of Those Terrible Years

Nobody believes I've really put the house on the market. Someone even said it was a monument. People seem shocked, and it doesn't seem to occur to them that I might have had enough. I'm not allowed to have any doubts or weaknesses, that's what it amounts to. People ask me what I'm going to do now, but they think I'm joking when I say that I used to share a small flat with a friend in Bloomsbury, and what I'd really like to do is move back there.

I'm not joking, though of course it's a silly idea. My flatmate – that's all he was, it was simply a convenient arrangement – wasn't pleased when I moved out, and we haven't kept in touch. But his habits were so regular that I have the feeling I could plot his progress from year to year.

Every Saturday he would tackle a new classic of French provincial cookery for a dinner party, working methodically through the regions. He liked to work alone, though if he had chosen a really ambitious menu he might ask me to do some simple preparation. And now I have the idea that with a calendar, a map and a copy of his chosen cookery-book, I could bring myself up to date, and arrive at what used to be our front door one Saturday night, bringing wines that would perfectly chime with each intricate course.

It's odd to have this little pang of missing a nest that didn't suit me all that well, and that I left with hardly a second thought. But I've learned to indulge myself when little fantasies like this occur to me, and not to mistake them for real needs. When I need help, I will ask for it.

It's three weeks now since Anthony died. I'm doing well. I can say the name calmly: Anthony. I seem to be going through a phase where I need to go out a lot, which you'd think would mean that I want to be with people. But if anyone tries to talk to me, I go all charming for a few minutes, and then I find some way of putting them off.

Things have changed since the last time I was in the habit of going out – long ago, before I had found myself a circle of friends. I remember a time when with a little effort you could look as if you'd put on the first thing that came to hand. Not any more. There used to be *sweaters*, pubs full of sweaters. Now you have to get everything right before people will even ignore you properly.

People do come up to me, and I should be grateful for that, even though they always ask about the house, and tell me how much they admire me. I look well, apparently. What I'm doing is marvellous. I suppose what I'm really looking for when I go out is someone who will give me permission to collapse, someone who will say, you're killing yourself, put your own needs first for a change. It never happens. Even when they know me hardly at all, people have a vested interest in my ability to cope.

One young man even asked me about Anthony. He was wearing a baseball cap and a sort of anorak, with a row of fluorescent green bicycle clips all up one arm. It was a shock to hear the name mentioned, of course, but it was worth it if this was a friend of Anthony's – though of course he wasn't, just someone who had heard about what had happened. He was roughly the same age as Anthony, I suppose, and I tried to take an interest in him, but it was an effort. Illness had taken Anthony out of his age-group, somehow. It often seems to do that. This young man seemed shallow by contrast, politely aware of an epidemic that had always been there in the background of his young world.

He wanted to know how I felt about Anthony dying in hospital and not in the house. It's no secret that I wanted to nurse Anthony to the end, and I expect he was only trying to be sympathetic, to draw me out, but I found myself getting angry. Every time he asked a painful question – and all his questions were painful – he took a long sip of his beer, looking down into his glass so he wouldn't have to look at me while I answered.

Then he asked me if it was true I was selling the house, and this time he looked at me squarely. He told me he thought it was out of character – as if he knew what my character was – and that I'd regret it. It's only a house, I told him, and it's *my* house. And who'll help when I can't cope? Maybe I will, he said, and he wrote down his telephone number on the back of a book of matches.

I dare say the urge to flirt was there at the back of my mind all the time we were talking, shamefully enough, but if so I soon suppressed it. I started talking about what Anthony had gone through with CMV – that's cytomegalovirus – and after that the conversation could only fizzle out.

I took the tube home. I used to find public transport exasperating, but I've spent so much time since then as a sort of amateur ambulance driver that riding on a bus or a tube is a real pleasure. I enjoy not being responsible for anyone but myself; if I'm late, that's my business. Let someone else take the responsibility. But it was also a tube journey, once, that changed my life. It was on a tube train that I started to face the changes of these terrible years.

I was going on holiday, not because I needed one but because it was time to take one. I worked for a well-established agency that specialized in representing musicians. We had a number of successful performers on our books, and even one or two outstanding ones. I enjoyed my job. I believe I was the only partner with no musical ambitions of my own. Certainly at the firm's Christmas party each year two of my colleagues would be led protesting to the piano to attempt some Schubert four-hands. Despite their protests at the stiffness of their fingers and the limited time they had had for practice, they were really not very good.

I think my being free of that kind of self-deception made me good at my job, although it also made it easy for me to leave it when the time came. What I most enjoyed, and what became my professional speciality, was overseeing the beginning of a young singer's career. When I heard a young voice for the first time, I seemed to take a photograph of it, but a photograph that was also an X-ray and a clairvoyant's reading.

I closed my eyes and I could see the characteristics of a voice, its strengths but also its temptations. I knew which singers were basing themselves on the wrong models, dreaming of a sound that was impossibly big or pure. The limitations of the physical apparatus must be faced squarely, but then transcended. It's actually the limitations of the voice's owner, rather than the voice itself, that most often impose artificial boundaries on a singing career.

I got on exceptionally well with the singers I represented, although our priorities were a little different. They thought that The Voice made them important. To me, it was The Voice that made them unimportant as people. Nothing in their personalities must be allowed to impede its development. But in practice our approaches were compatible. With as much tact as I could muster, I set myself to reveal the musical self that their selfishness would otherwise hide from them.

Why would I need a holiday from that? Well, perhaps I did. Since then I have discovered that people can be exhausted, and keep the fact a secret from themselves. At any rate, a holiday was not what I got.

I struggled out to Heathrow on the tube, leaving what I thought was plenty of time before my flight, though admittedly not the absurd stretch of hours that the airlines stipulate so solemnly. I had never had any trouble before. At Heathrow I was told that economy was overbooked, which sounded like good news to me. I'd heard from friends how much more pleasant a trip they'd had when they were bumped up into business class. Except that it turned out that business was full up by now, and they weren't going to start a revolution by bumping me all the way up to first. The woman at the check-in counter offered me the use of a tatty lounge until she could secure me a seat, and that was as far as she was prepared to go.

The tatty lounge was full of mood music, but it wasn't the music for my mood. Friends were expecting me in New York, but there was no urgency to that. I couldn't claim that I was being kept from some urgent appointment. I couldn't work up my irritation into something magnificent, but nor could I bring it down into evenness of temper.

I had also left behind my fancy camera, newly bought, in the flat, but I like to think I wasn't just going back to fetch it by getting on a tube heading eastwards, and I don't mention the camera when I tell people the story. If I was sure I was coming back to Heathrow, would I have carried all my luggage back to town, when I could have checked it in or left it in a locker?

At Earls Court a man got on the tube, sat in the seat next to me, and burst into tears. I recognized him. He had been a guest at one of my room-mate's regional feasts, though I didn't exchange more than a few words with him. I was on *bain-marie* duty that night, tending a beautiful smooth sauce over a flame so low it was more an idea than a fact, and ready to shout for help at the first sign of curdling. Then at dinner we were seated far from each other. I can't say I minded too much; I didn't find him immediately attractive. He wore his hair at a sort of compromise length, wanting to look smart and conventional in the office by day, and all bristly and animal in the clubs at night. Of course it looked silly both ways, whether he was dressed casual-smart, the way I first saw him, or in office drag as he was now, his narrow shoulders heaving beneath the pinstripes.

No one in the carriage was looking at the crying man. Why are the English so terrified of tears? Perhaps my upright fellow citizens were afraid that if they paid the man any attention he might tell his sob-story. Or produce a banjo, sing some show tunes and pass round a hat.

Since that time I have shed tears in public often enough myself, and have found that I am suddenly invisible. Once, in a café, I had cried enough to feel better, and I wanted another cappuccino, but I couldn't attract the waitress's attention. I couldn't get out of the well-mannered pit that had been dug for me.

Now, in the tube train, I put my hand on the man's knee. 'Hello
. . . Dougie, isn't it? What's the matter?'

Then it all came out. He was on his way to visit an ex-lover of
his, who had Aids. He didn't need to explain what Aids was. The
newspapers had just started to go mad about it all. This ex-lover,
Shawn, had discharged himself from hospital early after a bout of
pneumonia, because the ward he was on was the same one where
his lover had died three months before. Now he was at home
alone, which didn't sound a lot better psychologically, and in
need of looking after. Meanwhile Dougie's current lover, terrified
of infection, had forbidden him to do any visiting, and said he
would lock Dougie out if he was stupid enough to go anywhere
near the sick man. So Dougie was taking days off work, without
telling his lover, to do what he could for Shawn, but he knew he
couldn't go on for ever, or he'd lose his job.

I couldn't believe there was no help to be had. 'Isn't there
anything the council can do?'

'I keep on phoning. But the moment they hear what the matter
is, they say they'll phone back, and then they don't.'

'Isn't there some sort of charity?'

'There's one just starting up. They hope to have some volunteers trained soon. In a month or so. But I can't do much more for
Shawn, ex-lover or no ex-lover.'

I squeezed his knee. 'It must be very distressing for you.'

'Oh, it's not that,' he said. 'But he treated me like shit when we
were together, and he treats me like shit now. Sometimes when
I'm making up some Build-Up for him, he's just so horrible that I
want to pour it down the sink, and let him stay just as skinny as
he is.'

I don't normally have much patience with messy lives. Does it
sound smug if I say that I saw through the seventies and its
morality before most people? I can't help that. I tired fairly early
of people boasting about their open relationships, and then
complaining when that same openness let everything they could
have valued trickle away. The word *open* began to sound warning

232

bells long before it became apparent that people were leaving themselves open to more than bad behaviour. I would almost flinch when I heard the word.

Perhaps it was necessary for me to be out of step with the old habits to find my place in the world that came afterwards. I can live with that. I don't think it was any more sensible to have a different man in your bed every weekend than, well, to recreate a new masterpiece of French cooking every Saturday night.

But of course I didn't judge Dougie, as the tears dried on his face in the seat next to me on the tube. I felt for him very much, and for the situation he was in. This all happened a long time before there was such a thing as an antibody test, and Dougie's life, like the lives of everyone like him, would have been a nightmare of anxiety even if no special demands were being made of him.

But I wasn't considering Dougie's position so much as my own. Looking down, I could see arranged round me, properly tagged and labelled, all the burdens of leisure. On a hanger inside one of my cases, I remember, visible through a sort of cellophane window, was a navy blazer with gold buttons that made me look smart and even slim, but somehow never seemed right for London. I had turned my back on London, but New York wouldn't have me. The rejection was only temporary, but it lasted long enough to make me reconsider my trip. A few phone calls would dispose of the welcoming committee, and I would be free, if I dared, to meddle with a stranger's destiny.

I told Dougie that I would do what I could for his friend Shawn, for a few days at least, but only if Shawn agreed. I wasn't going to foist myself on anyone. We arranged that I would wait in a coffee shop round the corner from where Shawn lived, in Pimlico.

Dougie was back in a few minutes, and just watching him through the coffee shop window, as he walked purposefully down the street, gave me my first dangerous taste of feeling useful. He talked non-stop as we covered the short distance. He led me up some steps to the entrance of a large wedding-cake house, with eight buzzers by the front door, and showed me into a spacious ground floor flat, the walls thickly covered with modern paintings.

I had a moment of belated panic, at the idea that my body might harbour some final resistance I was unaware of, which would make me spin around in spite of myself and march back down the steps. But Shawn's hand as I shook it conveyed only the usual neutral human messages.

Shawn had put on a bow-tie in my honour, a task that had clearly exhausted him. I found my eyes drawn irresistibly to his Adam's apple, making its reflex journeys up and down an unrefreshed throat. He leaned heavily on a beautifully carved stick which might otherwise have seemed an affectation.

There were in fact, as I found out, traces of dandyism about him even in illness. He liked to wear a kimono during the day, if he was well enough. He had several, of an antique silk almost as fragile as himself, so that an awkward elbow-movement while he was putting it on could easily rip the luminous fabric.

Dougie took a couple of dirty glasses into the kitchen, and left. Then we were alone.

With the experience I have now, I'm sure I would handle that meeting differently. I would mentally set a time limit, for one thing – an hour, an hour and a half at most – so that I didn't unduly tax someone who was forever paying off an overdraft of energy. And I would find some tactful way of stopping him from playing the host, struggling to show me where the sheets for the spare bed were, when I could have found them myself with the minimum of guidance. But at the time we were both unwilling to give up the habits that defended our identities. We were in no hurry to mix our lives in together, by chance and in crisis.

It was only later that I realized how unusual it was for Shawn to strike up such an immediate rapport with someone. When Dougie paid his occasional visits, taking half-days off work or hurrying across in his lunch hour so as to keep his lover in the dark, he turned out to be telling no more than the truth. Shawn treated him like a dog. Shawn expected him to read his mind, and was always tetchily interrupting. I had beginner's luck. But I was also shrewd enough to realize that Dougie brought out all the sourness in Shawn, leaving me to deal with a character surprisingly sweet. I made it clear to Dougie that his visits were necessary to the running of the household, although he might think that his attention was repaid only with scorn. I don't know how long I could have gone on dealing with Shawn, if he had turned the sharpness of his tongue on me.

Shawn and I soon slipped into a rhythm and a routine. Though I had sacrificed my trip to New York, there was a stubborn atmosphere of holiday about those first weeks of knowing Shawn. Perhaps it was just the fact of sleeping in a strange bed and living out of a suitcase that made the experience perversely refreshing. I was being tested, certainly, but tested in unfamiliar ways. Oh God, am I really only saying that a change is as good as a rest? I was under a strain, but I felt it to be a beneficial one, as if lazy muscles were protesting against being used in the way for which they had, after all, been designed.

I went on paying rent for the Bloomsbury flat, but I was pretty much an absentee tenant. After my fortnight's holiday was up, I took another two weeks' leave that was owed me, and after that I explained the situation to my colleagues. They agreed with reasonable grace to let me work part-time. I stopped taking on new clients, and even passed one or two of my current ones on to other agents in the firm, but I didn't stop representing anyone I really cared about.

Life in the flat in Pimlico was surprisingly peaceful, even if it was the deceptive peace of physical decline. One day I remarked to Shawn about how quiet the building was. Wasn't that lucky, seeing he spent so much time there?

'Yes and no,' he answered. 'It doesn't have much to do with luck, actually. But yes, it is nice.'

'How do you mean?'

'Everybody's moved out but me.'

'Why? Is the house being sold? Will you have to move?'

He smiled. 'Hardly. But my neighbours didn't take to having Aids on the premises. Ideally they would have liked me to move out. As it is, they've all made other arrangements. The last one left two weeks ago.'

'But that's appalling. Couldn't you explain to them that they're not at risk?'

'My lover tried that, last year. He tried phoning round, and people hung up. So he visited the flats one by one. The whole building stank of disinfectant for a week.'

If I had been in Shawn's shoes I would have found it hard to live in a building so full of recent hostility, and in a flat so full of associations. His lover's clothes still took up one of the wardrobes in the master bedroom, and there were reminders of him everywhere.

Stacked above the wardrobe in the spare room, where I slept, I found a large number of paintings which I realized must have been done by Shawn. He had gone to art school, though his job had been running a gallery. He always referred to himself as a parasite, a fussy parasite but a parasite just the same. But the paintings in the spare room were not quite the standard art-student productions. They were in a wide range of styles and mediums, and the most recent of them had been done only a couple of years before.

Half-playfully, but also with a more serious intention, I started taking the pictures off the walls – starting with out-of-the-way places, in corners or above doors – and replacing them with Shawn's own. He caught on almost right away, of course, but I think he enjoyed watching in his quiet way as gradually the flat played host to his first and last one-man show, a private view – and in the West End at that, if you stretch a point.

More than anything, Shawn wanted to die at home. I wanted to help, but there was a limit to what I could do. I didn't have the skills or the facilities to make more than a little difference. At best I could make it possible for him to leave hospital a day or two earlier as each infection began to give ground, and to stay at home a day or two longer as the next one began to hold court among his ruined defences.

But even when Shawn was in hospital he wasn't a difficult patient. Our relationship still had texture and unpredictability. I have a vivid memory of him looking up at me from a bowl which he had already more than half filled with bright yellow vomit, and saying, 'This must be very hard for you.' I didn't know what to say. If his idealization of me made it possible for him to project himself beyond the confinement of his illness, it was best to say nothing. But why would he think his illness violated my nature, in a way it didn't violate his?

I just thanked my lucky stars that Dougie visited whenever he could to maintain the balance of our relationship, bringing his flowers to be disparaged and his cards to be tucked away in a drawer, or have orange juice spilled on them.

One day just before the end, Shawn rang for a nurse and asked her, 'When is D-Day?'

She blushed and said, 'I don't know, I'm afraid, June sometime,' thinking for some reason that Shawn was testing her general knowledge, when in fact he was asking in a veiled way about his death. Then he put his hand on her arm and repeated the question – I have a mental image of his kimono sleeve against her uniform. When she understood what he meant she tried to reassure him, saying that although he had been very poorly they were sure they could break this most recent infection. But of course he was right.

I don't know whether I was surprised or not when I learned Shawn had made me the beneficiary of his will. On one level, I couldn't imagine him leaving property to anyone else. I knew his parents were dead, and there was a brother in South Africa that he didn't have anything to do with. If there had been particular close friends I would have been sure to hear about them in the time I lived with him. I wouldn't have been surprised if there had been a conscience-money payment to Dougie, after the way Shawn had treated him, but there wasn't even that.

At the same time I did find it shocking to think that Shawn had summoned his solicitor to attend him in hospital, had dictated a will, and had had two nurses witness it. There seemed, irrationally, something hurtful about that, I suppose because it was exactly the sort of thing I used to arrange for him. I had got used to the idea of being indispensable. But there's no doubt Shawn did right not to tell me what he was doing.

I had never mentioned the matter of a will to him myself. It's realistic to make a will, of course, and it's downright stupid to die without one. But there seemed to be quite enough realism in Shawn's life to be getting on with.

What really did shock me, though it took a while to take it in, was just how much I had inherited. It had never occurred to me that Shawn might own the whole building in which he lived. His parents had bequeathed it to him. It made sense in retrospect that the tenants in the building had had no prospect of forcing him out, no alternative but to leave a situation that they in their ignorance found intolerable. But now I was puzzled by something else.

If Shawn was capable of summoning a solicitor to do his bidding, he could have done the same with an agent. Come to that, he could have asked me to find new tenants, if he had wanted them. All he would have had to do was fill me in about the true state of affairs in the building. So why had he left those flats empty? It couldn't really have been that he valued the peace and quiet.

It would be flattering to think that only the desire to reward me could make him bestir himself in his weakness – flattering, but not really convincing. I began to be haunted by the idea that Shawn was somehow freeing up the building, for me to do what I wanted with it. Then the horrible thought struck me that by taking his valuable collection of modern art off the walls, and replacing it with his own work, which had no market value, it must have looked to him as if I had already cast a beady, valuing eye over the contents of the flat.

I was able to suppress the second thought, clearly rooted in guilt at having been found worthy of the profound emotion that an inheritance represents. But the other thought persisted, the thought that Shawn had plans for me that involved the whole house. It even occurred to me that he might have evicted those tenants; for a resident landlord that would have been relatively easy.

I didn't take any decision in a hurry. I gave my room-mate in Bloomsbury notice, and I kept on working on a part-time basis. I noticed that I wasn't enjoying the work as much as I had used to, but didn't know what to put it down to, exactly. Was it that after nursing Shawn, merely nursing a voice and its owner seemed rather an inconsequential business? Or was it that because of my new financial status I lost the reflex of deference? Though in the past my deference had often been tactical.

It was Dougie who intervened in my life again, Dougie who made the decision for me. He had a persistent fever, and lost a lot of weight, and after that his lover kicked him out. I had room – good God, did I have room! – and I took him in.

Dougie was the house's first inmate under the new dispensation, but he turned out to be an uncharacteristic one. When he got better he stayed better. Away from the influence of his lover, and away I must also say from Shawn, who had hardly given him a flattering image of himself, he came into his own. When an antibody test for what was then beginning to be known as HIV became available, he took it, with what seemed to me to be astonishing courage. His test came back negative, and in fact he came through his ordeal with his health intact and his heart mended. He started a relationship with the male nurse, of all people, who had given him counselling before his test, and who really seemed to appreciate him – which must have made a change. In due course he moved out of the house to live with him. They still pay visits, from time to time.

But by then the house's new identity was well established. My first move was to install an industrial washing-machine and a drier in the basement. I remembered all too well the indignities that Shawn had suffered with night sweats, and how much difference it made to him to have fresh sheets, even though he would soak them through in a couple of hours. The house was a long-standing conversion, full of awkward passages and wasted space, but at least there were plenty of facilities. I installed handrails in the bathrooms and the lavatories. Later it seemed a good idea to buy a special sort of trolley that made bathing someone easier. I invested what seemed like an absurd amount of money in a proper hospital bed, and eventually I bought quite a few of them. The minibus is a relatively recent acquisition.

By this time, every gay man in London knew of someone who was in need of looking after, without quite being a hospital case. I realized that I would need to pick up some practical skills, and fitted in some paramedical courses where I could. Of course, by the time I'd learned how to lift a person safely, to give bed baths and so on, I'd done a certain amount of damage to my back, but at the time it was either that or leave people unturned or dirty.

I had to make an iron rule, early on, that I could only take on unattached men. This wasn't an arbitrary decision, and there were times when I had room to spare, and still turned people away, that it seemed like an unreasonable one. But if there is one thing I can say about myself it is that I have learned from my mistakes. Early on, I offered the hospitality of the house to a young man recently discharged from hospital, and although I have nothing to reproach myself with as far as physical care goes, I know that he sustained psychological damage during his stay.

His lover had visited him devotedly while he was in hospital, but although I had made it clear to him that he was to make himself at home without reservation, his visits to the house became less and less frequent.

I was changing the flowers on the sick man's bedside table one morning, when without a word of warning he said, 'I know what you're doing.' He solemnly informed me that I was trying to drive his lover away, so that I could keep him – in some unspecified and barely imaginable way – for myself.

I was astonished. 'What on earth makes you say that?'

His voice took on a paranoid harshness. 'You said his washing-up wasn't good enough.'

This was perfectly true, but it hardly seemed an unreasonable remark in context. There are few things more irritating than reaching for a clean glass or plate from cupboard or drying-rack, and finding it stained or even encrusted with dirt. And while I'm quite happy to do the washing-up myself, I do resent having to wash things a second time to put things right after someone else. If this young man's lover wanted to make himself useful, as he said, then he should do exactly that, and if washing-up wasn't in his line I'm sure we could have agreed on something else.

It was a horribly difficult situation, and of course I couldn't explain what was really going on. The last thing an invalid, freshly discharged from hospital with a purple cancer lesion on the end of his nose, needs to hear is that his lover is terrified at the prospect of having to look after him, and after appeasing his conscience that everything possible is being done by other people, is running away just as fast as he can, using any flimsy excuse that comes to hand to cover his retreat.

But of course I couldn't say that. I had to bite my tongue and go on with the business of caring as usual, changing the sick man's sheets, bathing him, trying to get him to eat, while all the time being told in this perfectly mad way that I had got what I wanted, now that I had destroyed my patient's emotional life.

Even with unattached men, of course, I made mistakes. I hated the idea that my hospitality was conditional in any way, but after one particular bad experience I had to set up a rudimentary sort of admissions procedure, some elementary cross-checking. I welcomed into the house a man exemplary in his lack of attachments, who had clearly been having a terrible time. He seemed to be carrying a little extra weight all the same, and I remarked that at least he showed no sign of wasting away. He replied dogmatically, 'I have sustained a considerable and irreversible loss of weight.' I said I was sorry to hear that.

But in fact he ate heartily, and it seemed to me after a while that he was getting positively plump. He claimed to be exhausted, and spent most of the day in bed. Eventually I became suspicious enough to contact the hospital where he had claimed to be treated, and they told me he was always telling them about some nightmare infection he had suffered the week before, but there was never anything actually wrong with him when they examined him.

Even before then, I was beginning to suspect he was reeling off sets of symptoms memorized from medical pamphlets and Government circulars – the line about the weight loss, for instance, was reproduced word for word. In a sense, he wasn't even faking, since he had genuinely convinced himself he had Aids. But even on a good day I was often out of my depth – I can admit that now – and I couldn't deal with mental illness on top of everything else. I had to get him out.

I tried to persuade him that he was getting better, and could for instance begin to help around the house. But he clung fast to his bed, and to his fatigue. Finally I had to cut his rations, saying that we needed to starve the organisms that were infesting his digestive tract. Then it was only a matter of waiting until he raided one of the fridges, and catching him red-handed with a bowl of rice pudding and a spoon.

I told him that he had broken the house rules by stealing food, and must go. He pleaded for forgiveness just as if the house was his only hope, and I'm sure he thought it was so. But I couldn't let him take up a valuable bed, and I had to see through what I had started, whatever I felt about it.

I don't want to give the impression that I had no help in what I did. The staff at the major hospitals were only too aware of the limitations of their resources. They were forced to rely on voluntary agencies of one sort or another to make up the difference, and over the years they learned to do so with a good grace. If I had medical questions, or needed advice on the practical matters of nursing, there were numbers I could call. I could rely on getting a good hearing from people who knew that we were basically on the same side. However busy they were, they could be sure that I too had a lot on my plate, and I wouldn't be troubling them if it wasn't important.

There were even doctors on the HIV wards at St Stephen's and the Westminster who would pop by in their own time. Relationships between doctor and patient tended to be much more personal on those wards than in more conventional ones, and the doctors liked to keep an eye on how their ex-patients were doing. But we also had a common interest – emotional on my part, more practical on theirs – in people spending as little time in hospital as was possible. This was particularly true when the HIV wards were full, which happened in strange cycles. For a long time there would be empty beds, and then suddenly there would be a wave of admissions. At peak times, it sometimes seemed that my house was actually a hospital annexe, with nurses delivering medication to the less acute cases, or else strong analgesics to those for whom nothing could be done. The house was large, but once or twice I and a couple of helpers ended up sleeping on camp beds in corridors.

Does it sound pathetic if I say that one of the great achievements of my life was to feed a young man, on his last day, a full portion of steak-and-kidney pie? I hope not. I encouraged him through the meal, mouthful by mouthful, knowing perfectly well – who better?, since I was nursing him – that he was profoundly incontinent, his poor ruined system retaining only the barest memory of how to extract the virtue from food.

But I don't want to give the impression that I was running a one-man-show. I didn't actually cook that steak-and-kidney pie, though I did put in a fair amount of time in the kitchen. I had plenty of helpers, and there were always tasks for them to do, God knows, whatever their particular skills or willingnesses. Helpers with any sort of medical training were of course a godsend, but naturally enough they were much in demand elsewhere, and I can understand that it would be more satisfying for them to put their expertise at the disposal of a more orthodox establishment.

It was particularly gratifying when the lovers or friends of people to whom I had given hospitality repaid their debt in kind, by offering their services as cooks, cleaners or drivers. Sometimes even former guests did so. It's only fair to say that my helpers didn't always stay very long, and often left before they completed the spell of duty they had set themselves. But until they try it, people don't realize quite how intense an experience it is to be faced with the continuing crisis of Aids. The atmosphere at my house could be very elevating, but it could also be taxing. I only hope that those who moved on before they had planned to don't feel they have let me down, or let themselves down.

Long before this time, of course, I had given up my job. The artists I represented said they would miss me, but what they really meant was that they couldn't imagine how I would manage without them. They paid lip-service to the idea that there might be some value in what I was doing, but they couldn't form a very clear mental picture of a life that wasn't focused on them. I get Christmas cards from one or two.

I gave up my career with good grace, and without agonizing overmuch over the decision. It was only a year or two later, when I met a French-Canadian who was touring the world in an aimless sort of way after his lover had died, leaving him with two cars, two motorbikes, a large apartment, a house in the country and considerable savings, that I found myself venting in front of this sympathetic listener an unsuspected rage against Shawn for his legacy. People forget that there are the Aids rich as well as the Aids poor, people whose lives have been wrenched out of shape by an unwanted affluence just as surely as others by poverty. I had my little rant of resentment against Shawn, and then returned meekly enough to the house and what it demanded of me.

Friends have always tried to persuade me that I should set up the house as a charity; I've always resisted the suggestion. I've barely been able to manage with things as they are, and the idea of making things permanent fills me with terror. I appreciate that after an initial period the burden would actually become lighter, once a structure was established that didn't depend so directly on me. But I know I wouldn't be able to keep going that long. I can only cope by living from day to day, not looking further into the future than the next small improvement in the house's running or equipment, a bigger microwave, a sterilizer, a hot-drinks dispenser.

It's certainly not that I'm awed by the Charity Commissioners. If I can handle undertakers, I can handle Charity Commissioners. I can hardly remember the time when my idea of a tough negotiation was trying to persuade the management of a concert hall to book an untried talent, or a young singer not to attempt the impossible cliffs of the repertoire. But soon after the house became a place of caring I found myself delivering an ultimatum to an undertaker.

Speaking purely personally, I can see no good reason for a person wanting to be embalmed. But if people want it done, or more likely their families want it done, then it should be done without question. That the deceased had Aids doesn't come into it. If the undertaker can't protect himself from infection, he should consider a different line of work. It really is as simple as that.

I rehearsed various approaches, all of them heavily sarcastic. *You can't offer an embalming service, and then say you've changed your mind. Embalming someone isn't a favour, you know. It's a business arrangement. It isn't a compliment you can decide you don't mean after all.*

Then it occurred to me that sarcasm was the wrong way to go about it. I didn't need to be wounding, because in a strange way I had power. I represented a sort of trades union of the dead. I had to be their spokesman, and make claims in their name. If I had to, I could boycott any funeral director who made difficulties, and I could make sure that the world heard about it.

In the end, I didn't even need to threaten this particular undertaker with a boycott. All I had to do was threaten him with complaints to his professional body (whatever that might be) and with the revoking of his licence (there had to be a licence of some sort). And I got my way. In fact the question has hardly ever arisen since then. But it was in its horrible way a point of principle, and a turning point. I don't think I was weak before, but I was strong after.

If the house was run as a charity the money side of things would certainly be easier. My desk with its wilderness of bills is a terrifying place for me, in a way that no sickbed will ever be again.

I still have a few items from Shawn's art collection left over, but the minibus gobbled up an awful lot of paint and canvas, and I'm keeping what's left for emergencies. As it is, I'm not above accepting small contributions from various charities to help with my running expenses.

After a death I'll sometimes be sent a cheque by the dead man's parents. I wish I could afford not to cash it, on those occasions when I feel that the cheque is being used to pay me off, to let the bereaved parents wash their hands in some way of their son's dying. I feel much more comfortable with a financial contribution when the parents in question have actually paid a visit to the house. I know it has made all the difference in the world to those parents who have nerved themselves to it, and have found that their son's last real home was a place both of peace and of a paradoxical excitement.

Often it has been a mother who has come on her own; never a father, on his own. There is something peculiarly painful about watching a family that is unable to settle its differences. I have had to watch many failures, not of love but of courage.

So if it happens that I open the front door of the house to a woman unaccompanied, I'm always careful to ask how she has travelled. Often it turns out that her husband has driven her to the house, but refuses to go any further, and is staying in the car. In that case I ask the mother to tell me the model and colour of the car, just in case, and I escort her to her son's bed, or if he is well enough, to one of the dayrooms. Then I go down to my kitchen and brew a nice pot of tea.

When it's ready, I pour out a cup, balance a couple of sugar lumps and a biscuit on the saucer, and go out into the street with it. Once I've located the right car, I go over and tap on the window. Maybe the man in the car has seen me coming in one of the mirrors, maybe he tries to bury himself in the newspaper he is reading, but sooner or later he has to acknowledge me and wind down the window. Then I smile pleasantly and pass the cup of tea across, without a word.

The first time I tried this little manoeuvre I had no idea what tremendous pressure it placed on the man in the car. It happened that he had driven a long way, it was a hot day, and I felt sorry for him, sorry mainly for the way he was impoverishing himself by disowning his son, in a way he would find hard to forgive himself for, later on. But now I recognize the deviousness behind my tea-making. I can almost say I glory in it.

By taking tea out to the father in the car I am acknowledging his right to keep his distance – which disarms him – while also making him feel foolish. Why is it, I wonder, that a cup should administer so much more effective a rebuke than a mug? I don't know. But at all events I prove to him that he has not been able to put himself outside the range of my welcome. Every father to whom I have brought tea has come into the house, and more than once I have hardly turned my back before I hear the sound of the car door opening, and the sound of the first footsteps on the way towards acceptance.

I think I can claim that my teapot has brought more families together than all the counselling services in London combined.

After a death, though, it isn't the families who dispose of the dead man's possessions. That falls to me. I have learned to do it quickly and efficiently, not letting myself think too much about the associations of each little hoard. I'm not going to linger over the task the way I did with Shawn's things. It was months before I managed to clear everything away. I had to steel myself to get rid of the kimonos, hearing Shawn's voice saying with reflex pedantry, 'the plural of *kimono* is . . . *kimono*'. He always gave the word invisible italics and three short syllables.

I left only the paintings that I had promoted to the walls. Oddly enough, I have never managed to disturb the wardrobe in the master bedroom, where the clothes of Shawn's dead lover are stored. Not having known him, I don't feel I have the right. That wardrobe is probably the only part of the whole building that has been left untouched in the quiet overturning I have visited on the house that Shawn left me.

It would have been good to hear from the families of our guests, after they had left us. But that may be rather a lot to expect. Families have their own way of saying goodbye, as we in the house have ours.

I've been careful to cultivate a good relationship with television and the newspapers, in the years since they first showed an interest in what I was trying to do at the house. There's only one aspect of the house's life that I prefer to keep private. I'm always aware that the media have their own priorities, and that I can't expect them necessarily to see everything the way I do. After all, the house has featured in documentaries about both the triumph of private enterprise and the breakdown of the health service, as a glorious example and a terrible warning. And there are some things that I simply don't trust them to see.

It sounds stupid to say that the first time someone died in the house, I was unprepared. Of course I had imagined the fact of death, but I hadn't given any thought to what I would do when it happened. What seemed more important than anything, though, when it did happen, was avoiding any feeling of taboo. So I simply gathered together everyone who was in the house at the time, and we sat round the bed and talked. I said a few words about the dead man, and then someone brought in a bottle of wine. Someone else put on some music. Nothing could have felt more natural. It would have been ridiculous to have covered our friend up, as if he had done something wrong. I think all of us in the room that night felt the strength that comes from facing things – and not just facing them for a few moments, by an effort of will, before turning away.

That was the beginning of our tradition. A farewell could never again be a spontaneous event in quite that way, but our farewells have become central to what we do at the house. I think the hospitals understand that. When medical complications or special circumstances mean that we haven't been able to take care of someone to the end, the hospitals know that he belongs with us all the same, and they release him to us so that we can take our leave in our own way.

A ritual like our farewell is important because it standardizes the emotions. It makes us express a uniform grief for those we have lost, when the truth is that we discriminate brutally from person to person.

Anthony was always different. Anthony was special. He had only been down in London for a few months before he became ill. In that time of accelerating weakness, he had made few friends. He was a bright boy, well-spoken and serious-minded, but he hadn't known what was happening to him, and things had gone pretty far by the time anything was done for him. To the house he brought only a spare pair of running shoes, a rucksack with a few clothes, and his personal stereo. He had four tapes to play on it, which he seemed to listen to, when he was well enough, in strict rotation.

Anthony wore his hair in a style that was severe but also rather complicated, and I had seen at once that it would be beyond the skills of our normal hairdresser, a volunteer who had mastered only the basic techniques, to maintain. So I bribed a local hairdresser to come in every now and then to attend to it.

I made sure Anthony was put in a bed near where I slept, so that I could hear him if he cried out in the night – which sometimes happened – whether or not I was officially on duty. Meningitis isn't exactly a novelty in the house – fungal, bacterial, we've had all kinds – and I'd always known that extreme sensitivity to sound was a common symptom. But only now did I set myself to keep the noise level in the house down, and I snapped at a volunteer who was singing, which I much regret. Singing is not something you can have too much of in a house like mine.

I could see how things were going with Anthony. After a time, you develop an instinct. Finally, one morning, before anyone else was awake, I took his hand, and held it. Anthony ran his other hand, almost dreamily, back and forth along the line between zones of his haircut. The line was as crisply maintained as it had been the day he arrived at the house, and I allowed myself to feel a little satisfaction at that. I had seen that in its own way it mattered, and I had done what I could to help.

I said: 'Anthony. If you want to fight this thing, I'm right with you. We'll fight it every step of the way. But if you've had enough, don't be ashamed of it.' I squeezed the hand I was holding. 'I can let you go now.'

When he spoke, his voice was thick with thrush, and he left long pauses between his phrases, but I could make out clearly what he said. He said, 'It's not up to you. *Old* man. Where do you get off telling people when they can die? Look at yourself. You've grown fat on other people's misery. With your television modesty, and your obscene birthday parties for corpses. But you're not going to get me.'

It was strange that he told me to look at myself, because he himself can only have been aware of my voice. The CMV had reached his eyes by this time, and he was blind. Strange, too, to hear him talking that way, when his temperature had come down so substantially since the meningitis.

On my way from the tube I try to slow my steps down, but when my thoughts wander my natural brisk pace reasserts itself – my health, with all its obligations, reasserts itself – and soon I am home. I must call it home. I open the door of the house gingerly, as if I might wake someone, the slightest noise magnified into pain in the roaring ears of the sick. But in fact this is one of those in-between times when no one is positively in danger. There's no one in the house at the moment who couldn't be moved, if it came to that. There have been one or two hiccups in the property market just lately, but I can't imagine that a large freehold like this, conveniently subdivided, would wait long for a buyer.

I used to think that the house wanted to throw off its partitions, its ungainly conversions, and start functioning again as a unit. I expect it's quite common for house-owners to have ideas of that sort, as if their property harboured plans for itself. Now I have different ideas. Now I think that the house can't wait to be properly broken up again, given over to people who will close their individual front doors, and not think too much about what happens on the other side of them.

TIME'S ARROW
by Martin Amis

Dr. Tod T. Friendly dies and then feels markedly better, breaks up with his lovers as a prelude to seducing them, and mangles his patients before he sends them home, in this ingenious novel that not only rethinks history but dreastically revises our notion of time itself.

"Splendid...bold...*Time's Arrow* is Martin Amis's most thrilling book...gripping from start to finish." —*Los Angeles Times Book Review*

Fiction/Literature/0-679-73572-0

FLAUBERT'S PARROT
by Julian Barnes

An elegant work of literary imagination involving a cranky amateur scholar's obsessive search for the truth about Gustave Flaubert, *Flaubert's Parrot* also investigates the obsession of the detective, whose passion for the page is fed by personal bitterness—and whose life seems oddly to mirror those of Flaubert's characters.

"A high literary entertainment carried off with great brio...rich in parody and parrotry, full of insight and wit...a great success."

—*The New York Times Book Review*

Fiction/Literature/0-679-73136-9

POSSESSION
by A. S. Byatt

An intellectual mystery and a triumphant love story of a pair of young scholars researching the lives of two Victorian poets.

"Gorgeously written...dazzling...a tour de force."

—*The New York Times Book Review*

Fiction/Literature/0-679-73590-9

THE STRANGER
by Albert Camus

Through the story of an ordinary man who unwittingly gets drawn into a senseless murder, Camus explores what he termed "the nakedness of man faced with the absurd."

Fiction/Literature/0-679-72020-0

IN COLD BLOOD
by Truman Capote

As Capote reconstructs the 1959 murder of a Kansas farm family and the investigation that led to the capture, trial, and execution of the killers, he generates both mesmerizing suspense and astonishing empathy. The resulting work transcends its moment, yielding poignant insights into the nature of American violence.

"A masterpiece...a spellbinding work." —*Life*

Nonfiction/Literature/0-679-74558-0

INVISIBLE MAN
by Ralph Ellison

This searing record of a black man's journey through contemporary America reveals, in Ralph Ellison's words, "the sheer rhetorical challenge involved in communicating across our barriers of race and religion, class, color and region."

"The greatest American novel in the second half of the twentieth century...the classic representation of American black experience." —R.W. B. Lewis

Fiction/Literature/0-679-72313-7

THE SOUND AND THE FURY
by William Faulkner

The tragedy of the Compson family, featuring some of the most memorable characters in American literature: beautiful, rebellious Caddy; the manchild Benjy; haunted, neurotic Quentin; Jason, the brutal cynic; and Dilsey, their black servant.

"For range of effect, philosophical weight, originality of style, variety of characterization, humor, and tragic intensity, [Faulkner's works] are without equal in our time and country." —Robert Penn Warren

Fiction/Literature/0-679-73224-1

THE REMAINS OF THE DAY
by Kazuo Ishiguro

A profoundly compelling portrait of the perfect English butler and of his fading, insular world in postwar England.

"One of the best books of the year." —*The New York Times Book Review*

Fiction/Literature/0-679-73172-5

THE WOMAN WARRIOR
by Maxine Hong Kingston

"A remarkable book...As an account of growing up female and Chinese-American in California, in a laundry of course, it is anti-nostalgic; it burns the fat right out of the mind. As a dream—of the 'female avenger'—it is dizzying, elemental, a poem turned into a sword." —*The New York Times*

Nonfiction/Literature/0-679-72188-6

BUDDENBROOKS
THE DECLINE OF A FAMILY
by Thomas Mann

Thomas Mann's first novel, published when he was only twenty-five, is an utterly absorbing chronicle of four generations of a German mercantile family. This acclaimed new English version by the award-winning translator John E. Woods deftly conveys the tonal variety, vigorous wordplay, and unfettered humor that previous translations missed.

"Wonderfully fresh and elegant...bound to become the definitive English version.... Essential reading for anybody who wishes to enter Mann's fictional universe."   —*Los Angeles Times*

Fiction/Literature/0-679-75260-9

ALL THE PRETTY HORSES
by Cormac McCarthy

At sixteen, John Grady Cole finds himself at the end of a long line of Texas ranchers, cut off from the only life he has ever imagined for himself. With two companions, he sets off for Mexico on a sometimes idyllic, sometimes comic journey, to a place where dreams are paid for in blood.

"A book of remarkable beauty and strength, the work of a master in perfect command of his medium."   —*Washington Post Book World*

Winner of the National Book Award for Fiction
Fiction/Literature/0-679-74439-8

THE CEMENT GARDEN
by Ian McEwan

Out of the blasphemous wishes and hair-raising games of four children alone in a world without parents or teachers, Ian McEwan constructs a novel that is all the more chilling for its offhand approach to the unspeakable.

"A writer of uncanny power."   —*Time*

Fiction/Literature/0-679-75018-5

A RIVER SUTRA
by Gita Mehta

Set by India's Narmada River, whose banks are said to contain four hundred billion sacred places, and inhabited by characters including naked ascetics and ecstatic singers, a millionaire monk and an erotically possessed businessman, *A River Sutra* combines Indian storytelling traditions with thoroughly modern perceptions into the nature of love—love both carnal and sublime, treacherous and redeeming.

"Enchanting...sometimes comic, sometimes tragic and always filled with insights.... A delight, bringing to Western readers the mystery and drama of a rich cultural heritage."   —*The New York Times Book Review*

Fiction/Literature/0-679-75247-1

THE ENGLISH PATIENT
by Michael Ondaatje

During the final moments of World War II, four damaged people come together in a deserted Italian villa. As their stories unfold, a complex tapestry of image and emotion, recollection and observation is woven, leaving them inextricably connected by the brutal, improbable circumstances of war.

"It seduces and beguiles us with its many-layered mysteries, its brilliantly taut and lyrical prose, its tender regard for its characters." —*Newsday*

Winner of the Booker Prize
Fiction/Literature/0-679-74520-3

LOLITA
by Vladimir Nabokov

The famous and controversial novel that tells the story of the aging Humbert Humbert's obsessive, devouring, and doomed passion for the nymphet Dolores Haze.

"The only convincing love story of our century." —*Vanity Fair*

Fiction/Literature/0-679-72316-1

OPERATION SHYLOCK
by Philip Roth

In this tour de force of fact and fiction, Philip Roth meets a man who may or may not be Philip Roth. Because *someone* with that name has been touring the State of Israel, promoting a bizarre exodus in reverse, and it is up to Roth to stop him—even if that means impersonating his impersonator.

"A diabolically clever, engaging work...Roth is so splendidly convincing...that the result is a kind of dizzying exhilaration." —*Boston Globe*

Fiction/Literature/0-679-75029-0

THE PASSION
by Jeanette Winterson

Intertwining the destinies of two remarkable people—the soldier Henri, for eight years Napoleon's faithful cook, and Villanelle, the red-haired daughter of a Venetian boatman—*The Passion* is "a deeply imagined and beautiful book, often arrestingly so" (*The New York Times Book Review*).

Fiction/Literature/0-679-72437-0

VINTAGE INTERNATIONAL

AVAILABLE AT YOUR LOCAL BOOKSTORE, OR CALL TOLL-FREE TO ORDER: 1-800-733-3000 (CREDIT CARDS ONLY).